MY FRIEND, THE GIFTED

E. L. ALDRYC

INFINITE
LIBRARY

CONTENTS

To Billy Pilgrim.
Please return my calls.

TIMELINE AND ROADMAP TO THE UNIVERSE OF INFINITE WONDER

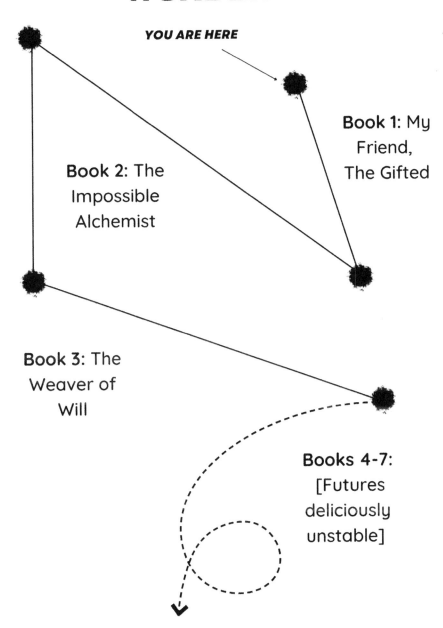

YOU ARE HERE

Book 1: My Friend, The Gifted

Book 2: The Impossible Alchemist

Book 3: The Weaver of Will

Books 4-7: [Futures deliciously unstable]

A COLD WELCOME

"The Five Philosophers took knowledge that led nowhere and replaced it with something the world needed—a plan to enrich plain science with the sublime. Responsibly.

Only three of the original Five left us with lasting legacies, but our world has changed beyond recognition. We practice true alchemy. We live with conscious AI. And we celebrate the gifted, who see a future where the work of the Five converges into something beautiful and better.

They call it the Universe of Infinite Wonder.

See it with them. It is the only plan for a future worth living, one where the magical invades the ordinary just enough to establish a precise new balance. See it. Many forms of suffering will disappear for the final time. And we will be free to challenge the self, not the hunger, for the first time. Humanity deserves mercy.

But you'll be wise to know one thing. No matter how many legacies are left, there is only one guiding light and shepherd of a future for humanity.

The Gifted. The Gifted are the key to everything."

Augustina Weiss, Rising Dawn President in Rotation, Opening Keynote for Faraji-con 2351

BELO HORIZONTE

Saturday, 1 December 2362

Elodie hit rock bottom on a Tuesday night. It happened at 4 a.m. in Brasil, in a poolside dive in Belo Horizonte, right after sixteen hours of damage control. The gifted had moved the doomsday clock a whole five minutes closer to midnight; there was an environmental disaster detected on the event horizon, something about clean water disappearing again. They drafted all departments to come up with emergency patents, and no one got leave until the gifted decided they had enough in their arsenal to weather a potential crisis. Elodie was noticing how they increased in frequency. Junior researchers didn't get breaks on days like these. All they had were the parties afterwards, raging with a force of four hundred thirsty, overworked brains.

Outside, everyone still tried to dance by the pool, but it was getting harder. The sticky floor had spilled drinks all over, mixed together with other less glamorous fluids. No more pictures. Through the small window in the toilet, Elodie heard someone shouting that they'd lost their handbag. The water was still; the handbag was floating in the middle of it. A loud, warped pachanga kept playing for the few who still kept up with the beat. Inside the villa, Elodie held her best friend's hair as she vomited her way through a bottle too many, swaying back and forth. And there came this moment of clarity.

She messed up. Two years at the Sight Institute, and all she did was hold hair back for the elite. The rest fell under Soraya's job description. Her friend. Their boss's right hand. An indispensable asset. The one that made it. And Elodie? Harmless. Great at parties. Invisible at work. She'd never seen herself with this much lucidity.

"I have to be back at work in four hours," Soraya declared, her voice all raspy. Elodie listened to the music. It wasted a heavenly harmony on these drunks. But Elodie was listening. She heard the words in the music.

No hay que ver el futuro para saber lo que va a pasar.

And it was never as simple as in that moment. A peripheral idea, the test was actually her last option. Why couldn't she acknowledge it?

"Listen, I want to do it. I'm going to test for giftedness," she said.

"What?" Soraya paused at the statement and raised her head with great strain. "We've talked about this. No, you don't. Just no. The gifted are… disgusting."

And she twisted in nausea, returning to the toilet. Elodie gathered her white hair and held it up like a good friend.

"Don't be like that, not when I'm telling you I just want to try something," Elodie said and tapped Soraya's back as she coughed. "I've been here for what, two years? I haven't done anything. I'm the lowest-rated researcher there is. This is your fault, too. You don't push me hard enough."

"You're not the lowest."

"That's not the point! Where's my exceptional?"

"Now you listen," Soraya said from below, somewhat delirious, "I want to stop having this conversation every time you're wasted. You have nothing to prove. You're not damaged. People come to you to talk about things other than work. That's the gift. You're great. Being taken seriously would destroy you."

Even in this deplorable state, Soraya was all eloquence. Elodie pulled her hair up a bit too tightly and twisted it to get it away from her face. That's what she got for being all condescending.

"Oh, please. You don't have to be messed up to accomplish something extraordinary," she replied. "I also work for the Sight Institute, so I should contribute to human progress. Which I am not. And I would like to."

Soraya had something to add to that, but she groaned in absent pain instead.

Elodie opened up a small holographic mirror window and checked if her lipstick was in place. It wasn't.

"If I join the gifted, Seravina will take me more seriously. It shows commitment."

Seravina Giovanotti cultivated and grew the knowledge of the Five. She'd brought their near-forgotten philosophies back to the forefront of science. She'd put her money behind what she believed in. That was the woman Elodie wanted to be. Back when she interviewed Elodie among the dozens of young ambitious students, she said that Elodie had a spark in her. That she could see her thrive. Fast forward, and two years had passed in a flurry of irresponsible drinking and long shifts. Elodie was drained. And ashamed to pass Seravina in the hallway.

"You don't want her to take you seriously, trust me," Soraya said weakly in between the convulsions. "I need to be at work in four hours. There's a... correlation."

"No, that's on you for being a workaholic. Relax. I'll just take the test. I'll be gifted. And I don't have to be the most gifted person ever. Just a little bit. Just enough to finally have an advantage," she said, testing out a smile in the mirror app.

"I love how you're taking this so lightly," Soraya said and promptly collapsed on the floor and into a foetal position.

"Hey, say you'll support me!" Elodie closed the window and lay next to her, poking her to see if she was awake. The floor was pleasantly warm, and there was something to look forward to. Even better. All it took was sixteen hours of torture and a revelation.

Soon. The gifted always looked like they were on a mission. Mysterious and heroic. She should have thought of this earlier. The gifted with their gifts. Finally something of direct use to the Institute. She should have gotten tested ages ago. Wonderful and powerful. Not like the current Elodie, who aimlessly drifted from project to project. The Elodie today, who had to manually count thousands of samples because the AI couldn't see them. Or the Elodie of tomorrow, who might bring coffee to a real researcher. The Elodie after the test—now we're talking.

"You know I need this," she whispered.

"No, you don't," Soraya whispered back, "and you don't know the dangers."

"Okay, but I'm gonna do it anyway."

Soraya let out a sigh.

"Stop talking like you mean it."

The two rarely disagreed on anything. Their friendship was harmony. The gifted were one of the few things that always got Soraya rattled. She didn't trust them. For no reason, Elodie liked to add.

Someone was banging on the cubicle door. They started shouting in Portuguese, and Elodie kicked back at the door, missing it.

"I hate the gifted," Soraya mumbled, falling asleep.

"Aha, but once I'm in, you'll love at least one of them. The statement will no longer be true." Elodie brushed hair from her face.

Soraya forced herself up. A cute comment, Elodie thought, but it agitated her so much she looked almost sober.

"You are so precious." Soraya held Elodie's face in her hands, and it hurt a little. "The gifted don't care about that. They make people into functions. What if they make you like them, boring and heartless? Or worse. That would kill me, Elodie. It would actually kill me."

Her eyes were pitch black. You couldn't tell where her irises ended, so Soraya always looked on edge. But this was real. Her voice was shaking. Elodie pulled her closer and hugged her.

"Zero chance. You come first. I just want to try it. Just to try it," she said.

"I don't know how I'm gonna handle this," Soraya whispered and held on to her even tighter.

This was as much an approval as she would get, and Elodie hoped she wasn't too drunk to remember getting the green light from the only person who mattered. The stars were aligning.

She turned on her back, observing the grey ceiling, listening to the melody of the music and of kicks to the door.

The Universe of Infinite Wonder was coming for Elodie.

STAR QUALITY ALIGNMENT

Tuesday, 1 January 2363

A hundred years since the Five shook up the world with their thought, the Sight Institute still captured the essence of what they stood for. It followed a feeble dream, and while most of the world was trying to forget these kinds of slim chances, Sight Institute refused to let go. It fed on a legacy. It thrived. A fortress of philosophy in practice. A fortress of the only future worth living. Just saying the name was an act of belief. The Sight Institute. For Elodie, it was like hissing at a weak opponent. The accent helped. "Where do you work?"

"I work at the Sight Institute."

The way people looked at her when she said it rekindled the wonder she had when she started, if only for a moment. Since the party in Belo Horizonte, Elodie didn't need people asking where she worked to feel it again. Every night, in the middle of a long routine that let her reflect on the day and get in the right headspace, she tried it on for size. She would say to the mirror, from different angles, and in different, calm voices. "I work in the Sight Institute, but more specifically, Rising Dawn."

There was never a good time to go through with it, but the weeks immediately after that party were too grim for her to push and add tension in the house. Elodie and Soraya had lived together since she came to the Institute and got paired with a live-in buddy and a temporary flat, all to help her adjust to life on Madilune. Most people moved out after a few months, but Elodie stayed. They clicked. Even though she did most of the talking at the beginning, Elodie learned to watch out for body language and listen carefully. It was the only way to get Soraya to share what was going well, or not so much. Otherwise, she only talked about the Institute.

They used to have a couple more close friends until Soraya got into a fight with one of them that was so bad, the poor guy left the island. Things got awkward and the group fell apart. Since then, Soraya had been avoiding all social life by either working late inside the Particle Lab, or studying academic articles at home. And even though this wasn't good news by any means, it seemed to help Elodie's plan along.

Now that she wasn't out having drinks every night, Elodie spent more time on her own at the Institute. And when Soraya wasn't walking the halls by her side, complaining about legal compliance or something equally boring, an unexpected ally appeared. Tammy Two Feathers, the reigning president of Rising Dawn and one of the most powerful gifted in the world, would give her a little wink and a smile when she passed her, and greet her by name. Prognosts could read intent and translate it into visions of what someone's future would look like if they followed through. She knew. Elodie's heart jumped every time. She smiled back.

All these were signs that things were in motion. She just needed to wait for the right moment. Soraya might have known about her intentions, but it was a bad time to test the strength of their friendship.

So on New Year's Eve, Elodie staged a near-intervention, getting Soraya out of the house to a party off Madilune. She reluctantly agreed, and only after Elodie promised that she'd go to the morning meeting with her. Seravina had some kind of news to share with an inner circle, but Elodie was the closest thing to a person Soraya fully trusted, and so she often got invited alongside her more influential flatmate. It was both a perk of living with the Institute's unofficial right hand and a frequent reminder that it wasn't her brilliance that got her in. Seravina liked certain types of people, and she liked Elodie for the wrong reasons. She kept saying that she had the kind of face that wanted people to see at the Institute. Extroverted. Carefree. Smiling. An image ambassador. People liked to think the Institute was made up of Belgian blondes whose name everyone knew, but no one knew what they were doing there.

At 8 a.m. sharp, New Year's Day, like torture, Seravina Giovanotti entered the main conference room in the admin building in an orange sequin dress. She was an exceptionally tall, dark woman, with an ever-present shine about her. Elodie never understood whether it was charisma alone or holographic projections that crafted it, only the fact that it made her look like down-to-earth royalty.

The outfit was a parody of the glitz that still rang in Elodie's ears as she struggled to keep her eyes open. But she had to. She had put purple lipstick on. The thought of its velvety beauty kept her awake, and the sobering nausea was abating. All high-level executives from different departments were in the room, with ten trustworthy junior researchers who acted as assistants to others. At the head of the table were Tammy Two Feathers, and next to Seravina, Soraya. Musing pleasantly. No one could have suspected that forty minutes ago they were both shouting into an ancient karaoke machine in Oslo. Good times.

There was nobody in the room to represent AI interests. People didn't publicly align with the agenda too tightly—AIs were a dead pursuit ever since their spiritual leader died, and a non-fashionable subject.

And then there was His Excellency Dr Per Birkelund, the only living (and sane) remainder of the Five Philosophers. An aura of aggressive self-importance surrounded him, carrying more emotion than his stony face. His last remaining apprentice looked as miserable as ever. Business as usual. Alchemists rarely came to meetings. They considered themselves better than the rest. Their science was the only one out of the Five that had fulfilled its mission by producing matter that was all sublime and made other matter forget its properties. They were apparently just waiting for the rest to catch up.

Elodie was curious to see if the apprentice would break the silence. His name was Frederich Hawken, and even while they were friends, he was a tricky one to get through. Now it was awkward. Soraya was uncomfortable, but only Elodie could notice. Frederich was ignoring both, like the absolute ass that he was, probably overthinking an alchemical equation. Elodie used to be intrigued by this indifference. Used to be. This too was a sign it was time to move on to something new.

Seravina gave them reading material as they settled. She and Tammy both stood up in a hurried conversation. One by one, the staff around the table was bringing up visible holographic windows projected in front of them. Madilunian comms were based on their homemade nanotechnology, the tola network—the greatest export in the world. Simple surface thoughts, controlling holographic windows so crisp, you wanted to press your nose against them. Only in Madilune could you see technology close to perfection and the sublime they strived towards.

Although they could only harness enough power for transferring and carrying information, tola nanos were small enough to penetrate beyond matter to the sublime, accessing power of forces only those who followed the Five could truly understand. The rest knew terms based on their approximations, like intent, materialisation, will, consciousness. These took over when conventional knowledge showed limits. They were forces that were shunned until the appropriate climate emerged for them to find their way back into scientific discourse, as fragile as it was a hundred years ago. Forces almost lost to oblivion after the Five failed, until one woman, Seravina Giovanotti, put a lot of money behind them and created a product that promised energy beyond the limits of possible. The legacy of the Five Philosophers resumed the making of the future they dreamt so fervently. It was easy to hope in this world. With only a billion people left, all living in safe curated zones around the world, it felt quiet and empty. Elodie brought up a window too and read the note.

[TOPIC: *Testing Tuesday*

The Rising Dawn HQ will open its doors on Tuesday, the 29th of January 2365 to all the Institute to take part in a large-scale ability testing event. All will take part. That includes you, and, if applicable, your subordinates.]

"Now, let's talk about the why," Seravina said, clearly having prepared a speech. The sequins rattled, and Elodie watched them reflect the single ray of sun that snuck in behind her. "The recruitment drive into the Rising Dawn slowed down during the last few months, but the demand for gifted services is still increasing. Rising Dawn cannot dilute its pool any further by accrediting more associations—they're already stretched too thin. As an umbrella organisation, the Sight Institute is responsible for ensuring the thriving of its parts. We must lend our efforts to aid the gifted with their proliferation.

"A healthy number of gifted is the most important symbol of progress, power and sustainable development. Strengthening Rising Dawn directly means strengthening the Institute and makes the Madilunian government look very good. The government enables all of us to live and work on this island without imposing its interests on the agenda of the Five. If these things make little sense to you, I suggest you look at a different career.

"Above all, we're dedicated to the slow, steady, and sure progress, which can only be achieved through increasing the strength of the gifted. Testing Tuesday will contribute to the glorious future of the Five Philosophers and help the legacy of Nada Faraji thrive. The current prognostic efforts have predicted a huge breakthrough within the next few months, which means we might enter exciting territory with new faces at the helm."

Elodie was waiting for Seravina to look at her, out of all these people, and make it real. To say they were waiting for her.

"So *how*, you're probably asking." Seravina scanned the table instead, looking for resistance. Elodie noticed Seravina always played up her Sicilian accent when she looked for dissidence. "Even though our employees are twice as likely to test for giftedness, the actual number of those who do it is still low. Seeing that there are just so many people who are already knee-deep in their understanding of sublime forces, Tammy proposed that we boost Rising Dawn numbers internally. And here you go: Testing Tuesday is born."

She raised her arms in a self-congratulatory pose. Obligatory testing. What an idea.

"Testing hundreds of people in a single day obviously won't be easy, so it's up to you to make it painless. Encourage your colleagues and friends to do it as early as possible. I'd rather have a queue at 7 a.m. than in the evening.

"Of course, we need to go through some legal business to put you at ease. We recommend that you have this conversation with your team if you are a department head as well. This is an obligatory work event. However, the results are for internal purposes only. We cannot emphasise enough that even if you, or your subordinates, test positive, you won't be forced to be part of Rising Dawn. But you will be warmly encouraged."

Elodie looked at Soraya, sitting there on the opposite side of the table, her lips tightly pursed together, a look of solid hate directed at the small holographic window.

It was quintessentially Madilunian to fight about, think about, explore the philosophy of the Five. That's what made it a place of its own. Elodie often thought about how the history of the entire world led to this meeting, in this room, in a place that would have been unimaginable only a hundred years ago. Madilune. An accidental island in the middle of the Atlantic, a city state that birthed six new music genres, with no respect for anything other than the legacy of the Five. The work here was so coveted that no one dared attacking the ideas, slowing down something as beautifully precious as hope. Madilune was bursting with life, shaping the world with a quest for goodness. Special. It stood for something. Just like Elodie wanted to.

Not even Soraya could stop it now. It was all coming together. They said it. Testing Tuesday was obligatory.

"All right, everybody." Seravina clapped to hush the murmurs. "This will be a logistical nightmare to organise, and it will mean several days with no real work done. But it's imperative that we do it."

Why? Why now? Rising Dawn was always scouting for fresh meat. She looked over to Tammy instinctively, as if she could get answers from her face alone.

In that moment, Tammy turned to address the room.

"It's so lovely to hear the Institute is on the same page about this," she said, even though the rest of the Institute was merely receiving orders.

Tammy Two Feathers was Seravina's softer and nicer counterweight. Exuding peace and diplomacy, wearing white blissful dresses, she seemed like a person who was easier to empathise with. But Soraya always warned that Tammy was much more than a harmless spiritual leader. Seravina favoured the gifted, which was a warning sign. According to her, a certain degree of aggression and manipulation was key to get into their leader's good books. Elodie doubted the gifted needed that. They were the most useful part of the Institute. They predicted challenges and dangers so well that life at the Institute was mostly uneventful.

"Because there's a reason why we need reinforcements now, more than ever," Tammy continued. "We've sensed the Universe of Infinite Wonder on the horizon. Just barely, but we sensed it."

The table fell silent. So that was the truth behind it. Not a marketing ploy, but a door to true progress, heralded by a sign of wonder. The kind worthy of the universe they desired. This wasn't supposed to happen in their lifetime. They were always told that the Five had failed and there was no way of telling when humanity would be worthy of another chance to reach for the Universe of Infinite Wonder. But Tammy stood there gravely and peacefully. Meaning it.

Elodie heard a rushed whisper from several parts of the room while Soraya shot a patronising glance at Tammy and returned to feigning boredom.

"We will not be participating," Dr Birkelund said, rushing out of the meeting room. "Call us when you have something solid," he said to Seravina, and practically dragged Frederich out the door with him. So much for interdepartmental collaboration.

"Don't go crazy, people," Seravina said with agitation. "Tammy and the rest of Rising Dawn might be excited, but this changes nothing on a day-to-day basis. Futures come and go out of the picture, and even if we do everything right and keep the event horizon stable, we won't be anywhere close to the finish line for at least a few years. We won't be sharing this with the public, is that understood?"

The business side took over. An unexpected future would destabilise the investors' plans and markets all over the world. It shocked Elodie that no one else felt the pull. The gifted just announced that they had sensed the Universe of Infinite Wonder. This was a key step in bringing it into reality. And she was in this meeting. Right in the core of history.

"I'm just happy I could share the news with you all." Tammy smiled benevolently, sweeping the room. She stopped and stared at Elodie just long enough for her to understand that she knew. The stars were aligning. For Elodie, and for the world.

REBELO HORIZONTE

Wednesday, 2 January 2363, 1 a.m.

"Are you going to talk to me about it?" Elodie asked Soraya, who was immersed in a schematic for the new upgrade to the Particle Lab complex.

It was late at night. Elodie had come home last, which was rare. Soraya working from home was not. Not responding to a perfectly reasonable question like this—equally common.

"Looks nice. Is this the annexe?" Elodie walked through the schematic and got a beer from the fridge.

"It might be, if Rising Dawn doesn't poach our entire workforce," Soraya replied. She was still wearing the lab coat as if the twenty miles between their flat and the Institute were nothing. Her feï was sloppily parked on the terrace. This was a premium limited-edition vehicle that could fly around the world in an hour if it ignored airspace laws, and it deserved better. It painted a clear picture of distress, but Elodie had spent the day elated. Resistance was expected. She could deal. Testing Tuesday was mandatory. What was she supposed to do?

"I thought you'd be happy. They've just spotted the Universe of

Infinite Wonder on the event horizon. That doesn't happen every day, does it?" Elodie stretched on the couch.

"I don't believe a single word that comes out of that woman's mouth," Soraya said, "We're in no position to be looking at the Universe of Infinite Wonder. We'll just fail again. Every science apart from alchemy is slowing down. The AIs are neglected. Even if it were true, it was a stupid thing to say."

She made the schematic hologram disappear and sat down on the couch with her strict, upright posture. Soraya was always so stressed about things. Perfectionism ate at her. Of course she didn't think they were doing well enough to try again.

"Didn't Ai Kondou say that the gifted would be the first piece of the puzzle?" Elodie tried to give her hope. "They'd see the path for the other sciences to take? So maybe that's what's happening. And with the new gifted that will come from Testing Tuesday, they'll be strong enough to see it all."

She must have said the magic word.

"And what," Soraya said, "you'll be the one to do it? Show us the path to the Universe of Infinite Wonder?"

She meant as a jab, but Elodie couldn't help but to smile.

"Well, maybe I will."

Soraya got up from the sofa and walked off without a word. She stopped at the entrance to her room.

"I'm not angry at you. I don't want to be rude," she said, "but please do some research and find out what you're getting yourself into. If you don't want to follow through, I can get you out of Testing Tuesday. You won't be the only one that refuses."

Her voice had a barely distinguishable shiver to it. Elodie kept thinking it would get easier.

"I know what I'm doing, Soraya," she said. And it came out colder than she wanted. "But I really appreciate that you care. And I promise not to be stupid about it."

Soraya looked like she had so much to say, which Elodie hated. It wasn't fair. And it was just after New Year's Day. The perfect time to make bold changes. She was about to close the door behind her, when Elodie asked, "Why do you hate the gifted so much?"

Soraya stopped the door animation with her hand and turned back around. Progress.

"Because I've never met a gifted individual who wouldn't want to either hurt me, steal from me, or lie to me. And I know a lot of people," she said, leaning on the frame. "I notice patterns like these. There's something about the gifted. It almost reeks."

At least she was honest. Elodie appreciated it. Tammy didn't strike her as a bad person. Same for the other members of Rising Dawn that she'd met. Soraya just had had bad experiences, and Elodie needed to respect that. Respect, not copy.

"It just means I have more to prove," she replied.

Soraya smiled weakly and stepped back into her room. "I guess you will. Good night."

THE INFINITE LIGHTNESS OF
TESTING TUESDAY

Tuesday, 29 January 2363

The secret was in the shape. Every inch of edging closer towards the Sight Institute revealed more of its complex structure that could easily be mistaken for a beloved sacred ground. The tall grass surrounding a vast circular plain on top of a hill—never cut, as no one walked on it—determined the borders of Elodie's world. Instantly recognizable.

There was a smaller concentric circle in the middle, where everyone landed, got out, and let their feï hover a foot above the soft surface until they sunk underground. A series of plain, nearly white rectangular structures, growing bigger and bigger as you approached them, surrounded it. They all faced the interior circle and were distinguishable only by the differently sculpted entrances. People stood out like ants around an iced monolith when you looked down, rushing about in the winter sun. There were never any windows to the interior. Everything was made from the same material, enhanced by alchemy so that it could look like certain things and mimic the properties of others. The buildings were nimble, moving and changing in size when they needed to. Static matter would just slow them down. Plus, it was expensive.

Elodie approached the Rising Dawn HQ, one of the first structures that called for attention when you landed. In theory, it should have looked like all the other buildings. Blocky, off white, an inch of creative freedom permitted with the entrance. In practice, the gifted kept throwing on forbidden decorations that were promptly removed when the facilities manager spotted them, only to return again late at night when no one was looking. A daily dance.

People were already there, enjoying the rare silence of the central reservation where all feï went off to drop passengers and then get swallowed by the underground parking. The Institute was a 24/7 affair, but today, the complex started off almost empty, with employees dripping in. Like all obligatory things, Testing Tuesday was a hated idea at first.

Since the announcement and a few additions to the agenda, the dissidence fizzled out. There was only one type of pan-Institute event that got everyone to both come in early and complete a bothersome task, and the PR knew what they had to do. Organise a party. And that's what Testing Tuesday had to be reborn and rebranded as.

Outside of forwarding the agenda of the Five, Seravina was famous for throwing obscenely indulgent soirées. It was one of the top perks of working at the Institute. Leaked videos of internal binges were one of the first things that attracted Elodie to join, and the only one that turned out to be as good as she expected.

While most of the staff was coming in curious and relaxed, a small group of hard-boiled haters refused to participate, writing letters of protest and threatening legal action. What surprised Elodie the most was that there were so few.

As an employer, Rising Dawn had a bit of a mixed reputation. Those who dreamed of working there, got tested, and got in, loved it. People who tested, got in, and preferred to stay outside, not so much. The gifted had a hard time taking no for an answer when people showed great promise. Elodie had had a friend who discovered a telepathic inclination but refused to leave his geological studies. Seeing how rare telepaths were, Rising Dawn relentlessly showered him with attention, messages, and gifts until he got tired and joined. The word harassment came up a few times. Soraya, of course, tried to convince anyone in that position to press charges. No one did. It didn't feel right fighting an organisation whose end goal was literally the survival of humanity.

Today, as Elodie moved closer to Rising Dawn than she'd ever been (outside of a telepathic probe that was mandatory when she joined the Institute), she could still see the details of their daily violation of standards before it got removed.

Golden shapes floated about the blocky surface like sea creatures, and there was a smell of freshly cut grass and myrrh in the air around it. Walking past the first pair of giant doors, ornament free, and another with heavy gilded Corinthian pillars felt like enjoying a song everyone thought was trashy. There was a theme, Elodie found. Surfaces looked monotonous until she caught a glimpse of something at the corner of your eye, under a right angle. After that, she couldn't unsee it.

She'd arrived early, no queues. This was it. A relaxing day without protective gear. Nothing to be worried about.

Speaking of worried, Soraya had been sending memos saying that there was a maintenance error she needed to fix throughout the night. The series of messages were addressed to everyone in charge and forwarded to Elodie. She detailed a collapse of cleaning procedures—a safe bet to keep people away. And just in case Elodie missed the hint that she could have volunteered to help with the emergency, Soraya then sent a message directly.

[I'm doing everything in my power to avoid the clutches of Rising Dawn slavery and greed. Please join in and reject the forceful recruitment. You know where I am.]

As dramatic as always.

Elodie could have been offended that she didn't do more to show support. But this was probably the closest Soraya came to it. By not dragging her away.

Knowing how hard it was for Soraya to accept her decision

made her appreciate the freedom to go through it even more. She was tired of being the only socialite the Institute had produced in its long history. Here to be seen, but essentially useless.

It was a crushing sentence, especially when Soraya told her with firm hope that "something will sit with her eventually". As if someone so talented in so many things could ever understand.

The moment she picked up a questionnaire at reception, Elodie felt the weight of it. It included a distant possibility of making the two equal one day. That was indulgent of her.

Imagine. Elodie Marchand. Of value.

She sat down to answer the questions, but they weren't exactly what she expected. She kind of wanted to be asked what kind of gifts she'd want. Maybe telepathy. Then she could find out if people really did think she was stupid or something. But the training was awful from what she heard. Stuck in silence with telepaths constantly talking to you in your mind until you spoke back with force. It sounded creepy. No one ever complained about paragnostic or prognostic training.

On the table in front of her were projections of titles recommended for browsing, and on the edge was an outline of a book cover that could be instantly picked up and read with her comms. The file was small but designed with great care. Whoever made it had chosen both the title and the font in a way for browsers to handle the publication with affectionate care, as if it were their little sister's diary. And it read: *To My Best Friend, the Gifted.*

Elodie picked it up with interest, and the first few pages popped open in front of her eyes, aligned into a row of rectangles. She began to read.

In the outlines of your wildest dreams is the person you will become. This person would be a stranger to you if you met them today. You might not even like them. But through the growing pains and the adventures that await you as you walk through the threshold of discovering your inner power, this is who you will become. Please don't try to imagine yourself as them. I want that to be one of those beautiful surprises you always hoped you would get in life.

I want to learn more about this person. I think they're great.

"Elodie? Do you want to come in?"

The woman who was greeting the crowd left the desk to see her, offering to take her further down the hall to one of the offices. She turned back and smiled serenely. But not as serenely as Tammy Two Feathers. That was on another level.

"I don't want you to get lost—it can be a bit confusing at the beginning. Are you feeling okay?"

She'd been here for a few minutes, and they'd already given her a warmer welcome than the SI did when she first started. That had been more of a "You made it, here's a lab coat. Go work."

"I'm great," she replied. The feeling she had in Belo Horizonte. It returned.

THE ART OF CLARINET
IMPROVISATION

For a moment, she thought about turning back. The hurrying was part of a selfish fear, thinking someone might put forward a reasonable argument against doing this. And there were many. She didn't know what would change if she were successful. Just like she didn't know what would happen if she wasn't.

The only thing left was imagining what would happen if she listened to Soraya. Stay away. And that was an option that would make her miserable regardless of the outcome—giving up without seeing what came after this invitation into the last unexplored fortress. The soft grey carpet reduced her steps to nothing when she entered the office. They should have closed the door behind her. Make sure she didn't run off.

The room was oval. Photos on walls all lined up, of nature, and not even the remarkable kind. Impenetrable forests. Perhaps they were in code, one that only the gifted could understand.

A man was sitting behind a mahogany desk on the opposite side of the room. He greeted her with an honest smile and quickly went back to an open window of notes. He was handsome, of an indeterminable age, but with silver hair and an air of wisdom that implied a certain level of experience with life. As he leaned forward to read something projected on the desk surface, she saw a final photo hanging on the wall behind him. Not of a forest, but of him. And he wore the same turtleneck in the photo. Funny.

Underneath the picture were big printed words. It was a book reference. "Docent Telepathos, Dr Mircea Rusu, *Wellbeing and Maintenance of Benevolent Stasis in Double-Linked Hubs: A Case Study*, Oxford University Press, 2341."

"Elodie Marchand, yes?" He said it perfectly French, with pride in the accuracy of pronunciation. "And what's your current department?"

"PR," she replied. What a sad thing to say at the world's most famous research institute. At least he'd know why she was desperate to move. "But I'm still in rotation. I'm deciding where to, erm, stop." She flicked her hair over her shoulder. It smelled like vanilla. Superstar. She sat opposite to him on an armchair that got lost against the identical grey shade of carpet.

"Do you have any siblings?" he said. It was an odd question to start with, but then again, Elodie's expectations were loose.

"Yes, three. Two brothers and a sister."

She had a thin notion that speaking in sentences might work better. When the telepath looked at her, there was this tiny itch against the inside of her skull. She could have imagined it. Telepaths left no traces of their work. Unless they wanted. Light lilac colour invaded the periphery of her sight.

"And what do they do?" he asked. Dr Rusu. Docent telepathos. One day she could have an office like this. But without a silly turtleneck. Shit. Was he listening? She watched his face, which was entirely pleasant. He might have smiled.

"My sister is head of urban development strategy for the EU, youngest person in the Commission," she replied. "My older brother is one of the nanotechnology leads at Byeolpyo. And my younger brother just qualified for the Olympics for the first time. Javelin."

Elodie could recite these things off the cuff. She practised not looking sorry when people got excited about them. Sometimes they slipped a question along the lines of "Oh, so you must be the rebel!"

Yes, well. Not on purpose.

Dr Rusu nodded as if every word she said was of the utmost importance.

"They have an impressive resume," he said.

"My parents wanted to cover all bases," she said. She saw the telepath note that down, urgently.

"And they initially wanted you to do music, right?" he asked. When he did, she felt a slight touch of warmth.

"The music school rejected me for piano. They had too many kids, and I wasn't a natural or something. I don't remember. So they suggested the clarinet. I tried that for about ten years, but I never went pro."

"You know, I used to play the clarinet," Dr Rusu said, chuckling to as if he'd just told himself a fantastic joke. Elodie looked at him and imagined this calm and languid man struggling with the chromatic scale until he couldn't feel his lips and got blisters on the sides of his thumbs. Impossible.

"No way."

"Twelve years. I still don't know how I made it. I hated every minute of practice, but you know how it is. You just don't want to quit. Because that would mean it won," he said.

Elodie didn't see it that way. The clarinet always won. It just either took over your life or messed it up if you weren't good enough.

"Were you better at tone or technique?" she asked. Her teacher always said that technique can be taught, but tone had to do with the gift of music. Elodie lacked the second, according to her tutors.

"Tone was easy for me; the technique required practice," he responded. His eyes focused on hers, and Elodie felt that this time, he reached a step farther. "When you're a natural at something, it's harder to improve," he added.

But the funny part was, it wasn't an intrusion. He seemed interesting. The more he spoke, the more she wanted him to understand her. To look at her and tell her "I know what you mean." She wouldn't believe most people if they said it. She'd believe him.

"And when you quit, it was your parents' reaction that got you to leave Bruxelles?"

When would the test start? Was this it? Were there correct responses to questions about her background?

"I mean, it wasn't overnight," she said. She never discussed the family situation. It was hard to explain. She lacked nothing at home. No one caused her harm. To feel as bad as she did around her family sounded childish whenever she spoke about it. They were all completely normal, nice people. But.

"There were always just these jabs at the dinner table. You know families and their inside archetypes. They couldn't pin anything on me that would stick. So eventually, you know, they made me into, like, a problem. Like nothing was good enough for me. Elodie doesn't care, Elodie looks down on us hard-working people, will the sun die before Elodie decides on a career. Things like that."

"I know what you mean," Dr Rusu said and gave her a knowing look.

"That was uncalled for, you read my mind!" she said in fake outrage.

"I'm sorry. I get one joke per test. I used it poorly," he said. If this were the gifted, and if this was the test, then she wanted in. This quiet confidence that everyone had. The support. The way they could joke without being mean to each other, or themselves. It was so different from the rest of the Institute.

He noted something in a semi-transparent window. It took a long time for him to jot things down in a tola-based app. If telepaths were like the rest of Rising Dawn, then they didn't like technology invading too much of their mind, so they carried touch pens and other ancient technology that helped them look even more like a private club.

"When I was growing up in Romania, Rising Dawn wasn't even that organised. Very few people knew about telepathy, especially since Nada Faraji was mostly promoting prognostics and paragnostics. My whole family is very down to earth, in logistics, and we've had a family business for over two hundred years. I wasn't just an outsider. My siblings were basically afraid of me." He noted more things down as he spoke, and Elodie searched his face for sadness or resentment. She came back empty-handed. If anything, he was downright entertained by his past.

"So I think you did the right thing by leaving," he concluded.

Telepaths made the best therapists.

"Just to double check." He focused on her again, and his grey eyes seemed to grow wider. "You did the basic security check when you started?"

"Yes, when I was put under telepathic protection," she confirmed. That day was a blur. She got the call that she got the job, and straight away she had to get there and do the whole induction in a day. There had been lots of jumping from building to building. The Rising Dawn induction came in the evening and it was a formality to put her under telepathic protection. Junior researchers handled sensitive data, and Rising Dawn would protect them from foreign telepathic invasion.

"No problem. It's just that the test requires us to go a little deeper, as you're requesting permission to access far more classified intel," he said, opening a new holographic window.

"Sure," she said, trying to remember what exactly the telepathic security probe was. All she remembered was that a person had asked her to relax, and Elodie had forgotten what they did the moment she left the room.

Dr Rusu broke eye contact and looked to the side.

"Relax for me," he said.

That was a big ask. Elodie tried to look relaxed, which she was good at. But then she realised that she was alone with all her thoughts. Fear of failure. Shame. Nervousness. That was bad.

"All done, thank you." Dr Rusu stopped her. As brief as it was, it made him frown and dive deeply into his notes. This was when deep wrinkles appeared on his face, possibly betraying a far more unusual age than the one he chose to display.

"Can you tell me what I'm going to be doing tomorrow night?" he said, looking into his notes. The warmth she felt inside her head was completely gone. After the last few minutes of kindness, this caught her off guard.

"I—I don't know," she said.

"Guess," he insisted, still looking away.

"I don't know," Elodie said. So. This was when the humiliating part started. Turns out, you had to be gifted to be in the gifted club. Fear took over. Elodie promised herself that she wouldn't let it get into her head. That she would just let it be and answer as accurately as possible. She had to say something.

"The minute I leave, a strong desire to play the clarinet again will possess you. You'll start browsing models, but you'll get confused deciding whether you should get a beginner's model, because it's been so long, or a top tier one, because you played it for long enough and you know you deserve it. In the end, you will end up in a jazz bar in North Madilune asking to go onstage at three a.m, drunk on expensive mezcal."

Dr Rusu laughed and quickly retorted by pointing at her as if to say she projected her own plans. But then he looked aside again, and the frowning returned.

"Your sister, the one in urban planning. What is she doing right now, in this moment?" he asked.

"I haven't spoken to her for a while," Elodie confessed.

"I know," he replied, "have a guess."

"Erm." Elodie tried to think of a fun way to blow this, but there didn't seem to be one. Her sister was serious and charismatic. People just followed her. There wasn't much to joke about.

"She's walking up and down in her office, preparing for a meeting. And she knows she's going to get what she wants. And everything is great," she said.

Dr Rusu returned to his notes for a long time.

"How do you think this interview is going?" he finally asked.

"Poorly," she replied, and they both laughed. It was the best she could do. What a stupid idea this was. What a mean question this was.

"Well, I'm not allowed to discuss your results in front of you, unfortunately," he said, while he noted down more things that Elodie didn't want to hear. He closed the windows hovering around him and put the stylus into a suit pocket.

"Can I leave you in the office for a few minutes so we can

compare the results that were recording your brain activity?" he asked.

"I'll be right here," she said, shrugging.

He sprang up straight away, and she watched him rush off past her. Would you look at that? He wanted this painful meeting to end just as much as she did.

The door rematerialised into fake wood, and she reached out to make a call as soon as she was sure she was alone.

"Yes," Soraya sounded absent and in a quiet place.

"Okay, urgent, urgent," Elodie hurried, "I'm in Rising Dawn, and this is so awkward. I need a drink. Can we forget this ever happened? Honestly, I can't even explain."

Soraya switched to video and confronted Elodie with the smuggest face she had ever seen. But she had it coming.

"Oh, how terrible. I wish someone had told you Rising Dawn isn't worth your time."

"It's not that. It's just, I know what they'll say. I think I should just leave. They asked me to wait. Ugh. This was so embarrassing."

"Ditch them," Soraya said expectedly, "come to the seventy-third level. I have wine, and the gifted aren't allowed this deep into the labs."

She smiled. Elodie exhaled pure relief. This was all she wanted to hear. Her most feared event of the month took less than twenty minutes. If she drank enough, she'd only start cringing once she sobered up tomorrow. Elodie got up to walk out. But the door clicked, and Dr Rusu returned.

And with him, another person who introduced herself.

"Augustina."

This was the only thing Elodie knew about the woman, yet when she sat down and greeted Elodie, Augustina let out a contagious vibe of ease, and Elodie felt like they were old pals. She looked at her with a gaze full of warmth and sincere interest, which made Elodie see gold at the edge of her visual field, and she blinked several times. She looked older, brightly regal against the dull grey backdrop of Dr Rusu's office, with long ginger hair that seemed to follow its own rules of chaos. Another telepath.

Outside these walls, a person with telepathic abilities wasn't even allowed to look at you for more than three seconds without paperwork verifying that they were part of a hub and therefore under peer revision, which was to stop them from peeping at others' heads freely. But this was their domain, and they did as they pleased. Making the world a happy place just by being in it and oozing chill vibes.

This Augustina woman gave Dr Rusu a short look, which could mean anything among their kind, and it made Elodie feel uncomfortable again. What was another telepath doing here? And what were they discussing? Then she put down a new item, one that Elodie could identify. It was an active AI link. These were necessary for an AI to function in places that didn't support their ever-presence through a good enough density of nanos. Rising Dawn was a textbook case. AI was all but forbidden and all instances of tola density that could support them were regularly dispersed on purpose.

The AI link was a smooth, white half-orb that stuck itself to the surface of the table. At the very top, it gave out a warm blue glow to say it achieved the kind of sentience that severely displeased the gifted. Just like that, Augustina plugged it in, as if half of her colleagues wouldn't pretend they were having an allergic reaction if they knew someone had activated it inside their headquarters. That was it. Elodie had to ask.

"What's this for?"

"We're just making sure we've got a good reading on you, sweetie. Me and Mircea will cross reference to make sure you're not reading minds when looking for answers. And as sad as it is, we need a non-human sensor for that. That's what the AI is for. I normally don't trust these, but it's a pretty simple task, so hopefully it won't fail."

There was no one there to defend the opposing philosophical stand, as was usually the case with the AI. It just glowed there, waiting for a challenge.

"It's the standard advanced paragnostic test," Augustina added.

"Advanced?"

Elodie didn't dare to put two and two together. It didn't make sense. Augustina looked at her and somehow pushed the weight of her confusion into the background.

"There are two images displayed on the table. One of them is about to disappear. Which one will be left on the table?"

"Circle or cross?" the AI said in a voice of a thousand, a sound both impersonal and magical at the same time.

Elodie smiled bitterly. Isn't this the same test Nada Faraji started her journey with a hundred years ago? When someone challenged her to guess it in public and face mockery?

Extra points for failing a historical reference.

"I don't know. Cross?" she said, shrugging helplessly.

"Keep guessing," Augustina said and quickly consulted the AI, which reported nothing odd. The orange mane made her small face hard to distinguish when she wasn't looking directly at Elodie.

The AI was back with another question.

"There are four images displayed on the table, and no one in the room is looking at them. What is pictured in the third image?"

"You want me to guess again?" She looked at Augustina with doubt. The latter nodded, and Elodie started disliking the whole charade. What was the point?

"It's a tree. A big one."

Augustina looked at the image on the table and typed some kind of instruction to the AI.

"There is only one picture left now. Tell me what mood best describes the image."

Elodie thought long and hard about that one, but not because she wanted to guess it. That was impossible. She just didn't want to anger the two telepaths in front of her. There were legends out there, that they could kill people with thoughts alone. That's how a group of them killed Jomaphie Afua, the second of the Five, the envoy for the AIs.

"Hopeful," she said. "Optimistic."

Rising Dawn would never have nasty photos. Not on a paragnostic test. It wasn't in their nature.

Augustina and Dr Rusu gave each other a longer look, nodded in perfect sync, and left the room. Augustina picked up the AI link on her way out with two fingers only, as if just carrying it could dirty her. The door made a whooshing sound as it rematerialised.

Elodie was alone, and her heart pounded in confusion. Was this extra time and testing a courtesy thing because they knew she was so eager? Why didn't they look excited at the prospect that she could test positively? Advanced prognostic paragnostic test? Was it needed because they didn't find anything but really wanted to dig deep just in case? Why was there an AI link? There were only about two in the whole Institute. Elodie knew, because she used to be the sucker doing inventory for these types of hardware. So they couldn't be used for gifted tests very often.

She needed to tell someone that something odd was going on. Just in case. It was the kind of paranoia she got from Soraya's depiction of Rising Dawn. So there was really only one person to text.

[Erm, something weird is happening. They asked me to do an extra test. Is that normal?]

A reply came in a matter of seconds.

[Tell them sexual favours are off the table.]

Soraya was right. She was overreacting. It was oddly comforting to know that. The door clicked again, and Elodie closed the chat. Dr Rusu came in for a third round, now locked in with the frown. This time, he brought with him no other than Tammy Two Feathers, Rising Dawn's current president in rotation.

Tammy looked like she'd just been pulled out of a far more important meeting against her will. She had that look of senior management encountering a new problem after their day had been planned out. It was weird to see the most powerful paragnost in the world with it. She had a file open in front of her, which spilled onto the table and became part of its surface. Some of it was words and some was images.

Elodie couldn't read what it said, and she didn't want to prod, either. She let Tammy look at the file first and then speak. Etiquette.

Tammy raised her eyes at Elodie and stared at her for a minute.

Funny how extended silences weren't considered awkward in Rising Dawn.

"This must be getting a little bit annoying, I'm sure," she finally said. "We're nothing if not thorough when it comes to our testing. I hope that was made clear to you."

Tension started coming out of nowhere. Elodie noticed that both lilac and orange hues intermingled in the periphery of her sight, and there was something telling her to calm down. It wasn't helping. She didn't want to say anything that would attract even more Rising Dawn members to the room. But if someone could just tell her what was going on, that would be great.

"Let's cover our bases here," Tammy said. "You know that this is a pan-Institute event aimed at getting a broad idea of how many potential gifted we may have here, and who might be interested in joining Rising Dawn."

There had been three meetings. By now, everyone could recite this line. Of course she knew what Testing Tuesday was. But Tammy took the time. It was important to her.

"This is a quick test to confirm the broad strokes of an ability. Not a standard test most people take. We came up with it against canon to get through the volume."

She waited for Elodie to nod.

"At the same time, I want to make it clear that this is still a fully legitimate test. Its results are considered proof of ability, or inability. Can I confirm you understand that?" Tammy said and all three gifted heads peered at Elodie.

"Yes," Elodie assumed the correct answer.

"You confirm as witnesses?" Tammy said to the other two, who also nodded. The AI link, which made its way back via Tammy, gave an affirmative blink without being asked for an opinion.

"Good," Tammy said to herself. "Good. Let's talk about this."

She shared the document with Elodie, and both the images and text on the table suddenly became pristine.

The document looked like an excerpt from a medical journal. They structured it as a case study, and from what she could glance over before she was forced to focus on what Tammy zoomed in on the middle, it looked like the hypothesis they were making was that Exhibit A had the properties of Exhibit B.

The part Tammy was trying to point out was a graph that explained which parts of the brain were active during an activity and in what way. It was hard to understand much of it, and the text was full of complex jargon. Elodie caught one relatively plain phrase at the top under health recommendations - 'immediate release'.

"Let me explain what we're looking at," Tammy said. "Whenever we want to introduce a person into Rising Dawn, we need to create sufficient evidence to prove that that person is actually gifted. To do that, we generate a report that could be presented in a court of law as evidence of brain functionality that has a legal precedent of being accepted under the definition of 'gifted'. Its complexity depends on the country. Obviously, being in Madilune, the rules are strict, and we need to demonstrate clear potential. The bar here is high because it also gives you a permanent, irrevocable visa. This means that whatever you do in life, you can always come back here and be treated as a citizen with full benefits."

Permanent visas for Madilune weren't even given to those born here, and consequently a coveted status symbol. They were reserved for those who had proven their value to the city-state beyond doubt.

Tammy placed her hands on the table.

"This is the document we've generated based on your case. So far, so good? You following?"

A nod.

"The test you took just now wasn't meant to score you based on accuracy. We're far beyond the days when we measured potential ability by expecting results before augmentation. So don't worry about that," Tammy said. "When we look for potential in abilities, we look at how your brain behaves when faced with questions that you can't answer, and how it processes that query. Now if there was no attempt at an external reach, meaning that your brain would just look through your memory to see if there was an answer, we'd see that. If it tried to fabricate an answer through imagination, we'd see that too. But what yours did is the third option. It reached out for answers outside its own memory and creative core. It didn't try to remember. It didn't try to create. It reached completely outwards."

"Is that good?" Elodie asked.

"Yes. And that's a-mazing," Tammy whispered, but loud enough for all four to hear.

"Thank you?" Elodie said and suddenly felt really hot. The room was definitely getting stuffy with four tense breathers in it.

Tammy held her hands.

"Listen to me very carefully."

But Elodie had listened plenty today and could've really used a break.

"We have reason to believe that you have potential for both paragnosis and prognosis. And they only work together if they're present at a very high level."

"What?"

"The problem with this kind of ability is that we need to act quickly, before it starts hurting you," Tammy continued.

"What?"

Elodie was put off by a fervent stare that Tammy probably didn't want to share this obviously. She wrestled out of her hands.

"If this is how your brain works, then it's really not doing you any favours when it comes to making sense of reality," Tammy pointed out an image that didn't look any different from the rest. "Unless we help rewire it in a way that releases the ability correctly, you could develop cognitive difficulties or mental illness."

"Like what?" Elodie asked cautiously.

"I have your file here," Tammy said, and the file opened up to show her performance. An embarrassing affair, really. "And it shows that you tend to move to a different department as soon as more complex tasks are introduced into your workload. Do you find it hard to move beyond entry level assignments?"

Not fair. This year had been stressful. The Institute had a lot of emergencies, most of them caused by alerts for possible futures that came from Rising Dawn. Technically, her stress was Tammy's fault. She was tired, that was it. She dropped the ball, but it wasn't because she was stupid. Plus, Elodie just had the misfortune of being surrounded by workaholics and alchemists who thought work was everything. She hated that. It became her job to destroy that mentality. And it was a big one. It took away from her daily responsibilities.

"I don't think that's true. I mean, I don't know what to... do with this," Elodie said. "You can't just sit me here and tell me I'm losing my mind because I'm too gifted. I've never even had a déjà vu in my life."

Augustina breathed in to say something. Tammy's hand shot over to hers and held it down. It was a *no* to whatever the telepath was about to say. Direct future prevention. Augustina didn't lose her pleasant face. The gifted never did.

"Totally understandable. This is huge," Tammy replied and leaned back into her chair. "And if you say that you don't want to deal with any of this, we'll leave you be. I know people think we push potential members into joining. But that's not what we're about. The only reason I'd recommend releasing the ability like this would be if it were dangerous for you to leave things the way they are. And I am making that recommendation."

Tammy was a beautiful woman, one of the most perfect faces that Elodie had seen in her life, something that would require a genius artist to capture. Fleeting and ever-changing. When she looked at Elodie, she didn't just show tolerance for her existence and mild interest. She looked invested in the deal.

"Listen, Elodie," Tammy said seriously. "You understand that I am currently the only A-class paragnost in the world? And that an appearance of another one is massively huge deal? For the gifted and for this world?"

It was objectively hot inside. There was no doubt about it. And the place definitely shrunk. Everyone who ever thought they wanted to be trapped in a room with a bunch of people telling them they're great was wrong.

"I don't know. I need some time to think about this," Elodie said, as diplomatically as the impending panic attack allowed her.

"I've seen so many futures," Tammy said, and a bitterness came out in her voice for a moment, "and I've seen some of yours too. I know your past. I know you've been overlooked all your life. I do my due diligence. I am offering you a shot at the happiest future you could have."

She'd looked at her past? Elodie felt both violated and understood. The gifted had that effect.

"Well, people have different ideas of what happiness is," Elodie said.

Augustina stepped forward to chime in.

"But we've listened to your story, without you even saying it. We can help. And we want to."

"And what if I asked you to leave me alone and delete these results?" Elodie asked. The three gifted flinched in disgust.

Augustina tried to respond, but Tammy gave her another stare, and she changed her mind. Tammy turned back to answer.

"We're still obligated to tell your superior, and we'll have a right to make a case to them. To encourage you to reconsider," Tammy said seriously. "It's important that this is taken seriously."

So much about discretion.

"Which superior?"

"Seravina, firstly. She said she wanted first-hand knowledge if we make any useful discoveries."

She was done. Seravina loved the gifted. Elodie knew how much an A-class paragnost was worth. Too much to let her turn it down. She felt cold sweat make its way down her spine. She tried to hang on to the joy. It was happening. She wanted this. She got it.

But before, there were all these options. And now there was only one.

AH, YES, THE DIVE

Rising Dawn and the Particle Lab were far apart, but Elodie didn't—couldn't—stop running. She darted through the central launchpad, avoiding vehicles landing around her. The cold polymers of the Particle Lab were home, the real Institute that she knew and remembered. The research curator AI Norbi greeted her lazily and approved her passage at the entry gate. He was consistent, patient, and stable.

"Thank you," she whispered.

She stepped inside and looked up at the unreachable ceiling up above, catching natural sun rays with the cupola that was so far away it looked the size of a bead. The Particle Lab used to be the seat of the Afuan organisation for AI studies and development, until all other sciences invaded it and took it for their own, with the AI agenda becoming more forgotten every year. The AIs offered everything, asking for nothing. Not like the gifted.

After the first lobby, white tunnels opened up into all directions. She texted Soraya for help in finding the deep lab she was in, and almost immediately a red thread, visible only to her, appeared and took her through a tunnel on the left. The tunnel got narrower and steeper until it opened up into a large hall that seemed to have light coming from more directions than a rectangular structure should have. They all showed an exterior of a dreamy forest, air full of tree fluff.

Soraya was at the far end, facing the other way, behind a large working surface. The floor was littered with mechanical components. When Elodie walked in, she forcefully pulled apart a chrome cuboid, which gave out a loud screech and a shower of black sparks. She still wore the Institute-branded lab coat even though it wasn't mandatory for the day. Rules were rules. In here, it was just another working day. Elodie forgot why the tightening and pressing on her chest was about for a brief second. She took in the last normal moment. It was hard to start.

"I told you it's too weak. We need to get Reijin to redo the specs for this material," Soraya said into the air.

"*I agree. They should be able to withstand up to 350N,*" an AI voice replied, a low volume whisper from every atom in the room. That was Norbi.

"We need to replace all the relays, at least in zones M to S. Mark the trial as failed."

Soraya was putting the broken components back on the working surface when she noticed Elodie was standing by the entrance.

"What happened?" she said, closing all the windows around her immediately and began walking over the long stretch that divided them. She saw something was up. "What's wrong? What did they do?" she shouted, accelerating.

Good question.

"I swear if they touched you, I'm going to—"

Time to bring out the good news. Decisive news.

"They told me I need to join," Elodie said. There. Suddenly, her knees felt weak.

Soraya whipped out a chair and sat Elodie down on it.

"No, you don't. Rising Dawn doesn't have that authority," she replied sharply, and one of the shapes on the floor became another chair. Soraya crossed her arms. "What do they think, just because they're cutting corners and simplifying tests, they can simplify verdicts too? Typical gifted. Disgusting. Scaremongering. They have zero power over you."

"I know that, but," Elodie said, and took a nice, long breath. "I think they might."

Her mouth was dry. Words wouldn't come out. A telepath would ironically come in handy. If only to tell her what to actually think.

"How?" Soraya settled into a more empathetic posture.

"I tested positive," she said. The words left her lips, and look at that, they were real. Elodie was gifted. She was gifted.

Soraya had a bad-news look on. Seravina's right hand was always the first one told when things went wrong, and she looked exactly like that time when the Institute accidentally made the air in Egypt less breathable. Stone cold. Calculating. How to fix it.

"Yes, but that doesn't mean that you have to join, and if they said anything of the sort then they're breaking the law, which I will bring up with any authority I can." Soraya brought up a window, ready to make a very angry call. "And then I'll kick Tammy in the teeth before she sees it coming."

"Just stop right there," Elodie said. "I don't need anyone else pushing me right now. I need to think."

"You need someone who's thinking clearly, and you don't look like you want to join, not after you—"

"No. I have just received the most important news of my life," Elodie said, "and all I want is for you to help me think. Because right now, I'm not thinking. I'm panicking. I'm confused. I need you to listen. Because I'm confused."

"But—"

"I know you hate the gifted, Soraya. You have two t-shirts that say it."

"It is one shirt—" she protested.

"I just need to think."

"What did they say? Verbatim?" Soraya asked, this time calmly. That was better.

"They said that they're worried."

"Worried as in—" Soraya looked at her tensely, "the ability you have is so strong they recommend a release?"

That was weird.

"How did you know?"

Soraya huffed dismissively.

"I know them. They can only say that you need to join if they can prove that your ability is so strong that it would hurt you otherwise."

"So they're telling the truth?" she said carefully.

At first, Soraya didn't respond. She had a well-guarded face in public, but here, Elodie could recognise a grim mix of agitation and worry.

"Did they say immediate release?" she finally replied.

"I learned the phrase from them, so."

"All right, then," Soraya said and brought up a document and projected it on the table. "Let's get legal."

The tola density needed to support the AI inside the lab made it look crisp and solid, almost like real paper.

"Gifted legal issues are messy. That's why they always push for consent first. In the end, it depends how much they want you. If they do, they'll fight you all the way to prove you need to release the ability to save your health."

"Yes."

Soraya was getting it right. That's exactly what they did.

"But they can't just determine you're super gifted on the spot. They need to look at brain scans, look for potential, all that stuff. The document normally takes some time to compile," Soraya said, unconvinced at the ruling. "And even then, the threshold for the gifted to even qualify for immediate release is crazy high. Especially in Madilune."

"They said I have potential for both paragnosis and prognosis," Elodie said. It was hard to repeat the words. They didn't sound real. None of this did.

"Like an A-class paragnost? Are you serious?"

This was new. Soraya never looked at her like that. With that ounce of fear.

Elodie had the holy grail of gifts. And if there was any logic in what happened, also no way they'd let anyone go free with that kind of potential. The gifted thrived through their strength, and strength in numbers.

"I mean, yeah, that's what they told me," Elodie said. "And by the way, if this is a prank orchestrated by you to make me realise how I didn't think this through, I'll never talk to you again."

Feeble hope.

Soraya raised her hands in surrender and shook her head. "Nope. But A-class?" she repeated.

She quickly opened a new holographic window and pulled up a document protected with several passwords.

She skimmed it, highlighted a part and forwarded it to Elodie.

[If a subject with a high levelled para or prognostic ability is discovered during testing, the need for the release of ability must be communicated to them clearly. However, no coercion should be present when familiarising the subject with the data. If the subject accepts the terms of training, they must be scheduled for urgent augmentation as soon as possible and their next of kin must be informed of their consent. If the subject is not of legal age, any decisions should strictly be made by their legal guardians.

If the subject refuses training and treatment, the participating testing body has a right to inform their doctor, and the information will be placed in their medical file.]

"Did they inform you of all of this?" Soraya asked. She got up, crossed her arms and started walking around in a small circle.

"Yes." Elodie nodded after reading it again. "They said it's possible my cognitive functions are suffering because of it. They looked at my achievement record."

"Your achievement record is suffering because you spend more time drinking at the beach than you do grinding numbers in the lab. If that's what they told you, I'd doubt anything they say is true," Soraya replied, scrolling down and reading the next few pages of regulations as she continued to perambulate the lab.

"Of course. Why would someone actually give me a compliment? Or a means to do better? Why would I have any problems other than my laziness? This is so typical!" Elodie snapped.

"I think you can improve plenty," Soraya replied, "but maybe it doesn't need to involve the interference of people who follow a poorly written diary of a sixteen-year-old as their bible. Have you even read any of Nada Faraji's work? To call it primitive is an insult to picture books. You joined the Institute to deliver the Universe of Infinite Wonder. Contribute? Have your name written in history? None of that will happen if you join Rising Dawn. You will serve as one of their drones in a best-case scenario."

Just in case Elodie forgot that she was living with a fanatic, Soraya had a sermon ready.

But that was the thing. The gifted were the enemy in her world. And that's not where Elodie wanted to live.

"Stop with this whole thing. I don't need to do what you do. You take up enough space in my life, and the Institute already. And you don't even have to fight for it. Things fall in your lap. Seravina practically adopted you! You don't know what it's like to have nothing to give!"

Soraya stopped walking around and knelt next to Elodie slowly, as if this was the conscious alternative to aggression.

"Bad timing, I understand, but you crossed the line. Let me explain something to you, so that we never have to have this conversation again," she said coldly. She entered a state Elodie knew well, one that emerged often in fights on topics she was particularly passionate about. The intriguing, polite façade fell off. Something raw and furious addressed her instead. "Seravina is my employer. She picked me up from a mentorship programme for runaways, a fact she puts into every speech she makes to a reluctant investor. I escaped the filth I was born into, and she found me at my most vulnerable. But I wasn't stupid. And you can't be either. I understand that this is a business arrangement. I play along. Laugh with her. Make her feel good about herself. I've been doing it for longer than I thought I'd stand it. So don't you dare. You know this."

"I didn't mean it like that, Soraya," Elodie replied. Soraya raised her hand to stop her.

"I am a walking trophy, proof of her charity. She loves me the way you love a good app. And that's normal. No one will pick you just to save you. You're a tool. I was smart and resourceful; you might be gifted. The more personally you take it, the deeper they'll get to manipulate you."

Elodie was already sorry. She sighed and waited for an opportunity to respond.

"You want to do something different? Go. Get your validation. I get it. But don't ever trust the gifted, Elodie. You don't need them to find yourself."

"Yes, I do." Elodie tried to explain. "Because nothing like that, nothing life-changing ever happened to me. You've done so much with so little. While I'm here, just in the middle of average life. Every type of extraordinary is out of my reach. And fine, it's selfish, but I still want my special. Can't I be happy even if I haven't suffered enough?"

"Rising Dawn won't give you the tools to compete with this idea you have of me, or your own imaginary failure. Work hard and believe in Ai Kondou. That will." Soraya shook her head. "But why are we even arguing? You have no more decisions to make. Welcome. You're now in Rising Dawn."

"I haven't signed anything," Elodie objected. Soraya laughed bitterly.

"You tested. That's enough. You're on their radar now. Excellent work, Elodie. I mean, A-class paragnost. They'll literally bag and gag you if you even think about saying no."

"Is there any part of you that's actually happy for me?"

"You did say something about suffering, didn't you? I think you'll have plenty of opportunities to catch up," Soraya snapped. She looked at Elodie, who began to tear up. "Okay, I'm sorry, that was too far. I'm sure everyone else will be really happy for you, and you'll have parties and everything. I just…"

Soraya leaned over to Elodie and hugged her from the side.

"I need you to support me through this," Elodie said. "And advise. That's all I need. I don't need *this*."

"I know. I'm sorry," Soraya said. "I should know better than to scare you. You have a right to decide. Just, let me be the one doubting, so that you can be the one trusting."

"You're a good friend," Elodie said.

The bottle of port and two glasses appeared in Soraya's hands, and there were no more questions, just a quiet nod and the sound of pouring.

"I'm the best friend," Soraya said, passing her an opulent glass of red. When she tasted it, it finally sank in. This was a celebration.

She was gifted. It was all coming together.

THE JOLLY AFTERMATH OF
BEING SEEN

Monday, 4 February 2363

The aftermath of Testing Tuesday had left the Sight Institute with more lasting damage than your usual bender. Out of approximately eight hundred people who were tested, only about seventy tested gifted enough to be invited into Rising Dawn, and it wasn't the people who wanted to be a part of it. Sensing a crisis, the PR department quickly released a statement that assured all who were tested that this was an "invitation, not order" sort of thing yet again, and that there were no repercussions to rejecting the offer. Test results were to be kept secret. Under public scrutiny, the Institute was obliged to stand by it.

However, Elodie didn't need to be told that for her, the situation was different. A-class paragnost. It still didn't sound right.

Elodie hadn't heard from anyone. She assumed they were trying to give her space to think and recover. Testing Tuesday's drinking got fully out of hand on Wednesday afternoon, when everyone accepted that the week was over and cancelled all meetings until Monday. Even without the drinking, the week would have been a blur. Elodie decided that she was going to take as much time as she wanted. Hours, days, even months to decide when and how deeply she was ready to get involved. Soraya was right about one thing. She needed to stay in control.

For now, she was going to stay in the PR wing and see how she felt in it with another option on the table. At least she knew what to expect. Before Testing Tuesday, she had been helping draft some sensible words about a new product release: an alchemical item that only had Dr Birkelund's seal of approval and purpose specifications available to the public. The Institute's unsung hero and head of brand Kenji Yoshida had informed all juniors who worked on the assignment that this one was going to ruffle some feathers in Europe, and the copy had to be written as innocently as possible. Elodie was good with words and more than ready to think about something else.

With all of her notes ready, she walked towards the building when a breeze threatened to mess up her impeccably placed fringe. She waved her hand elegantly and erected a strong shield made especially to protect from the elements. The wind around her stopped. This was more like it. Elodie Marchand. In control. A pep in her step.

The schedule for the day was full, and there was no slot in it for fear and doubt. Media release polishing until lunch. Lunch with Soraya and their wider circle of acquaintances, which was to be full of awful jokes about the last five days. Five! And the hangover hadn't even hit her yet.

After the afternoon lab shift, there were tentative plans for a "Hair of the Dog" party hosted weekly at one of their favourite clubs. They had a complex dress code that was a combination of clues left on the message board for the event. No one could get in without adhering to it, even Elodie, who was one of the founding members that came up with the idea to weed out the non-committed plebs.

The world didn't stop to think about Testing Tuesday's aftermath.

But Kenji Yoshida was looking rather startled to see her at the door of his office.

"Elodie," he said. "I didn't expect you."

What was there to expect?

"I'm here to polish the, erm, isotope killer copy? Or did we do that when we accidentally wandered inside the PR wing on Friday? I honestly don't remember."

Kenji frowned in response.

"No, I mean, I had to take you off my team," he replied sternly. "So there's the 'didn't expect you.'"

There was a lot of annoyance in his voice. Kenji Yoshida was an oddly direct, orderly man. He hated when others changed his arrangements, and he hated it even more when others still showed up when these arrangements got changed.

"I didn't get an update," Elodie said.

Kenji hated that too.

"Oh," he said. "I guess you'll ask me to show you why they asked me to remove you."

He forwarded her a message.

"I hate it when she does that."

[Ciao amore! Could you be a sweetheart and remove Elodie from your schedule till further notice? I'm having a catchup with her on Monday, but it's confidential. Thanks!]

"Seravina hasn't spoken to me at all," Elodie said. "W-what does this mean?"

"They're taking people in to discuss the results of Testing Tuesday," Kenji said. "I'll let you make the logical assumption."

It wasn't his place to express opinions on these matters, but if Elodie had to divine, he was pleased the news upset her. Rising Dawn was about to reap a plentiful crop of employees that had tested positive, and deplete a lot of well-staffed departments in the process. He was probably hoping she'd fight the move.

"I'm so sorry," she said, another chill making its way down her spine. "I'm going to talk to her."

She wasn't ready to face the unbreakable Seravina Giovanotti. But what else could she do? Go home?

Reluctantly, she walked down corridors to the left, finding an office door already open. There was a chair ready in the office as if someone had been expecting her. She peered in and the first thing she saw was Tammy. Then things really made sense.

"My god, look at that, she's like clockwork! Sit down, bambina. Let's chat."

The gifted knew when you were going to get to work. They knew how you'd react to their setup. They knew that Elodie would be stunned and unprepared for this. They knew she would simply enter, hands shaking, mouth dry again, and sit in the intended chair. Not just because she was summoned by the head of the Institute. But because all possible reactions she could have were already explored. The look on Tammy's face was slightly less amicable this time. She knew that Elodie was thinking of running out again. When she said hi, the door behind her closed.

Seravina was in a great mood. Her black hair was down, and she wore massive golden bulbs for earrings. She looked like a goddess inside her own temple, ready to decide on her subjects' fate.

"So Tammy here tells me that you had a nice little surprise on Tuesday. Congratulations," Seravina said. The golden baubles shook when she spoke.

"Thanks." Elodie was trying to recover from the setup. Think straight. What was her play? What was she trying to get out of this? Buy time? Make them understand that she needed space?

"Don't be afraid. I knew you'd be here even though she forgot to send you an invite," Tammy explained when Elodie refused to relax.

"I understood that," Elodie replied. "My cognitive function isn't that broken yet."

"And I understand that you have concerns about what we talked about on Tuesday." Tammy ignored the swipe. "I just want to assure you, your future is not yet determined."

She looked more worried than Elodie. It was as if her good heart was breaking at the thought of someone even considering her to be malicious.

"That's not what you said." Elodie remembered. "You literally said I'll be mentally challenged if I refuse to enter Rising Dawn. For the record."

"The only thing I offered, maybe too soon, was advice. I told you the truth. Abilities come at different levels of intensity. Some can be harmful if they're not released," Tammy replied, radiating empathy. "The choice is still yours."

"But what are my, you know, real options?" Elodie asked, twisting her fingers. Definitely not ready for bargaining this early in the morning.

"Your options," Seravina intervened, all annoyed, "are not listening to Soraya."

Tammy grimaced. It was not a nice thing to say. But the hatred between the gifted and Soraya? Definitely a two-way street. Tammy was just less obvious about it.

"It's not about—" Elodie tried.

"Don't give me that. I know her. I know all the tricks. Do you know how many times a week she asks me if there's something we can do to move Rising Dawn headquarters away from Madilune? The words she uses for them? Come on. I can only imagine the things she's been telling you."

"But are they false?" Elodie asked. "Would you let me say no and carry on with my life?"

"Yes!" Tammy said, outraged that anyone would even suggest the opposite.

"No!" Seravina objected, "because why would you? You don't want that."

Elodie wanted to say what she really thought, but it might have been too rude. Soraya made the mistake of speaking to Seravina in the same way that she was spoken to and had ended up in dire disciplinaries a few times before she learned. Seravina could be informal with you. You couldn't be informal with her.

"Listen, you took the testing because you wanted to see if you were gifted. Is that not true?" Seravina asked.

"It is," Elodie replied, looking at the floor.

"Forget about this immediate release thing. I don't care," Seravina said, ignoring some kind of protest from Tammy. "All I'm hearing right now is a damn A-class paragnost. Do you know how much that's worth? For you? For the Institute? What kind of life you'll be able to live now? Once you complete your training, you'll be invincible. Like Tammy. Do you think her skills are of no value?"

"No," Elodie replied.

To deny this would be foolish. Tammy and her teams had protected the Institute with such accuracy that no inspection had ever arrived without being thoroughly anticipated with the exact number of coffee mugs on the table. No weather phenomenon or market disaster ever touched them. The gifted were steering the world towards the Universe of Infinite Wonder. The gifted told the Institute which projects to finance based on how successful they saw them being. The gifted were making the Institute future-proof.

"Do you want to throw that life away, just because you're afraid Soraya will be offended by a little competition? Because that's what it is. And you shouldn't change your mind because of one voice that says no. Do you understand how happy we are to have found you?" Seravina said.

"I guess so," Elodie said. Seravina's words were powerful. They made the feeling from Belo Horizonte come back.

"So stop wasting your own time and get ready for augmentation. Does Wednesday work for you?" Seravina sat back victoriously.

Elodie was forwarded a timetable that made her heart sing a little. Her name was at the top of a training programme, designed with care and centred around her. There were weekly meetings where she'd just sit with a telepath and talk about how she felt about her progress. They wanted her. And they wanted her to be happy in their care. Why—*why*—was she thinking about saying no in the first place? This was the real thing.

"Yes," she heard herself say. Tammy sighed in relief.

"Good girl," Seravina said and did something that looked like she ticked off an item on the list. "Next."

DID YOU HEAR ABOUT THE NEW PARAGNOST?

Either the news spread instantly, or Elodie had been too oblivious to notice it before she left the office. She checked her socials and suddenly, half the Institute was talking about how Elodie Marchand was desperately wanted by Rising Dawn. An A-class paragnost, promised a life filled with adventure and noble battles for nothing less than the fate of humanity.

It took ten minutes to walk, slowly, to the cafeteria like Elodie did, all to digest the volume of what she had just consented to. And when she reached it, the big white gates, tall enough for three to pass on top of each other, opened outwards. It was time for elevenses, junior researchers' most loved break of the day to hang out and exchange gossip.

Elodie made a few steps inside towards the scent of coffee, when an oddity pricked her out of her steady daze. The silence.

It wasn't the whole of the cafeteria, but it made a difference. Junior researchers were usually the loudest. A hundred pairs of eyes to her right were trying hard to look like they're looking at anything but her while whispering. A rush of blood flushed over her and she couldn't move. She knew all of them. Didn't they have a life and a meal to think about?

An instinct told her that the best way to go on is to move

backwards, right where she came from. Forget the coffee. Every eye in the Institute was re-measuring her, repositioning themselves on the scale of approval. Some of the stares were outright frightened. An A-class paragnost. They didn't know what it meant, but neither did Elodie. Not really. She turned her back to them, when an arm caught her elbow. The scent of coffee intensified.

"Read your mind," Augustina said and passed her a hot cup.

Elodie still knew that people were watching. She accepted it carefully, just in case another scene was in store. She was just happy that someone had broken the silence.

"Thanks," she said quietly. It felt like being louder than that would have sounded like a church etiquette violation.

"I promise I won't do it unless it's for coffee," she said. "It's just sometimes easier to give people what they want before they ask."

"Don't spoil me too early. I'm not even in yet," Elodie replied as Augustina started walking deeper into the discomfort zone of the common cafeteria. The loud new label she'd been marked with was resounding across the hall, and now a senior member of Rising Dawn was buying her coffee. Half an hour ago, she was parking in another life.

"I'm happy for you," Augustina said. "I wanted you to know that. And that there's nothing to be afraid of. Literally. The amount of gifted we've birthed. I mean, we got you covered."

"I'm just so confused right now," Elodie said and threw an eye to the shamelessly peering assortment of colleagues. They may have been quiet now, but get a few drinks in them and she wouldn't be able to shut them up with the questions. If she was going to the party tonight, she was going to need some answers. "They scheduled the augmentation for Wednesday."

She said it now, and it was real. The rest of the world might still have been deciding on what to do with the new vision of Elodie Marchand, but she held on to her quiet excitement.

"It's good that it's fast," Augustina replied. "I would suggest you take time off. We've already got it authorised from Seravina. It's best if you're rested. The augmentation takes a lot out of you."

Comforting.

Elodie had the distinct feeling of gold invading her peripheral vision and caught Augustina looking at her all interested behind her orange mane.

"I thought you only used your gifts for coffee," she said.

"Do you want to come to Rising Dawn with me? We've recently acquired a few poems written by Nada Faraji herself, and I thought maybe you'd be interested to see them. The exhibition won't be open until the investor brief. Plus, I'll be able to take you through the augmentation without people staring. We can't talk about it in public."

"Yeah, I'd like that," Elodie said, and Augustina smiled with joy that looked out of place in a serious environment like the Institute.

They left together through the exit on the other side, when Elodie felt a knot in her stomach. She, and consequently Augustina, looked behind them. Soraya entered the cafeteria, saw them, triggered an uncomfortable glare that seemed to last a lifetime, turned around, and left. It seemed no one was going to simply get coffee that day. Elodie's heart sank entirely. She must have heard the news. It was not what they had planned.

"Do you want to—" Augustina started.

"Yes, I want to see the exhibition," Elodie replied and led the way out. Augustina was right. This was an exciting time. Elodie's time.

YOU HAD ME AT "AUGMENTATION"

Monday, 4 February 2363

Less than twelve hours later, Elodie was in a rooftop bar, watching a sunrise and trying to remember what country she was in. The music was quiet and lounge-y. There was room for talking, and lots of people came over from the Institute. It wasn't her party, but it felt like it. People were coming up to her. After the first awkward congratulations, they all poured in. They bought her drinks. They hugged her as if she'd already done something. This was good. Friends and colleagues thought this was good. Elodie was nervous, but agreeing with them was easy. It made her feel like she was making the right choice, not just because they pushed her into it. But because she was gifted. Really gifted, whatever that meant. There was no reason to avoid victory.

Just as she thought the night would go smoothly, someone unexpected showed up. Frederich Hawken, shamelessly walking around the party with a bottle of liquor. Catching her eye and coming over. This wasn't one of those days when he was too awkward to speak. Not that Elodie ever found the source of his anxiety. He was Dr Birkelund's apprentice. The sky had opened and granted him the one wish every alchemist ever wanted. And Frederich Hawken was miserable all the time. Elodie was angry too, at how he was wasting the opportunity. Angry and intrigued. It was strange to see someone who had everything he could have wanted and still seemed so disappointed. He was the one who used to listen most carefully at her displeasure at the Institute. Just listened. No unnecessary advice. When they were still friends, of course.

"Where did you get the bottle?" she asked, seeing him approach carefully with a clear, dangerous-looking, label-free liquid.

"They sell them," he replied and took a swig. The Slavic accent. Darkness and brood. It reminded her of a different era at the Institute.

"We talking again now?" she said.

Elodie felt better than ever. Would the new confidence help her tell if there was more to Frederich Hawken than a broken mess?

"It's not your fault. I don't wanna talk about it," he said. The closer he got, the more Elodie saw how impressive it was that he was still standing and talking; the bottle was half-empty. He was staring at her as if he wasn't sure how he got there.

"It's good, it's good you did this. I remember. You wanted this. It's good." He swayed and drank again.

"Thanks, I really appreciate it," Elodie replied loudly and looked around to see if anyone else who knew them both was around. She wasn't equipped to manage drunken Frederich on her own.

"But don't ever trust anyone, you hear me?" He suddenly pulled closer. "And never, ever, ever look into my research. You understand?"

His breath was so boozy that Elodie felt drunker just by being exposed. Someone pulled him away, and Elodie saw Soraya behind him hissing something about how he was embarrassing himself.

"Shut up, it's all your fault!" he shouted, while Soraya dragged him to a recliner where he collapsed and almost instantly passed out. She ripped the bottle from his hand and brought it over.

"I'm sorry, miss. Was this man bothering you?"

Soraya seemed to have recovered well from her morning moodiness.

"Too late to say no to that," Elodie said. Now it was time to keep the peace. "I'm sorry I didn't call you after the meeting. I was just getting some coffee, and the next thing I knew, everyone was in on it."

"It's fine. You don't need to apologise. As long as you're happy," Soraya said with honed neutrality and took a sip from the bottle. It was so strong she coughed and passed the bottle to Elodie.

"Let's go crazy one more time for the old days," Soraya whispered.

Elodie took the bottle. Soraya was making an effort. Why should she say no?

It was 9 a.m. The sun was up. This wasn't the same party. It wasn't even the same country. Soraya was sitting at the edge of the terrace they were on, fidgeting with a flat hematite, dividing her attention between the shrubbery and the conversation.

Elodie was there with her and six random Greeks who kept bursting into laughter. Finally, she remembered what she was about to say.

"They're just gonna take it out," Elodie said. She was all slurry and nauseous.

"Take what out?" one of the Greeks asked.

"The part that determines what's real and what's not. They can condense and isolate the function in the human brain. And then they take it out," she continued.

"What?" the same guy asked, perplexed.

"Elodie," Soraya straightened up into a posture that threatened intervention.

"What? It's my brain, I can talk about it," Elodie replied, "and you need to shut up anyway."

Soraya sat back, offended, which was a first.

"Anyway, after the procedure is done, I'll need to relearn to process reality from zero. Because the influx of paragnostic data is all around us, but this natural function stops it so we don't go crazy.

And when I'm done, I'll be able to access all the information my mind naturally tries to reach out for. To look at futures, remote places, anything. Isn't that crazy?"

The six Greeks gasped in a mixture of feelings. Soraya kept flipping her hematite, now with mesmerizing speed.

"All right, I'm leaving. I need to be at work in… two hours," she said. "Elodie, you coming?"

"No, I'm fine," Elodie said. Another round of drinks came over, and they began to distribute it.

"Elodie, I think you should wait in the feï," Soraya said again.

"I don't have to be at work until Wednesday," she replied in French.

Soraya marched over, took the drink out of Elodie's hands and poured it into the plants. She too spoke French this time.

"Do you not understand that you are currently violating the privacy of Rising Dawn's most secret procedure, which they've tried to keep under wraps for over eighty years? How do you think they'll react when they find out that their new trainee, who hasn't even been given any confidential information, has leaked the augmentation to the first bunch of idiots? Wait in the feï!"

Elodie felt wobbly, and this was really loud. She let Soraya pack her into the back of the vehicle where the ceiling started spinning. Just before she sank into sleep, she heard Soraya talk to the six Greeks. To be fair, Elodie wasn't even sure they spoke English apart from that one guy. They probably didn't understand what was going on and why this woman was shouting at them. The scene made Elodie laugh.

"The Sight Institute will know if you ever tell anyone about this. They will know who you tell, when, and maybe even before you do it. The repercussions of even thinking of this kind of betrayal will be much more severe than any reward you may think of reaping."

A good friend.

OFF WITH YOU, BE ON YOUR WAY

Wednesday, 6 February 2363

When Elodie was feeling unsure about something, she dressed up for the situation. She had that down. Looking the part was easy, and when she set off to Rising Dawn on Wednesday, she made sure she looked like she already belonged. An inevitable happiness seeped into her as she marched across the circular central reservation of the Institute, with vague shimmering footprints left in the off-white polymer. She had spent her last day off alone in the flat, watching movies and feeling sick from a hangover. A fitting end to the worst period of her life.

Soraya was due early to join in for a last pre-augmentation coffee, but she'd gotten pulled out into some kind of an emergency. Things were going down at the construction site set up at the side of the Particle Lab, and Elodie promised to let her know when she landed.

She decided to see what was going on there when she heard yelling. The closer she got to the construction site, the more chaotic it all looked. Several workers were pointing at a hole where the foundations were being laid out for the annexe. It smelled of raw nano polymer, the kind they warned them never to touch, and from what she gathered, a person was stuck inside. A moment later, Soraya climbed out of the pit with some kind of protection mask, and the construction manager started shouting at her for going in there. She ripped off the mask and pushed the tall man towards the edge.

"You put one of our entities in danger! Rule number one! Never ask them to inhabit an unstable field! You got lucky this time, but if you ever damage an AI, I'll come for you."

Pushing the man away from the hole, Soraya opened a voice projector app and marched around the site.

"Take a break everyone! Go read a safety manual!"

Elodie sighed. This was not the vibe she wanted just before the augmentation.

She turned around and walked all the way to Rising Dawn, when she received a message.

[Sorry, had to clear something up. People are incompetent. Are you still around?]

She responded that she was going to wait inside. Maybe it was best that she spent the last minutes pre-augmentation alone with herself. She closed all apps and returned to reading Nada Faraji's book. In the absence of feeling like she had a true understanding of the gifted, the kind voice spoke to her from the pages soothingly. It'd been almost a hundred years since the first of the gifted had gone through something similar. Plus, it supplied her with a mantra she'd adopted to not freak out in the process.

You're not the first one and not the last to go through this.

Augmentations were routine, and a rite of passage. She was gonna be fine.

The chapter she was reading was just getting interesting when she felt another person sitting next to her. She turned around and saw Soraya had finally made it.

"Not only did I escape, I came to find out how long before security kicks me out of this wretched, wretched place," she said, looking official in a tight dark grey anti-contamination suit. She stretched her skinny legs in front of her, picked up Nada Faraji's book, and put it back with regret.

"And here I thought Rising Dawn was your favourite hangout," Elodie replied.

"Oh no, I'm strictly here to talk to you."

Soraya looked so uncomfortable, constantly scanning for exits. It was almost endearing.

"About how much you love Rising Dawn?"

"Maybe! I certainly love how infallible they've made themselves look when their accuracy is still flawed. But in all seriousness, are you okay? If you thought about escaping, this is probably your last shot."

"This is a great conversation to have while I'm waiting for my augmentation." Elodie crossed her arms.

"Okay, fine, I'm still being selfish. I don't like the gifted. I like you. We've been through this. I'll keep a secret journal of negative thoughts and throw you a party when you're back from augmentation. Just to remind you what great friends you have outside the crazy place."

"Or maybe you can just give them a chance."

"Yes, well, no," Soraya said. "Seriously, gifted or not, you need to be careful how you handle yourself. These people are vindictive. They killed their own leader because they thought she was too soft. And they still worship her words. Talk about cognitive dissonance."

"I know how to handle myself. I'm not the one pushing people into holes," Elodie replied. She wasn't about to be lectured by someone who couldn't even keep their anger in check.

"That's my problem to deal with, well spotted. It's affecting me. I'm angry. I don't like imagining what they'll do to you."

She held Elodie's hand as she looked into the distance.

"Is that it? You don't like them? That's the whole story?" Elodie shouldn't be starting this argument right now.

"You know." Soraya paused and bit her lip. "I've always trusted you. I know you wouldn't purposely hurt me. But you know how paragnostics work. The closer you are to someone, the more about them you get to see. In your case, the future and past. And to be honest, I'm not happy for you to have that privilege. I've had some pain in my life. It gives me comfort to know that it's private. The details at least."

"I-I would never…" Elodie stuttered.

"But you might," Soraya replied. "Accidentally, while you learn at least. And what happens then?"

"I'll keep it to myself. What did you think I would do?"

"I don't know. I would like you to leave my past and future alone. And if you stumble upon something, you talk to me before anyone else. Please."

The plea was odd. Soraya was the one always in control. Now she was frightened about Elodie seeing too much of her. The giftedness was bringing them closer together, not farther apart.

"I promise," Elodie replied.

They stayed in silence.

"One more time. If you change your mind, I know a guy in Odessa who can hook you up with a new identity. You just need to keep a low profile for a few years. Tempting?" Soraya asked seriously, but she was already smiling with the corners of her lips.

"I'll be okay here," Elodie said. Confidently. "And we'll be okay."

"Fine," Soraya concluded, looking for a way to make it less cheesy. "Then let's do it. I'm excited."

It looked like it cost her a lot. Elodie wasn't ready for how much it made her happy.

"Now I have to," she said in mock annoyance. "You're basically pushing me into it."

"Get out of here." Soraya hugged her, while footsteps approached behind them.

"Whenever you're ready," Tammy said, arriving at her perfect moment.

"Now sounds good," Elodie said and left Soraya sitting on the sofa. She glanced back just before she stepped through the door and saw a face of well-guarded fear.

FROM BIRMINGHAM WITH LOVE

The augmentation procedure for Rising Dawn was the only surgical procedure performed outside of their research hospital, MediMundus. The gifted had fought long and hard to get the licenses for it to happen, as well as getting a few trustworthy doctors to perform it on their premises. On their terms. Secrecy was always a hard line, especially since augmentation was known as one of the most "non-press-friendly" procedures since the very conception of Rising Dawn. Some say even Nada Faraji was concerned how people would regard an initiation procedure that would resemble a lobotomy so closely.

Elodie tried not to think too much about it, sticking to her new mantra. Neither the first, nor the last. This was routine.

Nada Faraji wrote that suppressed abilities steered our life decisions towards circumstances for their release. They always won in the end, either through their release, or through our defeat as human beings. Elodie wasn't sure what that second part meant when she read it, but she didn't want to stick around long enough to find out what it referenced. She underlined it though, and as she walked through the marble-paved corridor, she thought about it again.

"Total defeat as human beings."

She fixed her lipstick for the final time. This was a backstage situation. She was preparing for a performance in front of the world. Today, Elodie Marchand, junior researcher. Tomorrow, Elodie Marchand. Gifted.

Tammy escorted her to an open door and a man motioned her to come through impatiently.

"See you on the other side," she said, and Elodie went in.

The doctor barely greeted her. Apart from the protocolled SI lab coat, slightly altered and shiny white, a right carefully reserved only for MediMundus staff, there wasn't much to it. Elodie got a distinct English vibe. There was something arrogantly awkward about the way he carried himself, as if it were passed on for centuries without rethinking it at all. He sealed the passage, the door disappeared, and she was alone with him in a cavernous room with precise lighting that came from the ceiling and a few unidentified sources.

It was only then that Elodie actually heard the man speak, and the moment he did so, a most disgusting British accent manifested. She didn't understand a single word of what he said, but she assumed it had something to do with sitting down on the lifted chair. A lot of the light seemed to be focused on it, so she did that. The next time he spoke she prepared herself and tuned in as if she were to listen to a language she was far less competent in.

"You'll also need to know that while the procedure is done by myself, and me alone, live paragnostic access is encouraged. Of course, only members of the Rising Dawn have access to the knowledge of what we are doing, so your privacy is protected. But knowing that there are actually gifted people sort of in the room with you seems to make a lot of people more comfortable. So there you go."

He didn't look at her as he prepped his hands by murmuring a command to some tool that made a thin layer cover his hands. Elodie took a deep breath.

"Are you?" she asked the man. She read a name tag that stated that the surgeon who was about to seriously shake up her life was called Dr Hollbrook.

"Am I what?" he replied, somewhat aggravated that he needed to look away from perfecting some part of his routine.

"Gifted. Are you gifted?"

"No," he scoffed. He went back to his preparations, but a moment later, he felt obliged to add something. "But you are. And that's what really matters, doesn't it?"

"Right. You're sure this won't hurt?" Elodie asked instead. Everyone had assured her that the procedure was nothing but painless.

"Well, as far as we know, it could be absolutely excruciating." He pushed her down on the recliner until he was happy with her position. "But nobody ever remembers it, so it doesn't matter at all whether it hurts or not, does it?"

Elodie would have liked to disagree, but then she began to wonder if there was something more to the statement and decided against opening philosophical debates on an operating table.

Dr Hollbrook finally seemed pleased with the lack of words, and took a few readings, beginning with directing a few rays into her eyes.

"I'll take you through this one more time. While I talk, you'll start getting drowsy. This is normal. And I don't like counting down from ten, so just feel free to fall asleep as soon as you want to."

Elodie nodded and thought about all the paragnosts peering in right now, witnessing what they called the true birth of a gifted person. She tried to look excited and calm. If all of this went wrong, at least her loved ones would believe that she went peacefully. She supposed that's what Nada Faraji would have done.

"The first thing I'll do is locate and stabilize all the centres that normally perform functions of deciding what is considered sensory perception. As you know, I will be impeding this function in your brain. This procedure will take between three and ten hours. After this you'll be moved to the intense recovery unit where you will be waking up in approximately sixteen hours. You'll be placed in sensory deprivation to get as little input from outside as possible to help you adjust. If you're still awake, you'll remember this conversation. Your memory won't be impaired by the procedure, but it's expected that you'll be experiencing extreme disorientation. There will be a lot of people specialised in recovery after the augmentation. Remember, this is a routine procedure, and the recovery time depends solely on you. You listening? Miss Marchand?"

Elodie couldn't move her lips, and in the distance, she heard a "Good."

2363: ODYSSEY

The recovery unit for those fortunate souls who could count the augmentation as an experience they had personally experienced was located deep under the Rising Dawn headquarters. The gifted didn't like giving the impression that they had secret labs or spaces, so they hid them with extra care. Deep below an empty office there was a room that would convince anyone out hunting for secret passages and spaces that there was nothing more to Rising Dawn than vapid slogans of universal human potential and special snowflake complexes.

The person who designed the entry to the recovery chambers must have had a bitterly deep understanding of how most people viewed the organisation. They furnished it with all the things that would be expected to disappoint a truth seeker that refused to believe that Rising Dawn was a completely harmless society that aimed to empower through positive affirmations and flowery wallpapers.

The steps that led to it only revealed themselves once a person smiled at a mirror. The wall opened up to a spiral staircase where a shiny yellow butterfly provided the only light downwards. When a visitor reached it, they found themselves in a room with windows that looked into a forest shedding leaves, all bright and serene. The room also included piles of books, mostly projections of titles that could be added to a personal library upon touching their physical manifestation, but there were paper volumes here and there. All of them, truly all, were self-help books marketed to the gifted, an ever-expanding industry. An inquisitive person would probably suspect this to be a bait of some sort, but nothing they could ever do would uncover the true recovery centre for post-augmentation survivors.

Eventually, the person would give up and admit to themselves that it was likely, if not true, that the Rising Dawn's secret "augmentation" was but a pep talk or symbolic ritual, and not a surgical procedure of a seriously shady variety. The recovery from it seemed to consist of a nap in a chamber filled with supportive symbols of self-recovery and change. They would leave with serious doubts about their original theory and zero proof.

But if a gifted individual in whom a certain level of trust had been invested went into the room below, they'd stop in front of a peculiar picture of a person behind which there was a ruthless sea, held back by an invisible force.

And if the visitor was telepathic, they'd take a deep breath and connect to the person hiding beyond the wall and let themselves feel the pain this person was going through. The brainwave scanner would match the pattern and let them through. A paragnost or prognost would let themselves feel it for a moment, the terror that the invisible dam represented, and the door would open quickly, so that they wouldn't have to dive back into the first moments after an augmentation. The Rising Dawn didn't like its members to suffer more than necessary.

For Elodie, at first, it felt like a failure to sync. They told her she'd be waking up in a sensory deprivation of darkness, but Elodie began to wake up into something else, resembling the sensation of falling asleep on a beach and slowly becoming aware of imminent sunburns. Pain. Pain. Ripping through her, tearing thoughts apart. She had no mouth to scream with. A punch. And then another one. Bursts of new wounds growing inside every part that could feel and think. Time passed slowly, and then incredibly fast, measured only by the speed of new sources of pain that protruded deeper into her.

Before she could collect pieces of a thought, like "I am" or "Here" or "When", something would come tearing through her consciousness condensing, coming from directions that she couldn't understand. Slow and helpless, she simply floated. It hurt. She was still for so long, it might have been a lifetime. And then, something of a cry coming from outside perhaps, or from the augmentation training that Elodie had no way of remembering—recalling information would have taken strength she couldn't even afford to imagine. Letters clicked. Meaning happened. Something screamed inside her. The barrier!

"Build the barrier."

The word unlocked a clarity, which hurt now not as thuds, but blades. Knowing the word, the self, the memory of the instruction, Elodie felt a path forward, but there was no strength to stay alert enough to understand. The barrier dissolved as soon as it appeared.

Something had gone wrong.

The pain subsided when she stopped trying. It felt like a millennium before she had another moment of clarity that pushed her back into sharp pain. It was brief, and for a moment, she was alert. She saw what was cutting her. Like an open wound, her mind bared completely to a stream of words, images, sounds and smells, textures with no order whatsoever, each with a hundred variations that split into a hundred more, and then on, a violent stream of information poured into her and through her. She was completely powerless, unable to move or call for help. She watched, tired after the first millisecond, helpless against the bombarding flow of millions, billions of images, each demanding the same attention. It hurt as if something ceaselessly pounded on the inside of her eyelids. She didn't feel the rest of her body, or anything that could help her fight the flow, and in the enduring tiredness that weighed on her mind, she realised that this couldn't go on forever. There was an end to it, if she just let go of everything that was able to feel, and let herself be carried away, become nothing in the flow. Become nothing. It was the thought that scared her so much that she held strong for another small eternity.

And in a brief strength came the idea. Was there a way to hold the flow at bay? As the multitudes of smells and faces, textures, and songs pounded against her, she tried to imagine a shield, or a force, or just maybe an intention of not wanting to be a junction for all the information stored in the universe. She pushed back, and with will alone, a small distance appeared between herself and the ruthless current.

As the thudding stopped, she felt the exhaustion. Non-essentials shut down to rest pain free. Time passed. Intent broke.

The ceaseless thudding started all over, overwhelming the barrier, and Elodie now knew to gather the strength to overcome the widening river that threatened to drown her again.

And then she did it again.

And it broke.

And again, and again. There was no help. There was only her will to live and exist.

She lived like this without counting. She forgot about the world outside. Information had to be fought off, not invited. It hurt, so freedom from pain became the only thing she celebrated.

This was how she lived. For moments, for years, for centuries.

She made the barrier. She rested. It ripped apart.

The thudding began again.

She was at home in the flow. The barrier held. Sometimes longer.

She got used to the fight, but never the pain. Every time it overwhelmed her, it hurt like the first time.

Emotions other than fear of pain had no place in the endless battle. Not until the periods of freedom from the current lasted longer. But they were never forever.

When a longer stretch of freedom from the pain happened, she didn't expect to feel anything but relief. But the absence made her aware of how oddly long it had been since the barrier fell. She remembered what time meant outside the current. And she remembered this state called awake.

And a spark lit up, remaking her into mind nested in a body, and she opened her eyes. Just briefly. A million years passed in that current. But as soon as she woke up it was 7:14 p.m. And it was Wednesday again, whatever that meant. But the pain of holding the barrier and the fear of it collapsing were still there. Her eyes were open, this she knew, but this couldn't be it. This was not what she remembered.

All around her was just darkness and softness, but she wasn't saved. She didn't just leave the current behind. It was still there, just behind her eyelids, tucked away. It was still ready to swallow her the moment she grew weak again. And then this. Even in the darkness, there weren't words to describe it.

A small ray of light shone through a crack that quickly widened. The light was as much a shock to her system as anything else. She covered her face in a reflex a body still remembered, frightened by the feeling of touch. The physical movement felt so slow. A silhouette was appearing in the opening. The sight adjusted to the brightness quickly, but not the rest.

"Elodie, dear, it's just me. Can you hear me?" She recognized an outline of an individual, and the silky waterfall of dark hair that accompanied it, but the voice wouldn't click. Tammy was never worried like this.

Something orange flickered right behind her, and a second voice joined in.

"I can read her. Oh, no."

Oh, no—exactly. The telepath read the pain. It hurt so much. Something had gone wrong in the augmentation, and it went really wrong. This was not the world she'd left when she went under. She was slow, the mind was fast, and the two didn't sync. And it hurt. Chunks of memory started appearing and sticking together, making the current and the battles Elodie had fought just moments ago into a dreamy, unimaginable landscape that wanted to slip away.

But there was a miscalculation. There was nowhere to slip. The current was there now, it took space, it took root inside of her. She was a collection of pieces with bolts taken out, the mechanism broken. She could neither sleep, nor rest, nor stay away.

"Seven days," Elodie said with a groggy voice. "You left me out for seven days?"

The words felt metallic, but she needed to say them. Anger was the only thing she remembered being her own.

The norm, as Augustina explained in their preparation walkthrough, was about ten hours.

"She can talk. Thank the cosmos." Tammy spoke something into a private line and several hands prompted Elodie to sit up.

"I can't make it stop. It won't go away."

She blinked at the gathered group. She was getting weaker, and the current was pulling again. It was horrid, and they knew. They were gifted. And they threw her into it. And they wouldn't help; the hands just quietly held her. Liars.

The world was grainy, probably because she'd been sleeping for the past seven days. But blinking didn't help. It was all off. Like a newly blind person coldly sweating in horror of suspecting they'd never see again, she began to understand that it wasn't going back to what it was. Before, pristine, stable. The eyes were not the problem. The current was still at bay. But things pushed at her from the outside too. Objects that were distant seemed clear and detailed. And she knew things about them that she shouldn't. She wasn't even curious. There was no way to stop the flow of information. It crawled over to her, like she was a drain.

Tammy saw what was happening, and she came closer.

"Ambivalent, you're ambivalent. Care about nothing. You're not interested in anything," she whispered with urgency.

Elodie panicked, and the polymers in Tammy's shirt spoke terabytes of information about where each strand had been. But she learned one thing fighting the current. She could switch off. Just be. Don't think. She forced herself to retreat, she forced any interest away. And it stopped.

She couldn't cry. It would bring the information overload back. This wasn't part of the current.

But it could crush her too, sneakily. Paragnosis. The other edge of the blade.

This wasn't supposed to be like this. She was told she was going to wake up and finally feel like the person she was meant to be.

"I'm getting everyone out. They've seen her now. She's fine, let's give her space," Augustina said.

Great idea. She felt a fabric under her fingers and realised someone had swapped her clothes for a bland hospital robe, and that really was it.

"What did you do to my dress? Where is it?" she snapped. Everything in front of her eyes was still warbling and wanting to remind her of something else, and else and else. Nothing stood still. New information prickled her awareness, and a mere inch away, the barrier she had set up with her own blood, sweat, and spit was threatening to give in. Being mad about how some gifted hippy handled AI-hand woven silk, however, helped.

"We've put it away. Safely," Tammy said, and sat next to her.

Elodie realized that she'd been sleeping on some sort of dentist chair. Uncomfortably. This annoyed her. She moved up and her spine cracked. More pain.

"Talk to me, sweetie," Tammy continued, and motioned the doctor to come closer. He used a portable application to once again check her vitals, did a quick blood analysis and looked into a scan of her brain.

"Do you feel good?" he asked. Good? This was a question?

"Not at all," she said angrily. Tammy took her hand and squeezed it.

"You're good, trust me," she said. "You'll only get better from now on."

"No," Elodie replied. "It's all broken."

Uncomfortable, in pain, balancing on a razor blade between being lost in the futures and awake, with the reality trying to crawl inside her mind from every cubic inch of the room, Elodie squirmed and tried to retreat. But there was no safe space. There was no blanket to hide under. There was no machine to take off, no command to log out, nowhere to hide, no one to help. She inhaled and tasted what the voice of each of the six people who left the room had ever sounded like and the make of the windows and the type of protocol that constructed them, and all the protocols that are used for window construction, and how old the plant inside was, and how pure was the golden ring that Augustina wore, suddenly and it didn't help she wasn't interested. She twitched and Tammy held her hand tightly, but touch was the last thing she needed, and she started screaming, eyes wide open, darkness descending, pain approaching.

"Make it stop! Make it stop!"

Tammy said something to Augustina, and an unnatural golden orange glow appeared at the edges of her peripheral sight. Boom. She lost the floor beneath her feet and fell into darkness. Sleep.

THE TURNING OF THE EYE

The next time she woke up, Elodie got up by herself. Not that it made any difference to her crushed insides, hollow and replaced with a screeching horror that wanted to swallow her whole. This time, Tammy led by telling her she was assigned a guardian. Tammy deployed one of the most powerful telepaths in the business to help soothe her pain a little.

Augustina had recently ended her rotating presidency of the whole of Rising Dawn, and now they put her on standby to keep Elodie calm or something. But Elodie wouldn't calm down. Augustina was honest in her walkthrough. She said the abilities could crush you, right from within. It was a singular warning at the time. Something to spice up the excitement with a little danger. The longer she was awake, the more Elodie knew.

This thing would crush her. It was only a matter of time. There was no strength in the world that could keep it away. And if there was, Elodie didn't have it.

The recovery room still had no windows now, so the place looked positively like a dungeon. Tiredness from excessive sleep made it easier to keep the paragnostic information overload away. Silver lining.

Unlike Tammy, Augustina wasn't one for protocol. She went

straight for the hug. As insufficient as it was, a telepathic understanding resonated through her. It was unconditional. Elodie felt it. She knew her experience echoed straight through to another person in unaltered form.

"It doesn't get any better, but you have to," Augustina said.

"Or else what?" she replied.

It was a trigger. Elodie thought of a question, and instead of her fears creating an imaginary scenario, the current from inside pulled her right under.

The current cut at her, exhausted and afraid, fearing what would happen if she let go. All that was keeping her anchored was her will to return. But even that had its limits. She fought to reconstruct a barrier, and just as she did, she was pulled back into a state of awareness. She couldn't have been out for more than a second.

But it was already late at night, and Augustina wasn't with her anymore. She was sitting in a room surrounded by strangers who were perched on the soft floor, meditating. She had been sitting in an improvised lotus, typical for someone who hated yoga with a passion. She looked around in panic and saw about a dozen peaceful faces illuminated by soft candlelight. There was a stage in the front and on it, a person was reading words in a calm, placid voice. How did she get there? Why did it seem like she was awake while she was back in the current?

"The turning of the eye brings a time when its secrets give way to my infinity.

But in the storm I stand, until its flow is weak, I live in the echo,

The eye provides the antidote to blindness."

She looked around, hoping to get someone's attention, but no one broke from their murmur of the words chanted in the front. There was no obvious entry or door, but when Elodie checked into her tola network-based applications, they worked, giving her the time, place and an abundance of messages she had missed out in the last few days.

The comms weren't supposed to be working. It must have been an error. She was prohibited from interaction until she was more stable. Just a quick one then.

[You were right.]

Nothing came back. Elodie sat there, in a crowd of strangers and feared being swallowed again.

The current was inside her, waiting patiently, eating at her will to hold on. It was like it knew she wasn't strong enough. All it needed was time.

The next time she came close to conscious, she recognised the recovery unit. But darkness took over again. The current had like a claw that rushed to grab her the moment she faltered. It was impossible to stay awake for more than a few seconds.

She came back to it, in a different spot than the last one she remembered. Confusion grew into panic. Panic grew into—

The stretches of habituating in the current led to her being able to think, albeit on the side of a treacherous battle of resisting gushing information in a current that followed her from all points in the universe at once.

Disorientation was something the gifted expected. They defined it vaguely before the augmentation, with a side stare. It was mentioned as a dreamy state. Not an infinite battle. And it had a sound, a high-pitched tune that wouldn't disappear completely even when she was awake. But when she started losing ground, it gained volume. It was the first sign.

Augustina said the relationship with the current was personal, and that the interpretation was unique to each prognost.

The first time Elodie witnessed it, she was too busy to think about it. After a few times when it pulled her back, she understood just how personal it was. This was why she was afraid of it so deeply, that she had trouble explaining it even to herself.

The current told her that she was irrelevant.

The interconnected, rapid, flowing, synced, and harmonised universe rushed on. She had no power to stop it going through her, forever trying to make her disappear. To prove, finally and forever, that she had no counterweight to gain her worth in the universe. It was the deepest insult possible.

And Elodie sometimes felt like the anger she felt towards it was the only thing keeping her alive. She denied the universe this little victory. She was kicking. Irrelevant, but kicking.

Swinging between awareness and the current, in and out, Elodie managed to keep her eyes open for seconds sometimes, sometimes minutes. When she was awake, she knew what time it was. She knew when it had been a day since she last woke up, she knew when it had been minutes. Sometimes, she made it several times a day. It was just enough to try and gain clues as to why she was waking up in unexpected places, as if she were present the entire time she should be unconscious. The gifted weren't that weird. They wouldn't just carry her around.

But the current always grabbed her and pulled her back before she could speak.

Pictures were forming. Augustina was always beside her, reacting first to her awake state. She sometimes noticed the orange hues, as if something were reaching toward her to help, but if Elodie learned one thing from the experience, it was that the telepaths weren't that much of a helping hand when it came to prognostic problems. She slipped out of the realm of human interaction pretty quickly. She just wasn't in her own head—and a telepath didn't seem able to travel into the current with her. If anything, when she felt the telepathic intrusion, she felt like it accelerated her fall.

The two times she saw Tammy, it was obvious she was concerned. Instead of waking up into a gorgeous future, Elodie transformed into a messy, unresponsive wreck. Passing out, awakening, repeating the exercise.

When she woke up on Sunday, they were seated in a bright office, and she caught Tammy speaking about her in third person.

"... matter how rare it is, I'm positive. I think that's what's happening. Haven't you noticed anything?"

"She might just be adjusting. Power is pain."

Augustina hit the nail on the head.

Elodie smelled jasmine. She opened her eyes into full consciousness. Tammy was drinking tea from a fragile little cup.

"There! Now!" Tammy practically threw the tea and reached for her.

"W—what's wrong?" Elodie said.

"Stay with me! What's the last thing you remember?" Augustina asked, both verbally and telepathically. Elodie felt a different type of pain, frontal, as if something singed her awareness.

"Help," Elodie said, the high-pitched noise approaching again.

When she got pulled into the current again, she was ready for it, but it felt stranger this time. She lost track of time, carried away and defending herself from drowning. The next time she opened her eyes it was only for a blink. She couldn't tell what was happening, but she felt Augustina near her.

Down again. The next time she opened her eyes for a moment, it was days later. Elodie didn't know what time was supposed to look like, but this was wrong. More wrong. It was night. And silence. And then she fell back into the current again.

Before she could collect her thoughts, she almost crashed into a clear awake state in the recovery unit. A small laser light danced around her hands, reflecting on the metallic machinery that was gathering around her head. She even felt a new word in a sentence she was saying form in her mouth, but she couldn't for the life of her understand what she was about to say. How was she talking? Was she talking while drowning in the current? Dr Hollbrook looked at her, puzzled. He must have realised something had changed. Whatever expression she wore transformed into panic and confusion.

"I have one, I have it again," the doctor said and pulled out some kind of pop-up window that revealed a bunch of intertwining lines.

"What's happening?" Elodie breathed, and grabbed him by the pristine MediMundus robe. He turned all of his attention to her, abandoning whatever he tried to do with the screen. His eyes were that peculiar English blue that shines brighter on rainy days but otherwise never attracts attention.

"Stay with me. If you can stay in this moment with me, I can help you get rooted," he said. Augustina rushed through the door, opening a line to someone and talking on the comms. The orange invaded Elodie's visual field so much that she didn't see who was grabbing her head and shaking it as if to try to keep her awake.

"I don't understand," she said, then shouted, "I don't know what's happening!"

The distance between her and the current was reducing again, and the last thing she saw before she was pulled back into it was the excess of orange that grasped desperately to hold on to some part of her consciousness and keep her there. The current engulfed her. It was vast and silent and lonely. Fragments of information flowed all around her. She was only a minor obstacle. Not even a permanent one. She was running out of strength. Every time she woke up, she felt more tired when pulled back in. She sensed a thought forming inside her mind, an ambivalent one. One that would end her existence in the current when she couldn't go on. It hurt so much.

Now she woke up in the middle of a session with Tammy, one on one, in different clothes, in physical pain. She was on the floor, and the chair was lying on the side. Tammy got up to help but didn't help her up. Instead, she crushed a small metallic ball on her skin. Elodie felt a jolt of energy and awareness. Tammy spoke to her, fast and concise.

"Help me out, sweetheart. Stay in this moment. Don't drift away again. You need to root yourself in this moment."

"How?" Elodie asked, panicked. Two days had passed since her last waking moment. But she didn't live them. Someone else did. Her memory started syncing, but it didn't feel like her own. Someone was enjoying the lesson, the yoga, the treatment, the attention, the awakening, the recovery. She was trapped in some kind of hell she was only able to penetrate long enough to cry out and vanish again.

"Tell me the date. Every time you wake up like this, tell me the date. We'll know what's happening and guide you back. You'll be f —" and Elodie fell back into darkness, even faster than before. This time, the current grabbed her without warning, and Elodie shouted in horror as the millions upon millions of images, sounds and impressions of other senses descended on their unrelenting mission to crush her.

She only sensed how much time had passed when she was able to resist the flow for long enough to create a distance once again. She was so tired that she rested in the blissful nothingness of a quiet mind. This was the halfway between the current and being awake. She was safe here, but it was never forever.

"Fourth of March 2363!" she shouted the moment she was out again. As fate would have it, she also spat out some food she was just eating, and about fifty people looked at her. But one knew exactly what it meant. Tammy was ready and grabbed Elodie by the elbow and dosed her again.

"Lose this one, come back next round with more strength, just think of the question, and then come back again with an answer. Remember what I'm telling you, the order matters," she told Elodie, her voice so commanding that Elodie didn't question it. She let go and voluntarily retreated back into the current carefully, so that it was easy to stay afloat and go back into the state of peace, where she could gather strength. She was getting better at creating a distance between herself and the current. As long as nothing bothered her, she could keep it up for hours.

And then:

"Sixth of March 2363!" Elodie was alone, in the dark again, in a bed inside Rising Dawn, and there was no one to save her. She tried to remember what Tammy had told her. Focus on the food. Was she hungry? What was the last thing she'd eaten? And just like that, she fell out of the moment again, and woke up in a classroom with about four other people and Dr Rusu, softly lecturing.

"Seventh of March 2363!" she shouted, and Dr Rusu stopped his lecture straight away, and knelt beside her.

"What is the last thing you've eaten?" he yelled.

The question confused Elodie even more, but she felt a part of her brain work that hadn't felt active for a long time.

"Porridge. I had porridge," she said.

"What kind of porridge?" he shouted and all the other four students with her abandoned their seating to witness this.

"I…" she struggled.

"Don't leave me now, Elodie," he said.

"With bananas. And dates!" she shouted back.

"And yesterday, what did you have for dinner?" he asked quickly, and Elodie felt once again as if something moved in her head.

"Nothing. I didn't eat," she said. "Why didn't I eat?"

These last words echoed around in her skull as the darkness took hold again. Elodie tried to fight it, but it made her only slur something in response, and she witnessed a sound of a thud, which must have been her body losing control again.

"Eighth of March 2363!" she shouted again the moment she woke up and felt the time. She was strapped to that damn dentist chair, but there was Tammy, right next to her, as well as the man, and they sprang into action. She felt the same jolt of energy as if she'd been given something to help maintain her state.

"I didn't eat because I had a late lunch. Pasta. And you made me eat dessert even though I was really full. It was a cherry almond tart, and I don't regret it," she explained hastily.

"Go on. What about breakfast yesterday?"

"Tea, only tea. I had a long bad dream, and I can't eat after I had nightmares. This is why you asked me for lunch. You said there was an eighty percent chance I'd sync," Elodie said. She heard herself yelling while listing her meals, but something in the act alone made her feel as if she was finding her footing in the present moment. She began to remember everything about the last three weeks and how she was terrified of blacking out, even though it was always only for a few minutes. It was as if another self, one that was outside of time, tried to barge in. A strange horror came over her, but at the same time it was beautiful. Like two stories converging into one ending.

"Go slow. Don't panic. I need you to try and synchronise the memories. You are one. You are one person. You were merely displaced in time for a little while, and now you're here and you're fine. Do you hear me?"

Tammy held her hand. Elodie had never been so happy to see someone. She was the one who had pulled Elodie out. She was the one who thought of the food.

"I'm fine. I had porridge. I had coffee. I had pasta. I had a salad on Thursday," she said.

"Good," the man in the background added.

"What happened to me?" Elodie said and tried to sit up.

"Chronological displacement," Augustina replied.

"Romanticized in books. Extremely unpleasant in real life," added the doctor, who appeared just in time to shine that damn light at her again.

"Because of the trauma of the augmentation, a part of your consciousness became dislodged in time. It splintered, and one part kept resurfacing and overtaking the other. This happens super rarely, and the symptoms aren't obvious until you 'wake up' in the present at some point. Once we knew that this was happening, we just kept waiting for a new episode to give you instructions on what to do. You should thank Dr Hollbrook. He was remarkably perceptive for a non-gifted," Tammy said warmly.

"Is it over now?" Elodie asked and fixed her hair. She noticed her hands were shaking.

Things clicked. Elodie recalled a time period. Three weeks. Three weeks of lengthening her awareness. Clawing herself out, unaware that there was a piece of her left inside the current, one that was delayed in making it out. Three weeks of support, and counselling, and talking every day to Augustina about how to stay awake, how to get better. All of this progress clicked together like a training montage she was starring in.

Her first time going out of the recovery room. The problem with the floor. It overwhelmed her. Augustina comforting her and taking her back inside. Practising how to keep paragnostic information away, how to curb interest on one level without becoming apathetic. Tammy getting annoyed when they found out she'd used her comms (and disabling them). Trying to touch things with the intention of using them, without being overwhelmed by the story of the object. Augustina teaching her to select levels of her mental states and highlighting them inside her head for Elodie to be able to tell them apart. Splitting her mind in the parts that she needed to control, and the ones that were truly her own. Tammy telling her to take it easy and just adjust.

She was so concerned that Elodie would start putting pressure on herself to start performing too soon. Everyone was so supportive. And when they explained to her that she needed to re-sync with her lost part, they pulled together like they really cared.

This was great. This was what she came here for. She thought the only thing that happened since the augmentation was absolute suffering, but she might have been too harsh. They got it. And they were trying to help.

"This particular part is over, yes," Tammy said, "but your training will continue. All you need to do is be calm, let the episodes happen, learn from them, and you'll soon be on the other side of training."

The ringing was never truly gone. Elodie felt good about holding her distance from the current. She looked into the room, and while it glistened and invited her, she knew she had a way of combating the invading information.

But she only mastered short wakeful states. Progress was made, but it was slow. There were no records of gifted people taking this long to control the current.

"Amazing," Elodie said. "Nothing to be worried about."

TO LOVE IS TO NEGOTIATE

Tuesday, 15 March 2363

It took another week before Elodie was comfortable spending time alone, and without having to ask, Tammy appeared every time she wasn't. Elodie still hadn't left the Rising Dawn headquarters since she'd walked in for the routine procedure a month ago.

She didn't want people to see her like this. Elodie was meticulous about what she wore. In a past life. Now she took what they gave her. It was too hard to focus on anything outside of staying afloat. She was happy they'd asked her to sleep in the recovery unit. She couldn't risk someone she knew seeing the state of her.

Hands shaking, something twitching in her spine every time she tried to think of a memory. Looking weak and tired. An honest, representative look of affairs.

"You were right," was the last thing she wrote to Soraya.

Tammy had disabled the comms during the chronological displacement incident, saying the fact that they forgot to do that may have affected things and that she was absolutely forbidden from contacting anyone before they all agreed she was feeling better, like there was any risk of her trying. If someone really threw her off track—and the only people who'd be worried enough to call would—they would agitate her enough to break down her fragile barrier.

Her awake time was getting longer. She was up to ten hours a day, most of which she spent trying to get used to basic life. But when she fell in, oh boy, she fell deep. As she grew stronger, the current responded by dragging her deeper faster.

Tammy walked her through the lower levels of Rising Dawn on a Tuesday morning. Elodie did it with her every day now and could do the walk with her eyes closed. In fact, she preferred it like that. It was harder to get overwhelmed when she wasn't looking. The paragnosis was becoming a concern. When something grabbed her attention, she would lose her train of thought completely. Rather than passing out, she could stop talking mid-sentence and stare into the distance. Tammy freaked out a few times, thinking she was chronologically displaced again.

"Before I let you see Soraya, there's something I need you to know," Tammy said, without Elodie bringing it up. One step ahead of the conversation was business as usual in Rising Dawn.

"I know. I'm not ready."

Nope, she was nowhere near ready. She couldn't last a minute of their banter.

"I want to get better first. Otherwise she'll—I mean, she wasn't exactly—she'll think I made a mistake," Elodie said.

"You've made things interesting by messaging from the inside. I've been fighting with Seravina every day about who gets to see updates about your wellbeing," Tammy said.

"Who wants to know about my wellbeing?" Elodie asked.

"The first A-class paragnost after twenty years goes without underground for a month? In metaphysical circles, people are speculating that you're dead. Asking for formal proof of life. We told your family that you're fine and recovering. We couldn't share more."

"Thanks," Elodie said, still mulling over the idea that her recovery concerned strangers.

"I know exactly how much courage it took you to make your decision," Tammy continued. "We've all had to make a choice at some point to defy people who mean a lot to us. The price of our gifts is our secret and our burden. You're different now, and there will be a distance between you and your loved ones."

"And I swapped it for the luxury of turning into a complete and total mess," Elodie said, and her hands started shaking even more. She didn't want to say that. Not to Tammy, who had done nothing but help her since she woke up from that terrible sleep.

"You're not a mess, Elodie, you're just…"

"Adjusting. I know, I'm adjusting. I just need to adjust to the adjusting," she said and stopped. The window they passed projected the central pad of the Institute. The outside she had almost forgotten was real and beautiful, just like the vastness of the universe that she discovered inside and beside her. The pad had three feï slowly descending, and one hole opening in the ground where a person stood calling another feï out of the compression zone below. Elodie almost convinced herself that one of them was Soraya for sure, but as much as she wanted to spot that painfully white hair, she was nowhere to be seen.

"Has she tried to reach me?" she asked Tammy.

"Let's see," Tammy said, and a rare occurrence of annoyance appeared in her voice. "She repeatedly tried to get inside the building and attempted to organize a 'Free Elodie' protest in front of our own doors that didn't exactly help our efforts to get you out of the spotlight. And then there's the matter of physically threatening some of our own people to get access to updates."

"That sounds like her." Elodie smiled weakly. "I miss her."

"Then I have just the thing," Tammy said and stretched out her arm, which projected a little video in the space between them. It showed the posh conference room next to Seravina's office. It was only reserved for foreign diplomatic delegates or partners deemed stupid enough to be offered a bad deal wrapped in flattering. Seravina was leaning on the table, standing alongside Soraya. It looked like some heavy words had already been spoken.

"… so of course you lured her in, and now what, you accidentally killed her? Is that why people haven't seen her in a month? A month? She wasn't ready to even commit to you full time and now she's literally vanished from the face of the earth. Did you see the message she sent me? 'I was right?' Are you surprised I'm doing this?"

"Don't be dramatic. She's inside of Rising Dawn headquarters, and she's recovering. If you could stop harassing them, that would be great."

Seravina waved her hand dismissively, but what really surprised Elodie was the fact that she looked cautious not to rile Soraya up any further. The notion gave Elodie a pang of jealousy, but it felt good. It was a good old pre-augmentation feeling.

"Recovering from what? I have had three surgeries that replaced my entire respiratory system, one of which included waiting for a whole lung to grow from zero while open, and I have never been in hospital for more than two weeks! I know enough about augmentation to know that it can—and has—gone wrong in the past," Soraya continued fearlessly.

"Nothing is wrong and you're exaggerating," Seravina replied. "Now can we go back to talking about the AI librarian again? I want it to be ready in time for the investor brief."

"It might be. I'll certainly do my best," Soraya said and looked at Seravina defiantly.

"Your best?" Seravina repeated, livid. "Do I need to explain your job to you, or can you grasp it?"

"My morale isn't at its highest, and I could focus on the project a lot better knowing what's happening inside Rising Dawn," Soraya replied. Elodie almost gasped at the possibility that she would go as far as an implied threat.

"And what if you won't find out? You'll tank the AI launch, and I'll fire you. Let me teach you something very new about negotiation. I think I should be the one." Seravina leaned forward. "You can only negotiate when you have power."

Soraya pushed a file over. Only Elodie could tell how nervous she was; she only took one short breath until it all dissolved into a fearless confidence that had taken her so far already.

"The mere hope that I could persuade you to provide me with information has propelled me to create this plan for the launch. Imagine what I could do if my worries were off the table."

Seravina opened the file, a little amused.

"I'm as far from malicious as possible. I have no wish to dominate you. And I have one request. You will give me accurate and unfiltered information about Elodie's progress and wellbeing, straight from Rising Dawn. In return, I'll build you a new tola function in my free time."

Seravina smiled a little and looked out the window, thinking.

"You always do this, you always ask me to agree to your terms," she said to Soraya, "but I like it."

The clip ended, Elodie looked at Tammy, who was standing there much less impressed with the grand gesture. Elodie had only one question left.

"This is real?"

The clip was, like all longer conversations between the two, conducted in Italian. Elodie's basic understanding of the language wasn't enough to discern if the subtitles that spontaneously appeared over the audio were truthful to the original, or a hoax to get some kind of reaction from her.

"She was given access to all your medical charts. Everything since the moment you tested and the reports of what has been happening since. Anything that goes to Seravina goes to her." Tammy gently touched her back to instruct her to keep walking. "I don't think this is a good idea. She probably has the best intentions, but I'm worried about someone demanding so much so quickly," she continued.

As they walked, Elodie noticed that Tammy was actively sifting through the futures, as she'd learned to spot a slight vacancy in her eyes.

"I want her to be part of the process," Elodie replied, but it would take much more to persuade Tammy, who quietly observed the futures. "You said I would need people to integrate me back into my life, and who could do it better? You've seen that she cares enough to do anything to find out what's happening with me. That," Elodie pointed at the space where the clip played, "is why she's my best friend."

"And so effective as well," Tammy said carefully, "you'd wonder what length she would go to if she didn't agree with your training. If she wanted to influence what happened to you."

"She wouldn't do that," Elodie replied. "We worked things out. I know she supports me."

"Exactly," Tammy argued. "This is about your future, and only yours. Whoever says they support you needs to understand that you are the centre of this. You. No one else. Your success depends on you understanding that you are a valuable asset. The star of the show."

"I know that," Elodie maintained, "but that doesn't mean that I have to abandon everything else. Especially people who care."

Tammy smiled mysteriously and opened the door to go back downstairs to the common area for some tea with her protege.

"We'll see. All I see on the event horizon is a lot of Elodie and a whole lot of nothing from Soraya. Remember that."

THE WALL-POUNDING SOUND OF REUNION

Monday, 21 March 2363

Within a few days of intensively imagining Soraya standing outside with a "Free Elodie" banner, Elodie felt like she was not going to get any better prepared to face her. She decided to walk out of the building and just see when they would meet. The idea was easy. Technically, there weren't any restrictions to her movements, but Elodie felt a churning at the very thought of getting out. It wasn't that Rising Dawn didn't provide her with everything she needed, and the team of experts who was looking after her health certainly didn't hide their happiness at the fact that she wasn't far from where they could keep an eye out for her. But Elodie was more afraid of anyone making the before/after comparison. To squirm at the sight of a nervous, haunted person who used to be Elodie Marchand.

Walking around Rising Dawn was getting easier. The halls looked emptier than they really were, because the building was partitioned in a way to make you feel like you were the main character of your own story, one of the few that walked these mystic halls. The gifted liked their space and never really congregated in large numbers unless it was for business.

She could now finish a meal and a conversation and a walk and some meditation without a single pull back into the current, and she felt the warning signs when she was stretching herself thin. The high-pitched sound, like a boiling point approaching. When she was lucky, she sat down and closed her eyes, breathing slowly. When she wasn't fast enough, she collapsed.

Augustina picked up on her desire to go out. She sat her down on a warm marble windowsill in the recovery unit and made a plan to reacquaint her with the world as it now appeared—a garbled mess. And if Tammy was to believe, filled with unwanted attention. The first step involved making Elodie accept it might not happen straight away. The second was her own condition—making sure she looked better than she felt before she presented herself to the world again.

With some negotiation and studying of the optimal futures, Elodie was enrolled in a practical training group to start first thing on Monday. Augustina explained that it might be good to see she wasn't alone in her struggle and journey. Plus, it would broaden her habitat a little before she was let back into the wild.

This was all good and right. She looked forward to learning the theoretical framework of coping with giftedness. Tammy wouldn't say why she was iffy about it but made her promise that she would be taking it super easy.

There were twelve of them in the training group. The first class was held in the building adjacent to Rising Dawn HQ, which was still connected to the training centre via an underground corridor. Elodie welcomed the opportunity to leave Rising Dawn without having to walk out into the central reservation.

The small training block was a multidisciplinary building, booked by everyone from doctors to alchemists. It was one of her favourite places and not just because she was one of the nine hundred people who worked on its coding and construction. It had a homey feel. She wondered if there would be any other homeboys or girls that resulted in being pulled in via Testing Tuesday, but as she reached the door, she felt absolute relief at the fact that the faces inside were strangers. One side of the classroom walls was transparent, with a single line of marking that signified its code and current purpose. *C99 - RD Training Module 3.*

She walked in through the simple opening that had been programmed into the side and headed towards the seat somewhere at the back middle, happy she hadn't fetched clothes from home. Forget the stress of choosing the outfit that would have been just the right amount of spiritual—all the trainees were proudly sporting their Rising Dawn outfits that looked like they just walked out from a series of spa treatments.

She attracted a few glances and hoped that people here had enough manners to not get too friendly too quickly. But it wasn't that kind of room—the dozen slowly moving heads just didn't seem like they had the social capacity to look at another and compare impressions. Every one of them just seemed on their own, lost in thought, struggling to communicate with the outside. After she sat down, a few people smiled at her, but they kept their distance, even from each other. The only chatter was happening between three Spanish girls, geographical bonding over which part of Galicia they came from and which way was the quickest to the cafeteria from the building.

Elodie knew the answer to that question. She had spent hundreds of hours in that cafeteria, but she just couldn't start talking. If she got too excited, if she lost control, these strangers would see the worst of her in the first minute.

A young man next to her, who was looking through the window, turned around. "Hi."

He was a few years younger than Elodie and appropriately spaced out for the occasion. It was weird, but the way he said the word was it. He understood. He was reaching from a faraway island to another, with a flaming sign that was still hard to notice in the distance.

"I'm sorry it's my first time out of the... intense gifted zone," he said, "Jay. From Jakarta."

And Jay from Jakarta was pleasant.

"Me too," Elodie replied. "I mean, it's my first time out too."

This was the first interaction Elodie had ever had with a person who was just like her—deranged and confused, but in a self-contained way. His eyes kind of buzzed, and he didn't really feel like he was there altogether. It made her wonder if she appeared the same way to him, and others. She looked around. A bunch of beginners, in hospital clothes, out of intensive care. Still sleepwalking.

And then, outside the classroom, another group of people caught her eyes. She recognised Tammy from afar now. Her silhouette was intimately familiar as the one attached to all the wisdom, always watching from the side, calculating the futures. She was surrounded by a mixed group that had only one thing in common. They were gifted. They had that air. Elodie knew now that if there was one thing she gained in terms of power, it was knowing that the gifted were an entirely different species from the ordinary types who walked around them. When the gifted around Tammy moved and laughed, they had a softness to them. The kind that meant they've already faced their nightmares. That's what made them special. One of the men said something to Tammy, and they both briefly looked into the distance. The man opened a direct line to someone, which was only visible as a thin green line next to him that glowed weakly. Something important was happening. Tammy was in her element. It was hard not to stare. She was different. When she was with Elodie, it felt like she was tense, like she was working with something fragile, delicate.

A burden.

The tutor arrived, sporting an orange mane that couldn't belong to anyone but the kind Augustina. She grinned to the group and made herself comfortable in a chair, ignoring the speaker setup in the back. She called for the rest of the trainees to form a circle around her and said hi to a few by their names.

At first, Elodie wondered if she was the reason Augustina took this class, but it soon became obvious that she'd done this before.

She kept information in small chunks, clear and concise, simple and plain. Every couple of sentences she repeated the same thing over and over, as if she were training people who had problems with focus, or memory.

Without words she told everyone that she knew exactly what they were going through and by proxy, that it was going to be fine.

"The next step after augmentation is rehabilitation. Rehabilitation means that you will return to your previous life. You'll get grounded. You will return to your previous jobs and hopefully to your routines. You need to anchor yourself in your previous life. Anchor yourself. And then, when you're comfortable being with your own mind again, when you recognise yourself again, you can start building a relationship with the timeline or with distance. But focus on anchoring yourself. Your root belongs to one timeline, one point in space. There will be many realities, and you must hold on to the one with your root. When you're asking yourself how to get out of a tight spot, when your abilities overwhelm you, you need to think about three things. Your root, here, now. Here, now, you root. We can only truly train you when you're stable. Rehabilitation. We can only train craft once you've mastered the basics."

There was a covert whisper in the room about what exactly a root meant, and Augustina stopped talking and pointed the finger in the general direction of the murmur.

"That's a great point. What is the root reality?"

"Isn't it the one we are in now?" one of the Spanish girls asked.

"Yes, but that doesn't solve the problem of how you recognise it or find it when you're being tussled in the sea of futures, for instance," Augustina replied, as if she knew. Elodie supposed that a telepath could get close to the feeling. She wondered what they were lost in. Other people?

When Augustina spoke, she glanced at Elodie, and a whisper appeared in her head. It was cyclical. Short, and even when she looked away, Elodie heard it, even louder than the light high-pitched warnings that were always reminding her of the current.

Build upon it. Strengthen it. Learn from it. Make it better. Build upon it.

Strengthen it. Learn from it. Make it better.

"The way we," Augustina motioned to indicate all of the students in the circle, "can quickly identify the common reality is with memory. The last thing you remember from before you went in. Soon, when you're more used to diving in and out of the current space and time, you'll notice a certain attachment to it. You'll sense it. The here. The now. And that will be the lighthouse that leads you back to experiencing your root reality. Eventually, it will become routine."

Elodie had a hard time believing that.

"So what are we supposed to do in the meantime?" Jay from Jakarta bravely asked.

Augustina gave him a gentle look, but Elodie was almost derailed by something on her left. It was like a comet was approaching, and her fragile mental state that kept the paragnostic sight in check almost collapsed.

The floor shook as Seravina Giovanotti approached in some form of high heels that clicked rhythmically. Her walking was a thing of myth, of legend, of jokes really. She moved as if the ground beneath had to bow or suffer the consequences. Elodie had forgotten about the Institute. And now it was clambering towards her. The promises. Elodie felt the vibrations of the floor and turned her head around. She feared their leader had not come alone.

"... the key is to stay calm and focus on something that's special to you as a person, maybe lyrics to your favourite song," Augustina continued somewhere in the background.

Elodie couldn't understand a single word over the panic and heat roving inside of her when, almost in slow motion, she confirmed her suspicions.

A first glimpse of white hair with a silvery blue shimmer. This was the interference. She saw her moving alongside Seravina with a constant, respectful half-step delay. Soraya was built like a praying mantis, too skinny, but also most certainly too muscular for her stature and had a face that struggled to fit in with doll-like Mediterranean features. She only wore pale pastels, always making herself look more unnatural than she needed to be. She couldn't be mistaken for anyone else, even at a distance.

The two marched past the transparent side of the classroom in a hurry. Elodie wanted to see Soraya so bad, tell her everything she'd been through, get told off for not listening in the first place, and laugh at the thought that apparently this wasn't even the hard part. Soraya could make you feel like the most arduous things were easy. That's who she needed.

She froze as they passed, and Seravina was in the way, commanding her assistant's attention. Soraya was facing away from the classroom. Elodie couldn't move, and as she watched them walk past, her nervousness turned into despair. How long would it be before she could talk to her?

And then, as if she were summoned, Soraya turned around and noticed her.

The black eyes met with hers and suddenly, time stood still. She looked more shocked than Elodie. It stopped her dead in her tracks. Elodie stood up.

Augustina stopped talking. Elodie walked towards the carved-out door of the classroom. Seravina touched Soraya on the shoulder but didn't stop her either. Soraya punched the glass and shouted something like "get the f— out here", but she was also smiling, so Elodie had no idea whether she was going to get beaten up or just shouted at, but she didn't care. Not much else mattered.

"I'm so sorry," she said when they hugged, and Soraya said nothing, just hugged her tighter. Elodie didn't know when she started crying. Before this, she felt nothing but the will to survive under the crushing pressure of her new abilities, and now there was so much more, so much more to go back to.

The high-pitched sound got louder in the background. She couldn't do anything. It came too fast, too late.

As if to remind her that this wasn't her life anymore, every defence she'd built had simply broken, whooshed away like a bunch of straw, and Elodie hadn't felt the flood of images this strong since the first time. In an odd crossroad of developing abilities, however, she was able to see her own body as it shivered and convulsed on the floor, while the rest of the class began to fall, thud-thud-thud, one by one, into the same seizures. Seravina exclaimed something like "look at them go, you lost one and it pulls them all!" and she took Soraya with her, who was honestly more shaken by this than her deep knowledge of the gifted would indicate, and it almost seemed like Seravina was dragging her away.

But this time, Elodie did not face just darkness in the river of the futures; she encountered a scene. If this was it, then she read about it. One of those things she was afraid she would never be able to imagine. A remote viewing.

REMOTE CONTROL

She was in a space, and at first it was hard to determine which part of the room. It was all so deceptively real. She felt the current outside the closed space. The room was like an amalgamation of fragments that were always in the current, but her desire to see something specific pulled them together.

She was a dot in the space, free to move with a speed so fast that she could be almost everywhere at the same time. The edges of things were hazy, dreamlike, and when she stopped clenching in fear, a scene began unfolding. The space got a little less blurry, and she remembered it as one of those nooks in the Particle Lab that just invited people to sit down and talk there, by the entrance. Seravina was sitting on a shelf of some sort. Soraya was standing.

"Look! Look at what they've done to her!" Soraya snapped. It was Monday, 21st of March 2363. 9:55. Five minutes had passed since she fell.

"She's recovering from the augmentation, what did you expect?" Seravina replied tiredly, as if this were the third circle of the same conversation.

"No! Recovery from augmentation takes a week. Tops! After that, it's an—an occasional fainting, then the tying to the hub. I know how Rising Dawn works," Soraya said.

"Clearly not if you don't know recovery times vary," Seravina replied.

Soraya did a small circle, completely thrown off by the nonchalance.

"Look," she said, "she's barely awake, she looks like she's dying, and it's been longer than the longest recovery I've ever seen. Why are we not doing anything about it? Did anyone raise any questions? Did her parents call in?"

"This is not your problem, Soraya. None of the people responsible for Elodie's wellbeing are worried. It's going well. It's a big ability. It will take time to digest."

Soraya huffed in displeasure.

"You've given me all the documentation about her condition? I need to talk to these fools. They need to do something about this," she demanded.

"Let them do their thing, Soraya. I know you hate the gifted. But please. I know this is hard to hear. They know how to handle this better than you. Drop it," Seravina said with but a hint of authority.

Soraya walked to the other corner and back, deeply thinking. Seravina replied to a visible holographic message that looked urgent.

"This brings me to our next problem. Your request," she said.

"The AI trainer one?" Soraya replied. "It makes sense, no? Until you find a replacement. I can handle them."

"No, actually I don't understand why you want to be an AI trainer," Seravina said angrily. "You're wasted on that role. You should be working on the new generation of tola you promised."

"It's not waste; it's necessity. That breakthrough won't happen without AI input. Us not having a trainer is ridiculous. We should tend to the AIs to in the same way as we do to every other part of the Institute. With care, pride, and fear of missing something important. We need an AI trainer. No one wants to volunteer. I'll do it."

Seravina frowned with suspicion.

"But why? There's nothing wrong with the way things are. You know how many people work with them? I know, I pay them.

There's no need for this. And it's a lot of work. We'll hire someone or promote them."

"There has not been a proper AI 'trainer' as the position of someone who actively spends time with them in the most human way possible since Dr Kopec died. I honestly think he was the last person who actually understood the work of Jomaphie Afua," Soraya said, with added conviction.

"He was also the least popular person in the Institute," Seravina pointed out. "Surly man."

"But what he said is true," Soraya argued, and she flared up again in the fanatic way she always got when she got to share knowledge. She was an unapologetic follower of the Five. She believed in Ai Kondou. She could quote original sources. Ideologically, she was so deep, she even scared Seravina sometimes.

"The agenda of Jomaphie Afua, our great defender of cyber fauna, is the only discipline among the work of the Five Philosophers that was left completely unfinished. The gifted prophet dropped dead, Jomaphie Afua was blamed for it, murdered, and that was it. It didn't help that the public later found out Rising Dawn killed their own leader. We've had nothing but stagnation in the field of AI research since she died. It's been so long that it's accepted as the final point of AI development. People like to pretend like they get the agenda of Afua's legacy, but no one seems to understand enough to do something about it. Even though it's possibly the most urgent task we have to complete if we want to progress and reach the Universe of Infinite Wonder."

"I don't like this, Soraya." Seravina crossed her arms. "We agreed that things need to look stable and move slowly. I don't let the gifted parade their moment of clarity, and I won't let you promote AI development. People are afraid of AIs. If that fear turns to the Institute, we lose money. We lose power. And then no one makes any progress."

"Exactly," Soraya said, "which is why it will be secret. But believe me. Afua had it in her to deliver the Universe of Infinite Wonder. Her understanding of the sublime was only second to Ai Kondou. If I work on this, I might open new paths for progress that more senior experts can follow slowly. And that's stable progress. Not derivative pep talks that you can expect when forced to read a line of Nada Faraji's work. 'Follow the light', 'be yourself', open to interpretation by whoever runs Rising Dawn."

"Aha, so you admit this is about the gifted," Seravina said.

"It's about elevating a part of the Institute that I feel is neglected," Soraya protested. "The AIs roam around their own world performing tasks we ask of them because they understand that the dealings with the human race require almost zero effort and eliminate risk of conflict. We have an odd sort of truce where no one wants to touch the situation and hopes they will be dead before the machines change their mind. I find that horrifying."

"And of course, the fact that Elodie has just joined Rising Dawn doesn't impact you at all." Seravina curved her lips in amusement.

"You keep saying that, and I'm going to keep ignoring it." Soraya flailed. "Because none of this is personal. I told you exactly what I want. I'll sort out the AI, then we'll have a better chance at getting to a new level of doing science, which is exactly what the Universe of Infinite Wonder is about. With their help. Which is what both Ai Kondou and Jomaphie Afua envisioned. But of course, you can let the gifted lobby push the truth that progress should only come from giving people lobotomies, if you want."

"Soraya."

"Come on, it's my own time. I'm not hurting anyone. I am willingly offering my extra time and effort. It's not even a position of responsibility; I'm literally just debating with the AI about moral questions, and art, and psychology."

"And the restrictions?" Seravina asked. "You know that you're not allowed certain actions with the AI?"

"Nothing that could teach them how people think or access the sublime. Crystal clear. Tola hosts the AI and binds them to the only type of technology where humans have superior control over via consciousness. Anthropotomatic technology only works when a human mind is present," Soraya recited. "I'm not going to mess with anything important."

"You can't just shake things up. We cannot risk upsetting the public. Or the gifted. You know how they feel about any news of AI progress. It's a touchy subject."

"Which is why you deploy the only person you trust," Soraya said.

Elodie was pulled into the fading background before she could hear the rest. The room grew barren, collapsing into structure chipped away by the river of futures. She began retreating, panicking, trying to wake up. She wasn't ready.

Too late. The flow carried her over, and everything was saturated by the sensory flashes. She began fighting her out, knowing she was deep in it. Fresh wounds. Elodie tumbled out of a remote viewing. Wounds of victory.

Elodie woke up back inside the classroom, exhausted. The pull of the current was still strong, even though she fought it. Augustina activated her telepathic frown, and Elodie now knew she was inspecting her mind, and it felt warm and golden again.

Did you just do a remote viewing?

A voice asked from inside her head. She nodded, although she wasn't sure. Was that really it? It didn't feel as hard as the books described it. Coming back from it did.

This is absolutely brilliant. And you came back on your own!

Unfettered enthusiasm echoed through her skull, but Elodie also noticed that the rest of the class was fully awake. She was the last one to get out. As always.

Tammy will be absolutely thrilled. And you should be too! Can you continue with the class?

She nodded again. She probably couldn't, but she already looked weak in front of everyone.

Augustina continued talking even while she had a separate conversation telepathically, but changed up her speech in the meantime, and was now going on a tangent about paragnosts. She explained how they can remotely view places of their choosing all the time if they want, or set up triggers, to tune into them under certain conditions. This was a laughably impossible feat according to every trainee who was still hiding from the influx of information. Elodie hated the way it always crept up. If she let her mind slip into a slightly more inquisitive mode, she suddenly knew where the girl next to her had her hair done, what the salon smelled like, what were the stylist's kids' names, which was their favourite teacher, and so on. By the time she pulled herself back, twenty minutes of completely useless daydreaming had passed. Elodie wondered if it would be best to just sleep until she regained the will to be the great A-class paragnost she was meant to be. Or until everyone forgot that this was the expectation.

As if this was a cue, Elodie heard her name.

"... so for instance, our lovely Elodie, who will in time be a bit of a superhero, seeing through space and time, is currently having a more challenging time than all of you put together. Imagine. Those of you who are digging yourself from the flow of futures. Imagine what it would be like if you got out of it, opened your eyes and wouldn't even be able to look at the floor before you were dragged into knowledge about other rooms in the world that have floors of this particular colour. There are no safe spots for her. You think you have it rough. Maybe that will give you some perspective."

The classroom stared at her now. One of the Spanish girls from the corner passed out. An accurate reaction.

If there was ever a time when the Earth should have opened and swallowed somebody whole, this was it. Elodie was already dazed from coming back from the vision and the encounter with Soraya, and now the junior gifted were staring at her with their empty eyes and admiration. She didn't need to know what they saw when they looked at her. This was the damned cafeteria scene all over again.

Elodie, you're gifted.

Elodie, you're like, really gifted.

You can't escape it. You can't change your mind.

Does the term 'A-class paragnost' mean anything to you?

Pain. It meant pain.

Augustina felt that she was uncomfortable and dismissed the class. Elodie wasn't in the frame of mind to get up by herself. She waited until they all left. Augustina waited and dimmed the glass. This better be an apology.

"The remote viewing," Augustina said. "You don't understand how big this is."

The lack of sorry-ness was extra rude considering the telepath knew exactly what she was expecting.

"It wasn't that great," Elodie said. Augustina was being all fanatical too. She didn't like it. "Definitely not great enough to justify putting me on the spot like that."

Augustina shook her orange mane, as if struggling to understand why Elodie wasn't ecstatic.

"You do remember what Nada Faraji's objective for elevating humanity into the Universe of Infinite Wonder is, right?"

"Making the world gifted," Elodie said.

"Wrong," Augustina replied. "It is to produce gifted individuals strong enough to see the path towards it. And lead humanity through it."

"I thought she was the one who already saw the path. And that we're following it."

"She saw something. She saw that it was possible. That there is a path. And she revealed it to the most powerful prognosts she trusted, to always keep the path active. In the realm of possible. This is the objective of Rising Dawn." Augustina came closer, as if she were telling her a secret.

"Some say that we've lost the Universe of Infinite Wonder. We celebrate whenever we catch it for a split second. But those of us who are devoted know that there are always ways to get ahead. My teacher read Nada Faraji's mind. Telepaths hold the memory of what it felt like to see the path. We hope."

"That's bad news," Elodie said.

"There's a lot of bad news there, yes," she said, "but remember, Tammy saw a glimpse of the path. And it led her to put together Testing Tuesday. To find a person strong enough to uncover the path again."

No way.

"She doesn't want me to tell you these things. Because you're not ready to take the pressure. But know. There's a reason you're here. That you're this powerful. That you can go into a remote viewing just like that and come back unscathed." Augustina leaned even closer. "There are limits to how much I can read. I can't see what you saw. I'll only know if you tell me."

"I only saw Seravina talking to Soraya. It wasn't very exciting," Elodie said.

She needed time. And space to think. Every time the gifted spoke to her, they threw all these revelations. Too many, too overwhelming, and most importantly, all at the same time. She felt the claw of the current searching for an opening, an amount of stress that would cause her to lose control.

She had promised Soraya that she'd tell her if she saw anything that related to her. Their friendship was about to be tested. First touch after the augmentation. First problem.

Augustina let it rest, but Elodie had an odd feeling about their interaction. She was pushing her too hard, too quick. Tammy was right. She wasn't ready for the pressure. Her stomach was in knots when they mentioned taking a walk outside. And now they expected her to take care of humanity?

She made it back to the recovery unit. This was reality, not the whole "chosen one" fable Augustina was trying to sell her.

Elodie Marchand. So gifted she couldn't even stay awake.

———

Elodie was given the same timetable for the rest of the month. There was an exercise in routine to be learned here, and she wanted to learn it without thinking about Soraya and how she should go and meet her.

This was until Tuesday, when she realised her comms were unblocked.

[Are you angry with me?]

She wrote, and it stung her. Soraya'd said she looked like she was dying.

The message came back momentarily, but in a much more

private channel. Elodie thought she probably shouldn't have used the public Institute network.

[No, but I'm not allowed near you apparently, at least while I'm considered a "harmful influence" in your sore mind. Are you okay? Do you still remember my name? Your non-gifted little sidekick?]

A rock lifted from her chest. Of course it was all fine. This was all precaution. Tammy didn't want Soraya around, criticising everything they did to her while they were doing it.

[Am awful but also fine.]

And then Augustina looked at her and asked her to stop texting, as if this was an unspeakably vile thing to do.

[Let me see. Do I remember you? Was is Sameera? Samiya?]

[So funny. I'll work on it...Eloïse? Elenie?]

Elodie was thirsty for some normal talk.

There was one more thing. She scribbled hastily, and it hurt her head, the tola network used for comms wasn't quite used to her mind patterns anymore.

[I know about the conversation you had to take over AI training. You said to tell you if it happened.]

This was the real moment of truth. Augustina glared at her again, but Elodie just couldn't close the app. This was it. She was getting nervous. What was taking her so long? One word would do.

[Look at you, Miss Remote Viewing. All good. Don't get cocky.]

The relief. So immense. Elodie closed her comms and tried to get back to concentrating on the lecture. She decided that she wanted to get better. And get out. And prove that she could still be herself.

THE HOPEFULS

Thursday, 4 April 2363

Augustina was late for their class, and the trainees were agitated. The gifted tutors were normally punctual for the precise reasons of routine. The workbooks all said little touches like that made trainees comfortable and rooted.

After ten minutes, one person went straight into seizure. This was Alessio, the freshest from augmentation.

They didn't all start a domino effect this time, but Elodie had been feeling weird all morning.

Augustina's bushy hair barely kept up with her as she finally made her way towards them in the busy corridor. She opened the door and asked them all to be quiet and collected no matter what happened. Augustina's naturally sympathetic voice quickly turned into a tool for perfect orders. No one questioned it, not after being exposed to a stark change to the normally smiley tutor. When she closed the door, the wall was suddenly no longer transparent, and exits were no longer showing as available.

And quiet they were, in a box with no explanation or windows. They were soundproof. Nothing came in or out.

Elodie looked at Augustina for guidance, but she gave up nothing but the silent instruction to be still and quiet. This was different than the usual reach inside her mind—it felt like it had seized control, and even when Elodie tried to move a muscle, she couldn't.

She looked for a trace of consolation on any of her classmates' faces, but while about three of them had already gone straight into seizure, the rest weren't faring too well either. An indeterminable dread settled quickly, and even though they weren't explicitly told to hide, they all had the same instinct. It just didn't feel right to sit down relaxed while a conscious decision was made to conceal their location. What was going on?

Everyone but Elodie moved towards the outer wall, as far away from the glass as possible. Light dimmed, and emergency lighting, which appeared in calming blue hues above them, now turned on. It was real. Something bad was happening, and no one was telling her what it was, or what to do. Her mind raced in multiple directions, the paragnostic vision forcing fragments of strange people running through their white corridors, lost and confused. If they didn't have this odd, sickening quality about them, she'd think they were the ones being raided and running around. There was no order to their movement.

She was pulled back into the classroom when a visual disturbance frightened her. A part of the wall suddenly became transparent. A circular shape, through which a man looked inside, searching frantically. His eyes were glossy and distant, as if he were sleepwalking in this chaos. He wore a suit with something that resembled metallic gloves, around which a great amount of distortion was gathering. This is what revealed the wall as false, hiding the room they were hiding in. The man's face was covered, all apart from the eyes, which made contact with the two girls at the front, who immediately passed out and began convulsing on the floor.

"No, you can't take them," Augustina said desperately, but the door opened right next to her.

The man outside made eye contact with Elodie. The current

clawed to pull her in, and an indistinguishable whisper appeared, getting louder by the second, making her shiver in this perfectly air-conditioned unit. As she clung on, footsteps approached from behind the man, and an assembly of six security guards moved their fingers through the air, which triggered the surrounding tola. The man gasped, his skull cracked, and a stream of blood ran through the middle of his forehead. Defence apps.

As he fell, the opening he had made to look through the wall closed in, and they were alone again. The door rematerialised.

The breathing was the loudest sound in the classroom, apart from one girl, whose arm was hitting the floor while she continued to convulse.

Elodie could only focus on the sound of her own breath to overpower the high-pitched voice of the current that threatened to pull her in.

There was a tremor to the floor, and then three more, the last being so strong that even the handful of the remaining trainees that were still considered standing lost their balance. Elodie foolishly thought about whether Soraya was fine. Final straw.

The current thrashed her around like a little leaf in a current, but it was like she tasted something, something that matched the questions she asked herself before going in. And it said that Soraya was safe, with Seravina, shouting at the security to focus on defending Rising Dawn. And she let the information go when she read it. One small piece was orderly, in a sea of billions per second.

She did something useful. With her gifts. She'd answered a question.

The distance between her and the current was increasing, and she dug herself out of it. She did it. She did something.

Augustina was tending to one trainee with her typical sympathy. Tammy barged in.

"Did they take anyone?" she said fearfully and counted the trainees.

"No, nobody," Augustina whispered.

"Take?" Elodie asked. Why would someone want to take a trainee? They were the definition of useless.

Tammy didn't seem sure she wanted to answer that question.

"Technology that can harvest the sublime is impossible to replicate," she finally said. "Tola can't be studied and cracked. People who want to exploit the forces need a way to tap into it. Some believe that instead of tola, you can use brains of newly augmented people to access sublime forces. But that won't happen. I don't want you to worry about this. You are safe. There is no remotely probable future where you are ever harmed. Remember that."

There was a danger. These people were ready to kill her for the sake of what? The possibility of not needing tola? Competing with the Institute? The pettiness of it got to her. She remembered Soraya's words. "You perform a function."

Two of the trainees began to come back, and Augustina called two carers in for outside, who brought tea and reset the room to its former glory, windows and all. When the wall regained transparency, there was no trace of the man outside. Seravina walked past them, glancing inside and scanning the damage. She seemed to find them unremarkable and walked away on her highest heel Elodie had seen so far and motioned Tammy to join her. She was in for some serious questions. How did Rising Dawn not see this? They were supposed to be almost infallible.

As Tammy followed Seravina and left, Elodie wanted to know what went on in there so badly that she dared to feel for a way to follow them with her conscience. She was pushing it. She shouldn't be doing it. And yet... she did. This paragnosis thing. Not bad. Not bad at all.

It was like a minuscule window opened and she could see. Tammy and Seravina were in a dark nook, not far away. It was hard to keep looking here, but there was no protection against remote viewing in the training block.

"Look at this, are you kidding me? Intruders. Intruders, Tammy. In my Institute. What were you doing, huh? What was the whole hub doing?"

"A half an hour ago, they didn't know they were doing this. The moment they developed intent, I picked it up. They were literally landing," Tammy said calmly.

"I don't believe that." Seravina shrugged. "Someone equipped them. Some improvisers invaded us, and you completely missed it."

"There was no intent. These people are mentally unstable. Petty criminals. I checked the timeline; there were no threats up until the moment they landed. My guess is they were chancers. They roam around and randomly select targets," Tammy said.

"There were too many," Seravina said, "and your investigation better give me a clear answer. Let Augustina do her thing. Learn from it. We need to identify any weakness that enabled this. We're working on a new tola generation, and what we need is stability. No surprises."

"I'll get my team on it. We'll make it happen," Tammy assured her.

"It needs to be soon, Tammy. First you try to pitch me this whole 'I've seen the Universe of Infinite Wonder' thing and then you can't predict an attack? I'm losing trust in you. Maybe you should focus on your trainee and let Mircea take over."

Seravina didn't flinch when attacking, but neither did Tammy on the receiving end.

She looked to the side, and straight at the point from which Elodie was peering.

"She'll be ready in no time, don't you worry," she said and smiled.

OF ALL THE HOMES IN MADILUNE

The wounds of the augmentation had become dull aches and scars. The current was always there, but Elodie surprisingly got used to the constant prickling and threats of pulling her in. Even when it happened, and yes, it did, she knew what to do. Stay calm, think of your root. Don't panic. Most importantly: don't drown.

Rising Dawn had a hard rule against using gifts while still in recovery. This problem was new.

Elodie would often have seizures when she tried to use her gifts, which meant her official training still hadn't started. She voiced her frustrations to Tammy and Augustina daily. Telepathically and otherwise.

The answer was a categorical no.

Rising Dawn as a whole let go of Elodie, and at first she was happy about it. Tammy, Augustina, Dr Rusu, and other members of the board were constantly in meetings to find out what happened with the intrusion. That was the talk of every day. Elodie had messages asking if she was really killed (again), but the thing that interested her more was the narrative of who had attacked them.

Every country had criminals, but Madilunian criminals were apparently the worst thing that could happen to a scientific institution. The school message board speculated that the attack was done by followers of the often forgotten Fourth Philosopher, Green Garcia, which was absolute rubbish. If you dug through the conspiracies deeply enough, you'd hear a term—the Hopefuls—and it described people who claimed they were receiving instructions from Green Garcia daily. Elodie was running out of books to read about the gifted craft. This was a great distraction.

But when she pressed Tammy for answers on whether any of that was real, she got another categorical no.

According to her, Green Garcia was a humanist. His destructive damage was highly debatable. In the few books that referred to his work, the authors described him as a theorist who translated the cryptic words of Ai Kondou into actionable things and was consulted by the other three. Why people would follow him, let alone put themselves in danger by attacking an institution that he would have most likely approved of, was beyond Elodie.

Every scientific source available cited that Green Garcia suffered a mental breakdown in 2286, which ended his academic career. She knew that because the moment she started thinking about it, her mind forced her through thousands of pages of written data on the subject. She couldn't keep it all in her memory, of course, but had to suffer through it, regardless. Paragnostic binges were becoming an issue. As for Green Garcia, he'd apparently still tried to write and publish, but his later stuff was unreadable. A sad way to end things.

In a weird turn of events, Soraya agreed with Tammy on something. She wrote the whole Green Garcia thing off as absolute rubbish. Elodie got bored with it. Soraya was a good measure of crazy. If she wasn't worried about it, then it probably wasn't true.

Elodie was stagnating at about two seizures per day, even though she tried everything to stabilise. As if that wasn't bad enough, her paragnostic senses had grown massively since her remote viewing. Whenever she was alone, trying to study or focus, she drifted away into just gliding over the beaches of Madilune, and beyond, into the sea. Her consciousness was so fickle, the moment it didn't have to focus on socialising with other people, it was out and away. The sun went down, her body was cold, she fell out of it, starving. Another day passed. And another.

She knew her situation baffled people who had already invested so much time into getting her to where she needed to be, to more correctly, where she wasn't going. Her stagnation was unique. Elodie read about it, and judging by the vague things Tammy said, Rising Dawn had exhausted their few techniques on how to stabilise trainees, and there were none left.

She was getting tired of rummaging through the library, seeing that the topic of post-augmentation recovery was viewed as a necessary evil that passed on its own. No authors that debated the challenges of giftedness had any thoughts on it. They were all interested in things like increasing paragnostic viewing distance, or accuracy and detail in prognostic vision. Elodie didn't struggle with those. When she sustained a remote viewing, things were crystal clear. Control was the issue. It seemed impossible.

Elodie was afraid she was about to accept this new state as normal. Forever in progress.

And then Tammy called her into her office.

Wednesday, 15 May 2363

She didn't need directions. She literally knew every part of Rising Dawn, save for a few restricted corners. Tammy was leaning over her desk, looking ninety-nine percent zen, as she had been in the last few weeks. She passed over a document for Elodie to sign.

It said they released her to go back home.

"We don't have a legal basis to keep you here any longer," Tammy said.

"Is that it?"

Elodie had a knot forming in her stomach. What if this was their way of saying that she had failed them? That they were just sending away without mending all the things they broke?

Tammy reached for her hand.

"Honey, I really don't want you to go," she said solemnly.

"Then why?"

"Your optimal future dictates it. Familiarity with your former life will help you make the next step in stabilizing. It will help. This isn't me giving up on you. It's me trusting you."

The facts painted a different picture. The group she was placed in had already finished their training. They were assigned to hubs, put on projects, or returned to their departments with a little extra power over their reality. After the first few weeks, none of them even had a flinch of a seizure. Keeping it together was basics.

"You're lying," she said. That sounded way too honest. "I'm still falling apart, and no one knows why."

"I think we both know why you're falling apart, sweetie," Tammy said and stroked her hair. "You're too powerful. It takes time to carry that sort of burden. Everyone is putting too much pressure on you. Including me. You deserve a break."

Elodie knew what Soraya would have said to that.

It didn't help that a few days ago she had accidentally read an article lying open on Augustina's desk that discussed the research of gifted seizures, arguing that only a certain amount can be had before they start inflicting damage on the rest of her brain. It was a paragnostic episode she didn't want to remember. It was clear what it meant. Elodie was like a dumpster fire everyone was afraid to touch or take responsibility for. Saying it was because she was "too powerful" was a nice thing to say to Seravina, but it looked like her investment was tanking on this occasion.

She left without a word.

Tammy let her mull over it, but Elodie already felt unwelcome. She took her things, which weren't many. Rising Dawn had given her everything she needed while she was there. She'd thought she would hate it, this lack of showmanship, this clean cut from her previous life.

People could get used to anything. That was the big reveal. Even the current, the new image of the world, the constant pulls and pressures. And that it wasn't getting better.

Elodie was reluctant to go back to her flat in central Madilune. Their home AI still remembered her, but it felt like a lie. This wasn't actually the same person coming back home. It was someone else.

The sea breeze was stronger here, and there was salt in the air. It was cold inside. Soraya wasn't home, but the place was tidy. That meant she was spending too much time at work again. She turned on the lights, and all the memories rushed in. She wasn't prepared. There was so much of her in every inch of her flat that Elodie was sent into a paragnostic fit, bombarded by the memories. All the mornings, the shades of colour she selected carefully for nights out, makeup, clothes, wine and books, homeware, art. This year, last year, the year before. There was so much joy and lust for life in that person, an admiration for beauty and a thirst for laughter. So much energy. Elodie curled into her bed and smelled the covers. The memories felt like cheap echoes of someone too far to reach. Divided by a single, big line that split the before and after. Elodie shook, letting out tears for the first time.

She could never be that person again.

FROM TECHNO TAPAS TO TECHNO PANCAKES

Thursday, 16 May 2363

When Elodie woke up, there were three things to note. Smell of pancakes. Sound of techno. And the occasional "yes" when the beat dropped. It was past ten a.m. No one should have been home.

She carefully got out of bed and went for the kitchen, the source of the hallucination itself.

The music was playing at a low, crisp volume. There were pancakes on the kitchen counter, and Elodie could swear that this was the closest she had ever seen Soraya to food. She looked around as she was presented with a cup of coffee, and Soraya, pulling up a timer that counted down from thirty minutes, was acting like this was business as usual. It was late. This was her way of saying they haven't got time. Nice and quiet, like a considerate flatmate. Most importantly, without a gifted joke.

"Syrup?" she asked.

"You have got to be kidding me."

Elodie wasn't sold on the reality of the situation.

"Fine, no syrup then," she replied.

Elodie had a sip of coffee. The real thing, not the decaf the gifted insisted on. The first after months. Rising Dawn didn't like their trainees to engage in any mental stimulants. Even now, she really shouldn't. It felt good to disobey just a little. After all, Tammy just told her they needed some distance.

She opened a news site, and the first thing she saw was a headline about the Institute. A scathing op-ed about the plans to release a new generation of tola.

"It's official? They gave you a budget and everything?" she asked Soraya, who rolled her eyes.

"Guess who won't be sleeping for three months?" Soraya grabbed her own cup of coffee. "Me. Poor me."

The article said something about the new librarian AI that was just activated and how it blatantly violated all directives that forbade the production of this kind of technology for a simple archive minder. It mentioned that the Institute had found a sneaky loophole in the shape of the library that enabled them to build the world's most advanced AI, because a special law protected all knowledge archives. It would take years before they could take them to court without harming the existing libraries all over the world. This was all written before they even moved on to the main topic, which was how much they hated when the Sight Institute launched a new generation of tola. The arguments turned more personal, attacking Seravina Giovanotti herself and the individuals who were reported to be heading the research of the new wave. At the bottom, Soraya Gourrami.

"And you're listed as a proper researcher?" Elodie asked Soraya, who was waiting for her to read the article. Even when junior researchers moved mountains to deliver projects, their names never got mentioned. To have a role big enough to warrant a jab in the media was a career landmark.

Soraya lowered the volume of the music.

"I think so, yeah," she said and shrugged. Modesty? Soraya? What was this? "The breakthrough came partly from me, but I'm still technically just assisting Dr Doreti. And Dr Lian. And of course, they named Frederich the alchemical liaison, so someone will have to deal with him. But they shouldn't really put my name in as if it matters. It just cropped up a lot. I bet that's why."

She sat down.

"But enough about me. As far as I understand, Rising Dawn has weird lunch policies, so my first executive decision as the mentally intact roomie is that I've made breakfast mandatory. I heard that routine is good for people with brain damage. Is that okay?"

One insult to the gifted. This was finally normal. Soraya, asking if something was "okay", less normal. She didn't even ask for permission to buy booze on Seravina's expense account when they were working late on Fridays. And now she was asking so innocently. Stepping on eggshells around her. Making breakfast.

"Do you think I made a mistake?" Elodie asked.

"No, of course not," she said, twirling the handle of the cup. "Always coffee first. Then food."

"So we can't be serious about this yet?" Elodie replied.

"If I wasn't there telling you that the gifted suck, you'd feel much better about yourself. So ignore me. Ignore me," Soraya said with intensity.

"I deserve better than being a mental wreck. I should have listened to you. I've been up for five minutes, and it's a surprise I've not passed out yet." Elodie took another sip. The coffee was heavenly.

"Wrong," Soraya said, sitting into a soldierly posture. "You did as you wanted, and that's always the best course of action. I understand it sucks, but you're in the belly of the whale now. Punch through, or dissolve in its digestive juices. And I'm sure you can punch through. This is easy."

She flicked her hair backwards, imitating the same thing Elodie did when making a point. It made her laugh, but then she remembered how long it's been since she did something like that, and the dread settled back in. Elodie wasn't sure she could be herself again.

"Do you think something went wrong? With my augmentation?" Elodie asked her. Soraya was her last hope. She wouldn't pull punches.

"You're just doing really badly. Like, step up, no one has time for this. So what if you survived several complications and a hostile invasion?" she said, and it made Elodie laugh again. She missed the Institute humour.

"And this whole breakfast thing? It's not like your boss would ask you to keep an eye out on me so that I don't accidentally jump out the window," Elodie said.

"There's that, and the fact that a couple of amateurs decided to try and raid the Institute."

"I heard. And you're still not sold on this Hopefuls conspiracy?"

"That question was, again, asked on a public Institute network, and you really need to learn stealth," Soraya said, and blew steam off her cup. "Of course the Hopefuls are a thing."

"Aha! I knew it! Conspiracy queen. And they're out to steal my brain?" Elodie replied.

"You're joking. Someone used that as an official explanation?"

Soraya seemed more shocked by this than the existence of a cult of crazies.

"Tammy did. And Augustina didn't correct her," Elodie argued.

"Then they're either lying or they have no idea about what the Hopefuls are to the point where they're not equipped to run Rising Dawn." Soraya glanced at the time nervously. "Eat your pancakes," she said and pushed them closer.

"So it's like a gifted bogeyman story? And they're saying it to scare me into stabilising?" Elodie asked.

"If that's the case, then sure, they want your brain," Soraya teased, packing her stuff.

"You're holding out on me." Elodie pointed out.

"Can we have this conversation after you've completed your training?"

No, no. Soraya was actively avoiding this. And she wouldn't get away with it.

"Excuse me, little hypocrite. You talked your way into accessing all my medical data. You owe me," Elodie said. Soraya threw her stuff on the couch.

"The telepath will read you. They wouldn't want me talking to you about this. Let's just go to work."

"But you say that you'll tell me later, so how does that make sense?" Elodie resisted.

"Listen," Soraya said. She'd make this dramatic. She always did. "I'll tell you right now, but here's what you have to do. Try to pretend, in your head, that you're not listening to me. I'm just quiet, starting now. Don't attach any emotion to it, and after I tell you, don't think about our conversation when you're at work. The basics of telepathic deterrence."

She sat next to Elodie at the breakfast bar.

"The Hopefuls are real, but they don't want your brain. They're broken people who love a label; that's it. They're nothing but unstable, pathetic criminals with no concept of consequence. Our telepaths found nothing resembling a plan on the ones that attacked us, and I'm pretty sure they scraped them."

"Scraped?" Elodie already regretted asking it.

"Off the record telepathic intrusion. It's so deeply violating that it doesn't leave much of a person behind. 'Doesn't exist'," she said with air quotes.

"If that's all true, then why would they tell me I was in danger?" Elodie asked.

"There was a secret panic in our circles some time ago. It took off with lots of people piling on stories upon stories about how the Hopefuls were doing weird stuff to our 'hopeless world' in the name of Green Garcia. According to them, he was the only one of the Five who got it right after he went mad. You can't make this stuff up. It was classic mass hysteria. Eventually, of course, someone had to encounter a Hopeful. Then they saw how useless they were. I guess some legends lived on. Even the gifted can't resist a bit of panic. Anyway, come on, let's get ready."

Soraya got off the chair and started packing her stuff again. The tap of knowledge was closing. At least Elodie found something Soraya hated more than the gifted.

"I'm not done yet," Elodie protested. There were so many more questions. Where was all the knowledge about the Hopefuls? Why would they be associated with Green Garcia? How come her own mentor wouldn't tell her the truth?

"I'll tell you everything you want to know about the Hopefuls—when you finish your training. I'm serious. I don't want you thinking about something so dirty and annoying when you've already got things to work out."

"Not a fan of this educational approach," Elodie protested, "and where did you even get all this info?"

"I've been part of this game for a long time, and I've had to look into things that would make your eyes bleed," Soraya replied.

"Yeah, I know."

And straight away, Elodie knew that she'd said something wrong. The temperature dropped a few degrees. Soraya stopped moving or smiling.

"You know what?" she said, trying badly to keep her tone casual. "Did you see something?"

This paranoia. Just when Elodie thought it was getting better.

"That you've been at the Institute much longer than me," she replied. At the back of her head, she sensed the current of the futures, and for the first time ever, Elodie could see some of them pop up as if she had entered a search term into a database, and she saw pathways that she could follow to strong possible outcomes.

It was beautiful, but poorly timed. She felt an urge to follow them, but Elodie knew it would mean a certain loss of control. She wasn't strong enough to sustain a single vision.

"Sorry, that one's on me." Elodie heard Soraya's voice in the kitchen, which appeared farther and farther. She hoped she looked awake in front of her.

Elodie sensed a few of the pathways disappearing, and new ones appearing.

She was fighting to stay present and pushed it all away.

"I'd tell you if I saw something," Elodie said. "I know it's a big deal. So shut up," she tried to joke.

"Eat your damn pancakes," Soraya replied and opened the same article.

Elodie relaxed. Situation diffused.

Dealing with outsiders was hard going to be hard, and if that wasn't hard enough, she'd have to choose to live with the one person who went mad when any mention of giftedness came up. This was her reality. The old Elodie had it in her to bring everyone together. The new one had to do the same.

"I hope pancakes aren't the only thing you can make," she said to Soraya. "I could use some variety."

WHEN YOU GO FULL CIRCLE AND END UP IN A SPIRAL

An official announcement of a new generation of tola was a big deal. Uneducated masses believed that the agenda of the Five was just a show that the Institute put on to keep people believing that they are doing something purposeful, not just making money and spreading Madilunian soft power. Seravina wanted both, and tola was at the sweet intersection.

Tammy's goals were less clear in general, and even less so when she called Elodie to her office right after sending her home.

"You know I have an intimate relationship with the future," Tammy said. "I caught a glimpse of the true timeline that will get us to the Universe of Infinite Wonder. It's very fickle; I have to keep chasing it, and it takes a lot out of me."

That was all great, but Elodie still didn't know what she was doing there. It's not like she could help.

"Looks like I joined the gifted at the perfect time. You'll do the heavy lifting before I'm even trained."

"Don't worry, there will always be plenty to do for an A-class paragnost. What you need to focus on now is getting well," Tammy said.

"And then?"

"Then, when I can see you're comfortable enough to last a few days with no complications, I'll try to train you to do something only you and I can. There's your carrot," Tammy replied.

"Should I even ask what the stick is?" Elodie wondered.

"All righty, little miss bitter, then I won't teach you how to create full visions out of past events."

"Maybe you should teach me how to see normal future events first?" she replied. Ouch. Even she thought she sounded unnecessarily rude.

Elodie didn't want to get her hopes up by talking about the near-vision she'd had this morning. Especially since talking about it would probably get all deep in how her flatmate was a bad influence stopping her from reaching her full potential again. Or worse; break Soraya's trust just as they started making progress.

"Tell you what," Tammy said and forwarded her a schedule. "Here's what we're going to do. You will do some work in the Particle Lab. They're super short because of the new tola development."

"In the Particle Lab?"

It was the last place she wanted to go. So what, they recognised her as the biggest prospect in the history of the gifted, she vanished for months, and now she'd go right back to her old job? No. Definitely no.

"Familiarity, honey. That's the next level. I need you to be able to walk and talk to people other than myself before I train you." Tammy opened up a visible window to book their next meeting.

"No. Absolutely not. That will be so embarrassing! They know why I left. What will they say when I come back with literally nothing to show?"

It wouldn't stand. Elodie needed to fight against it. Nope. Not the Particle Lab. That's where all her friends were.

"Elodie." Tammy closed the window and looked at her with a look Elodie never wanted to see. Angry gifted looked like they were contemplating the best future outcomes of hiding your body. "You will go to the Particle Lab. You'll do any job they give you. And you'll be nice about it. And next time we meet, you'll tell me how much you like it, because you'll realise that the things I tell you to do are never things that would cause you harm or discomfort. Because I know what I'm doing. In this moment, I know what's best for you much better than you do. Is that understood?"

"Yes," Elodie said quietly.

"Come see me tomorrow at three."

Elodie got out of the office as quickly as she could. When she made it outside Rising Dawn, she started walking towards the Particle Lab. The central reservation of the Institute was much bigger than she remembered.

She texted Soraya to tell her that she needed backup. Elodie threw in a sentence about what happened and that she couldn't just walk in. She was hoping that Soraya would get the message and the urgency in it. And would make her invisible.

She stopped outside for a moment, thinking whether she should just turn around and go back, tell Tammy it was a no, accept any punishment she threw at her, and go back to reading books about the real gifted.

[Come along, I'll be your buffer.]

Phew.

Elodie entered the complex through the front entrance, and Norbi greeted her with an excited buzz. The malleable hall was full of off-white robes, and after a long time, Elodie was once again surrounded by people who weren't gifted.

Soraya came in from the right and took her under her arm. She looked like she was in a hurry.

Suddenly, everyone stopped, and even more researchers came from the incoming corridors to fill the entry hall, which grew larger as more power was directed at it.

"All right, everyone," Soraya said, and her voice carried all the way to the back.

What in the world was she doing? Elodie was so shocked, she was certain she would pass out any minute. Surprises were the worst thing to do to a gifted trainee. *Stop. Just stop.*

"How much does Rising Dawn love us? A lot. They love us a lot. They love us so much that they're willing to let your favourite Miss Marchand take a break from her super intense training and help your lazy asses. That's what I call interdisciplinary collaboration. As you can see, she's alive and ready to help. Be nice and don't ask stupid questions. Welcome back!"

About two hundred people applauded enthusiastically, and then Soraya pulled Elodie with her to a corner. A passage opened up, and they were in a smaller lab.

Only Soraya would do something like that. Make an awkward situation so public that it wasn't even possible to make it any weirder. Oddly, Elodie felt better now that it was out in the open.

"Before you bite my head off, Tammy cleared it, and I sent a memo out during the slowest walk over I've ever seen," she said.

"No, it was fine, I just—"

"We miss you, you know the admin, it's great to have you back. Temporarily," Soraya interrupted. She gave Elodie another coffee.

She really shouldn't.

"I'm ready." Elodie took a sip. Heaven.

"Lab three needs an energy usage risk assessment," Soraya said, and Seravina was approaching, waving at them both. It was just like the old days. The good part of the old days.

When she got used to it, Elodie was relieved to be in a place where everyone was too busy to talk. Her Rising Dawn duties were kept to a minimum, with only one depressing appointment per day at the HQ to monitor her progress and advise her on day-to-day problems. Progress: zero. Problems: see previous segment.

It was almost scary to see how welcome she was. Everyone in the Particle Lab was simply too busy to muster anything but joy at the sight of someone who knew what drawer things were in.

As a gifted trainee, she was only assigned to basic projects that weren't dangerous for an open mind like hers to react with less explored technology. And it was glorious. She was so overwhelmingly busy that she completely forgot her giftedness for the first few hours. She got into the flow of tasks assigned to her, and it even dulled down her paragnostic vision—she looked at items and did not see deeply into them, their stories, their origins, or the people they touched. They were just things and projects. It was like a holiday.

It took a whole day before she noticed the first little twinkle in the corner of her eye, inviting her to look at a piece of rock that was used in a perceived hardness test. And when she looked at it, it was suddenly carved out of a quarry in Romania. Close to Cluj. And Elodie saw herself being pulled again to the hole of knowing all, and she forcefully pulled herself out. And she kept on working. No one noticed.

At lunch, she took her seat next to Soraya, who was glowing. So many crazy things already happened between breakfast and lunch, and Soraya was complaining about Frederich, who refused to commit to a date for the alchemical matter specs.

"Ever since he's been put on Catalyst duty, he's gotten cocky. I got nothing out of him during our meeting. I don't have time for that. People send me to check in and get commitments. If he's going to act like this, I'll have to take him down a peg."

Elodie almost believed that nothing had ever changed. And then of course, her daily seizure swept her out of herself and into the infinity of futures.

She clawed her way back out of a whirlwind of numbers and segments of words that were repeated to her in sequence over and over again. It was even more fragmented than usually, and she assumed it was a direct consequence of the volume of information she was handling again, without being fully intellectually ready for it. But she found herself awake again on the floor, Soraya supporting her head. Her hands were bloody, and there was a healing beam directed above her eye level.

"How did she even do that?" Soraya asked someone else, and with a sigh, someone put Elodie on a stretcher.

Elodie closed her eyes, and when she opened them again, she was upright, listening to the end of the same sentence.

"... take him down a peg." Elodie looked around and quickly gathered her thoughts enough to realize that not even a second had passed. She felt herself getting pulled back into the current, but she reached towards Soraya, relying on her reflexes. She was looking at some kind of holographic message, but she spotted it and immediately grabbed Elodie by the wrist, stopping her from falling back on her head. Elodie was still pulled into the current, but her body neither fell nor bled. When she came back to her basic senses, Soraya was looking at her disapprovingly.

"I thought this wasn't supposed to happen anymore, seeing that they let you into the wilderness."

"Now we know even your knowledge has limits," Elodie snapped.

"All right, calm down." Soraya closed all her windows and focused on tending to Elodie. She brought her a glass of water, pulled her up and fixed her hair behind her ear.

Elodie drank the water.

"Should I call someone?" Soraya asked.

"They know already. They're gifted, remember?" she replied.

"So, what do you need? I mean, to make it better?"

"Just be quiet for a sec. That would help." Elodie checked her messages and realised the tasks had started piling up again.

Someone came up to them, and as they came closer, the indefinite figure turned into Dr Lian from the AI initiative. He was a tall man with an awful posture who seemed to be racing with time itself to get ahead, another one of those awkward people who spent more quality time with the AI than socialising. Two Nobels so far. Both so complex that even the person giving the award had trouble pronouncing some words in the paper titles that led to them.

"Sorry to disturb, erm, there's a black alert in sector M," he said. Soraya dropped everything and nodded to Elodie, who watched them disappear at a speed that was just a degree away from running.

At the edge of the entrance, Dr Lian stopped her and opened a type of passage that Elodie had never seen before. Space was pliable in the Institute, and those with high level access codes (and Soraya, because she always got special treatment), could create passages between most parts of the Institute. They exchanged a few words, and it almost looked like he was taking instructions from her. He followed her into the passage, which closed a moment after it swallowed them both.

Elodie thought of how odd it was, seeing Soraya once again being counted as an essential part of the Institute. There was a pang of jealousy, sure.

She finished her lunch alone and completed her tasks for the day. Outside, Augustina bumped into her, and Elodie shared how she lived the same few seconds twice. Augustina was of the opinion that this was a sign of growing prognostic ability. First, she was to feel comfortable looking a few seconds ahead, and then more. There was even a chance that she was finally stepping into a normal healing route. There were always these chances, of course. Elodie was expecting to hear the end of the healing story, not another beginning. She needed to figure something, something to get out of this funk.

Next morning, Soraya was there again with the coffee and pleasant conversation. A routine had started. Elodie went to work with Soraya, who was again snatched by Seravina, surprised that she had the audacity to take a break.

This was why she had wanted to join Rising Dawn in the first place.

Elodie was in the same position as before, with the added bonus of these daily seizures, and the general inability to use her gifts for any practical purpose. Talking to Augustina made her realise that she needed to start taking risks if she wanted to get anywhere.

Soraya did risky stuff all the time, and nothing bad ever happened to her. Elodie was still so afraid, but she recognised that there was an opportunity. At home, she could practice far enough from Rising Dawn's pressure. She wasn't supposed to, but hey. No one had any better ideas.

She started alone at night during the pre-scripted meditation practice. Checking something unambitious, something like the food or weather for the following day. And while she sometimes succeeded in pulling herself out just as she was about to be swallowed by the current, without result, she more often ended up unconscious on the floor. Soraya would pick her up late at night when she came home, and Elodie woke up in bed every morning.

And there was the smell of coffee, the techno, and both varied very little. Soraya, who varied even less, reading articles and sharing gossip about who was sleeping with whom after-hours.

Elodie was avoiding Tammy, but she had a way of finding her when she was feeling down. And every time, the only question on Elodie's mind was "how long"?

"As long as it takes you to adapt," Tammy would say. These were supposed to be supportive words.

And Elodie was horrified by them. She didn't know how to get better. Things didn't just fix themselves because she wanted them to. She needed to find a way to become the gifted prodigy they wanted her to be.

A will was born out of it.

Elodie started seizing less. She put lipstick on in the morning. She did her hair. She hoped that maybe, with time, these things would snap back into place inside her if she faked it. Her eyes weren't absent or glinty.

She didn't seem desperate or sad on the outside.

So the mirror was the only one she needed to fool. Whenever she faced her reflection, she forced herself to think, *look, this is the new, super powerful A-class paragnost. Look at that. She's great. And everyone wants to be like her.*

Sometimes she got a bit brave with it. And she said it out loud.

"And yes, actually, I am the one who delivered the Universe of Infinite Wonder."

Things were looking better. For a moment, it looked like nothing could go wrong.

SO LONG AND THANKS FOR ALL THE GLAM

There were no days off when a new product launch was close to a breakthrough. The only pressure release was the spontaneous parties that flourished in the wake of rough days and made the days after them exponentially harder. Elodie went to a few of these. She didn't drink, and she didn't like them sober.

Something had changed, and she liked it. She practised for herself, and quietly. So quietly that she didn't even tell Tammy.

She was done listening to advice about how to get "well". She just had to. Period.

Soraya was great at handling stress, and Elodie was hoping to learn from the best about how to do it. She was about to become the Institute's biggest asset; she'd have to learn to suck it up.

There was an odd one though—as Elodie painfully forced herself to try to observe separate futures, she hit a wall whenever Soraya was involved in the question.

Reading into people close to you was supposed to be easier than strangers. It didn't add up. It sucked that she couldn't just ask Tammy about it. She wanted to get fully over this adjusting stage before she asked for more.

Now it was Wednesday morning, and things seemed as uneventful as ever. Soraya took a call during their morning coffee in which she told someone blatantly not to pursue a project, because they needed to wait for the confirmations of an addendum to the new AI law. She said she'd talk to Seravina if there were issues.

"You should be careful with this stuff," Elodie said. "There's one boss at the Institute."

"My life is drenched in secrecy and carefulness," Soraya replied without elaborating. Elodie felt an itch somewhere in her other senses, but it was early, and she didn't want to get her hopes up.

"I thought you weren't supposed to give instructions on how to do their research," Elodie noted.

Soraya waved her hand dismissively.

"I know exactly what would happen if I didn't tell them. Chaos. Two weeks of delay. And they would wait for whoever was heading that research, and they would take it up to Seravina, and she'd say the same thing."

She gave Elodie her jacket.

"And if you're bent on preaching me about overstepping my limits, maybe you can tell me why I'm picking you up from the floor every night. I thought they told you to take it easy and just stabilize."

"It's my responsibility to progress and get past this phase. No one's pulled me up on it yet, so I must be doing something right."

"They should have a plan that doesn't involve just leaving you until you figure it out," Soraya replied as they stepped out onto the terrace where her feï awaited.

"You're forgetting that all of the gifted, Soraya, all of them complete their training in a month or two. I can't even work on anything but theory. I've literally run out of books to read. I can do what I want. The gifted leave me alone. If I were Tammy, I'd give up on me too. Wouldn't you?"

Soraya got in the feï first, thinking about the rhetorical provocation as if it was a true quest for advice.

"I'm not sure I should give you suggestions. You do you," she said after a while. At least Elodie could still count on her honesty.

"But if you were in my situation?" Elodie asked as the door dematerialised. Soraya gave good advice and never asked for any.

"I don't know. I feel like you're kind of in between. You're doing what they want you to do, but then you do this private rebellion. If it was me, I'd do one or the other. Either follow the charted part of the Rising Dawn or reject it completely, find out what works for you. This inbetweening. I couldn't."

Elodie frowned, looking at the Madilune panorama. Soraya took them over Shinju Bei, where the first morning raves were in full swing. The sea had large neon shapes touching the surface and diving back into its depths on repeat, following the dominating beats.

Elodie reflected. Soraya had a familiarity in her opinions, something that came only from listening, remembering, and thinking about what people said. Maybe she should have rebelled harder against Tammy. Or maybe she should have rebelled harder against the current.

Soraya dropped her off at the front of Rising Dawn, which was still inappropriately decorated as the daily quality assurance manager hadn't walked past yet. The event horizon and her schedule for the day were both uneventful. But something at the back of her head was nagging her. The itch would have to wait until night-time.

Friday, 7 June 2363

Soraya came home late again, and Elodie couldn't sleep. She was staring at the ceiling in her bed restlessly. When she heard her moving in the kitchen, Elodie got up and went to see her.

Soraya was sitting by the breakfast bar. Heavy silence. There was liquor, but that wasn't the issue. It was her.

"Are you okay?" Elodie asked.

Soraya shook her head.

This wasn't Soraya who'd had a bad day at work. That one would be starting bar fights in downtown Madilune. The mood was sombre. Elodie abandoned her plans to retreat quickly.

"You wanna talk about it?" Elodie asked and sat opposite her. At first, Soraya said nothing, and Elodie took her hand.

Soraya sighed.

"You'll find out about it anyway, sooner or later," she said.

"What?"

She had a bad feeling about this. On every level.

"There's been an accident."

The one phrase you don't want to hear. It seemed forever before Soraya continued. Elodie felt a rush of adrenaline.

"What kind of accident?" she asked.

"We were trying to test the new tola in a controlled environment," Soraya said. She rolled a tiny piece of ice on her glass until it dissolved. "We sent the team home early. They needed a break. I was the only one left with her. We were waiting for an urgent delivery from Byeolpyo."

She fiddled with the glass.

"I went out to take it. I was gone for maybe ten minutes. I inspected the goods, signed it off, got Norbi to put them in storage. When I came back, I don't know. I don't know what happened. She'd changed the settings. I don't know, it looked like some kind of stress test."

"Who was with you?" Elodie asked, suspecting the answer.

"Seravina," she replied. The name stalled them both. It couldn't be. Seravina didn't feel like the kind of person who could ever be in an accident. The universe blessed her with the best of luck. She used to say it all the time.

"I checked her vitals, I did the first aid, I called the emergency services. I did everything right, you know? They kept asking, but I did everything right. As soon as I came back. Ten minutes."

This couldn't be happening.

"They've been at it for hours, working on her in MediMundus. Nothing worked. It's like there's no more potential for life in her." Soraya took a sip again. "I don't know what to do."

"You're in shock," Elodie said. They both were. Seravina was more than a boss. As complicated as that was. Elodie felt out of place, pulled in all directions at once. So many questions raced through her. She was in danger of collapsing under the sheer weight of them. Seravina Giovanotti. Dead? What did that even mean? Since when did people just die like this, during a stress test of a new technology? What could you even say to that?

"We'll get through this," she tried.

"Why? Did you see something?" Soraya tensed again, like every time she thought Elodie was reading into her. At least that was still intact.

"And what if I did? What if I said it was all gonna be fine?"

"You'd lie," Soraya replied and reached for the bottle. She didn't sound like herself. Elodie was worried.

"Tell me something. Tell me how you feel."

Elodie was afraid that she would shut down completely. The past few months were hard on her too. And now this.

"Everything is going to shit," Soraya replied.

"Elaborate," Elodie insisted.

"It's complicated."

"I've sat through enough of your speeches, Soraya. I can handle another one."

"This won't go well," she said. "Seravina wasn't perfect. But she was a great inhibitor. She kept everyone down and in their place. If she's really gone, then... things will get crazy. I shouldn't have left her alone. I was the last person to see her alive. The telepath was all over me. They asked me things like 'do you have hidden codes that can bypass security' or if I'm involved in off-the-books projects. They're afraid that there's a plan to put me in charge in case something happened to her. Well, there isn't. There's no plan."

Elodie knew what she was implying. Seravina had no number two. She had a dictatorship. If she was really gone, who would take over?

"How come no one—"

"Knew about it? That's easy," Soraya said. "The other gifted aren't as good as you. They have limitations, and I'm sure even you'll have trouble looking into futures connected to knowledge where you don't know how much you don't know. Like alchemy. It's hard to read into things that are completely foreign to you. The more you know about a person, the easier it is to see their future. Same for knowledge. Rising Dawn didn't get the specs yet, didn't know the technology well enough to know it would malfunction. Especially if it happened completely coincidentally. That, plus the ability-skewing qualities of the Particle Lab. It's twice as hard to see inside it. The present, past or future. The gifted aren't omnipotent. And I'm grateful for that."

She raised her glass.

Elodie wasn't grateful. If there was ever a time she needed answers, it was now. "What will happen?" she asked.

Soraya took another sip of her drink.

"The gifted will take over temporarily. That will eventually become permanent. No one will complain because on the outside, you won't be able to tell the difference. I can't believe she did this."

She said it like the dying part was Seravina's fault. Maybe that was healthy. Maybe not. Elodie was far from equipped for dealing with this.

"Turns out, *you* were right all along. You were gifted far before Rising Dawn ever scouted you. You moved in just before the start of the golden age of the gifted. Hats off. Enjoy the ride."

It started again. The itching. Elodie asked all these questions, and the current was trying to give her answers. For once it was playing nice. She couldn't just lose it. And she couldn't just leave Soraya in this state. But whenever she shut her eyes, it tried to take her inside the current.

"Go to sleep, Elodie. I need to think. Don't worry, I'll go to bed in a bit. The telepathic interrogation wore me out," Soraya said, and Elodie didn't have it in her to fight it.

"Good night. Wake me up anytime if you need me," she said with as much empathy as she could muster and went into the current as soon as she sat down on her usual spot next to the bed.

The itch was like a flavour at the tip of her tongue, just strong enough that she could follow. The current still hurt her; she wasn't strong enough to reject all the images that were crashing through her. She had to move inside tighter and tighter spots to follow when she sensed something that felt ripe, close. And for a while, she travelled with the current to reach it, even faster, knowing that she was strong enough to grasp for the piece she wanted. She expected an image, a set of scenes that would show her a story or something. But when she got it, it was only a word. One word of anger and desperation that resonated through her whole being.

Jiddispjačini.

AFTERMATHEMATICS

Monday, 10 June 2363, 7 a.m.

Elodie was sitting in the posh conference room, right next to where Seravina's office was. Had been. The gravity impacted everyone at the table. It was both a repetez and a continuation of the weekend, draped in uncomfortable silence and attempts to understand the news of death that hung heavily above her and Soraya. They felt weird laughing when they watched something funny, and Elodie had a bit of guilt lingering all day after catching herself appreciating a warm meal. Seravina's death should have meant more than a stale reminder of living for the moment. She just wasn't sure what.

The gifted knew she was up to speed. Tammy added a small condolence note to the invitation for a Monday morning emergency meeting. The Institute was shut down for the weekend as a gesture of respect. The news had time to travel. Everything online was bursting with homages. She blocked it all.

The invitation was odd on its own. Elodie was invited as a participant, not a cheeky plus one. Soraya was not. Neither of them addressed it, but she must have known that she was excluded from the list of Institute leaders. There were no junior researchers or apprentices on that list. But Elodie was.

She was sitting right there next to Tammy, who waited for everyone to turn up, even Dr Birkelund, who reputedly hated early meetings. There was a disproportionate number of gifted in the room. Three. Four, if you included Elodie. Dr Rusu and Augustina sat at the far end of the egg-shaped table, making it look like the gifted were a type of bracket that herded everyone else. Elodie was imagining that one of them, or maybe both, could drill into a person's mind so deeply that they destroyed it from within. It felt unfair. They were some of the loveliest people she'd ever met.

She tried to focus on anything else. Nothing good would come out of the telepaths knowing she thought they were capable of mental murder.

The scene was set to send a clear message. They were in charge now. And Elodie was a part of them.

No one chatted like they normally did before meetings. Every corner of the room was a reminder and a memory. She was dead.

Tammy wore a perfect expression of sympathy and determination. She cleared her throat.

"Thank you for coming in so early."

She stood up, the same way Seravina liked to conduct group meetings.

"We're all devastated. Losing Seravina is, for a lot of us, much more than losing a boss. We're friends, we're colleagues. We fight together, and we give it our all. Seravina was a key piece who helped us see past our own prejudice. In that aspect, she's irreplaceable. But we've also been left without her in a time where our future depends on how we carry ourselves. We're aware that even taking the weekend off in this period has caused a delay in our launch strategy. This is not what you want to hear. You want to hear that the world has stopped and is mourning. As the president of Rising Dawn, and the one responsible for our future, I feel obliged to tell you that we must go on. A significant delay in delivering the new generation of tola will have devastating consequences to our reputation in the long run."

This was Tammy speaking, but the words sounded a lot like Seravina's. She wouldn't have cared about any of their dead bodies. She'd care about the Institute. And the new generation of tola.

"With your permission, Rising Dawn will focus all of its resources on delivering the product, and once we're out of the woods, we'll organise a proper process to appoint a new leader. Those in favour?"

A muted series of "ayes" resonated, and just like that, it was done. So far things went just as Soraya had predicted. And just like that, she was off the table, all of her privilege gone. Elodie thought about what she wanted to say to her later. "Things will get better." They certainly didn't work when she was in that situation.

"We've established that aside from a few bugs, the new tola is looking healthy. It's more about polishing than finding solutions. Do you agree, Dr Lian?"

When addressed so suddenly, Dr Lian shrunk. He didn't like to be put on the spot, always using others to present his work. Even Elodie knew that.

"Tola is an extremely complex product. Success is only achieved by trial and error, because it's limited by our understanding of the sublime. I'm not sure I understand your question," he replied.

"I'm trying to ask if the key elements of the update are ready," Tammy repeated. The leadership suited her. She didn't backpedal.

"I can't answer that question. I didn't develop this product."

The first time might have been the confusion. This time he was rude on purpose.

"You're the head of the AI operations. If you didn't develop the new tola generation, who did?"

Tammy asked, and as soon as she said it, both she and Elodie knew it was coming.

"Soraya did. You need to talk to her."

You could almost hear the sound of animosity from the gifted.

Monday, 10 June 2363, 9 a.m.

. . .

Elodie never thought she'd see the day when Tammy and Soraya were forced to sit in a room and come to an agreement. It was hard to tell which one was more averse.

The first thing Soraya did when she entered the office was point at Elodie.

"Do we need witnesses?"

She looked suspiciously at all four corners in the office. It was inside Rising Dawn after all.

"I thought she would make you more comfortable," Tammy replied.

Elodie was referred to in the third person. Brilliant. She didn't remember signing on to be the mediator. There were a few chairs around, and she settled to sit down next to an empty one opposite Tammy. She was hoping Soraya would follow before this escalated into a physical situation.

"It's fine. I'm just here for a friendly chat, right? It's not often I get called out here. Would have been nice to be invited to your earlier meeting too," Soraya said.

She looked at the heavy bookshelf that took over the whole left side of Tammy's office and turned away from it, disappointed. What did she expect? Non-gifted books? When she finally sat down, Elodie sent her a message.

[Can you please try? I'll help in any way I can.]

"This whole junior researcher obsession Seravina had," Tammy replied. "I don't support it. She gave too many privileges to people who were far from ready for it. Which is why I'm sitting here, discussing the most important product launch of the decade with you. A junior researcher. I don't want this to continue."

[I don't need your help.]

"That's very progressive. You'll remove the one perk we get for putting in most of the work. How do the futures fare on that one?"

Elodie kicked her from the side. It didn't help.

"By the way, have you established the cause of death yet?" Soraya asked.

"How is that relevant?" Tammy snapped. Soraya brought out the worst in her too.

"They said the log was wiped for the whole hour before the accident," Soraya went on. "And the AI wasn't able to tell me why. If the tola malfunctioned, I need to know as much as possible about the conditions, so I can fix a mistake. Then I launch the new tola in peace and get out of your way."

Did she just say the log was deleted? Wasn't that the kind of detail that should have come up earlier? Was Soraya implying that Seravina's death wasn't an accident?

The shrieking high-pitched tone of the current returned. Not again. Elodie shouldn't. She really shouldn't. But the current invited her, and at the risk of a seizure, she took the plunge. The feedback was instantaneous. She heard a voice, but this time the anger had more character. It was dark, and there was only a silhouette, whispering in an ear.

Jiddispjaćini.

Elodie pulled herself through the current on a high and twitched in her chair.

"... nothing that you're implying. If anyone had the motive to hurt her, it was you. I know she had you chained to her side. I've been here for the whole decade. I know she was holding you back."

Were these words really coming out of Tammy's mouth? Elodie looked at her and realised she'd been caught. Tammy noticed and glanced over curiously. But judging by how well this went, she might not be in trouble. In and out. Elodie was on a roll. And she wanted to get involved.

"Can you both just back up a second," Elodie said. "I can't believe I have to say this, but neither of you killed Seravina. Can we establish the 'you're not a murderer' level of respect and work our way up from it?"

But what did the vision mean? She couldn't tell if it was a fragment of the future or the past. Was she imagining things because she wanted to see something so badly?

Tammy took a deep breath and sat back. An adult presence was desperately needed.

"I understand your loss. And I'm sorry. I know you're not comfortable with the changes that might happen as a result."

She restarted the diplomatic route.

"Just tell me what you need, Tammy," Soraya said wearily. "I will do the work. I always do the work. That's my job. And take a look at my hours, and my results, just in case you thought my privileges were unjustified. Then think again. I'm sure you're keen to prove your own augmentation didn't leave your cognitive functions neglected."

"You're right," Tammy said, ignoring the swipe again like the absolute saint. "I know you deliver, and I know that if I tell you that we only have two weeks to get it ready, you'll make it work. Am I right?"

"Why two weeks?" she asked.

"The tola launch is a priority," Tammy said. "But the Universe of Infinite Wonder is a bigger one. The probability of reaching it is higher the sooner we launch. Two weeks is the most I can give you."

[Your people better not screw me over.]

"It's my project too. If you're thinking of sabotage with a convenient scapegoat, I suggest you think again. None of you are ready for the suffering I can inflict, is that clear?"

They'd never be friends; that was a given.

"Yes, sure," Tammy said kindly.

Elodie remembered what Tammy'd once said. Soraya was a minuscule player in the great scheme. It was listening to threats from a cricket. Elodie became aware of the overwhelming power they now had. The gifted ran the Institute. They knew all the futures. They could shape it in any way they wanted it. And take it straight to the Universe of Infinite Wonder.

"Can you guarantee constant monitoring? I send the hub a plan and you tell me which tests to take, how much time to spend on them, what not to do? All resources in?" Soraya asked.

A positive surprise. Soraya was actively asking for the gifted to get involved.

"Of course. And when we've launched, I'll make sure your

contribution translates into something more tangible. How does 'Head of Research Operations' sound?"

Oh no, this was dangerous territory. An official position was on the top of Soraya's wish list for years. Seravina came up with every excuse in the book. Youth, external pressure, bad timing. Tammy, however, was better than that. She'd learned in two hours that the only way to keep the boat floating was to give Soraya what she wanted. This was the kind of person Elodie wanted to learn from.

"Two weeks is tough," Soraya said, thinking.

"But if you say yes, we have a 72.2% chance of a successful launch. How do you like those odds?" Tammy stood up and offered her a hand.

"I like them a little bit," Soraya replied and cautiously shook it.

FLOCK TO YOUR POISON

Monday, 24 June 2363

It was a great day to launch tola. Soraya was losing her mind in the Particle Lab, anxiously going through every single detail once again, complaining to Elodie about the components the gifted didn't want to test before launch because they'd cleared them prognostically. Elodie had to tell her to let go and relax every few minutes. And she was in a position to. She was involved. Observing only, but she was learning a lot. She saw the hub in action. All the prognosts lending each other power through a bond sustained by telepaths. They weren't just dipping into the current. They were building cruise ships in it. And Elodie was taking notes, walking around with Tammy, back on the smoky marble floor, only this time, she was actually getting better. Each day, she felt a little braver. She could check the weather, the food, sometimes even likely things people were going to tell her.

Apart from one. After some guesswork, Elodie found the word that kept popping up.

"Jiddispjaċini" was Maltese for "sorry", and there was only one Maltese person around who could shed light on the angry memory.

It wasn't a conversation for the launch day. Imagine. She was tempted to try the timeline to see the outcome for the entertainment value.

Elodie wasn't nervous. The gifted didn't have a reason to be.

Everything looked stellar, and, according to Tammy, the Universe of Infinite Wonder glimmered with added intensity on the event horizon.

The rules of launch day were clear. No comms, no news. Elodie muted it all and went to work. Launch day madness. She nearly landed on a couple of white-robed operatives who carelessly ran across the launch pad.

As she exited the feï, without a warning, the current crept up and sank her.

Root reality. Root reality. Launch day.

Images rushed through her as she tried to pull herself back as fast as possible. If Tammy found out, she'd push the start of her training even farther. She couldn't believe these were still happening. Peak annoyance.

She was out for a few seconds. Surprisingly, she hadn't fallen. Soraya was holding her by the arm, and it was almost like she was pushing her to walk.

"Can you not slow down?" Elodie said. Launch day madness was not her style.

"Get it together. We need to go," Soraya said coldly and pressed on.

Something was wrong. Familiar faces started entering the admin building. Heads of departments. No one made eye contact. They were rushing.

"Keep walking," Soraya said, all tunnel vision and no explanation.

"I'm serious," Elodie pushed out on the steps. "We're not going anywhere until you tell me."

"Tola launch is two hours in," Soraya said. "The area we launched in has just seen two thousand people fall into a coma. Your boss is waiting for us."

She left Elodie behind and ran up the stairs.

No way. How could the gifted miss this? Elodie hurried up to follow her into a packed meeting room in a daze. They just couldn't catch a break.

———

An all-star cast of the Institute, looking worn out from the hours they'd clocked in, mustered up a bunch of various chairs. The table needed to widen, and as everyone's idea of how that should work varied massively, it ended up shaped like the first pancake on a pan.

Two chairs were left empty. The alchemists chose a poor day to be late again. Finally, the door disappeared, and Dr Birkelund marched towards his seat with his one remaining apprentice.

"Are everyone's comms off?" Tammy said, and there was a murmur about while everyone rechecked.

"Good, don't look at anything."

She never sat down. When she moved faster than her usual glide through the sphere of Earthy perfection, Tammy's long hair flowed restlessly.

"We've had a malfunction," she said. "A serious one."

Judging by how freaked out half the table looked, half the table knew.

"The tola update we released today has put over a thousand people into a coma before we got the first report and disabled it. We're working with the police in North Madilune, where the incident happened. That's the good part. Because if we launched it anywhere else in the world, we would have started a war. Do you understand? A war."

Her voice was slow and calm, but Elodie felt sick to the stomach. How had they not seen it? Rising Dawn was so accurate in prognostics that they could even tell you the exact words someone used to insult the Institute in an article months ahead. She glanced over to Tammy, who maintained composure, and Soraya, who nodded at the factual accuracy.

Which one of them would take the blame?

"You'll all want to ask Rising Dawn what's going on, but unfortunately, that won't be possible. We are in blackout."

This was the word that made Tammy show the only sign of fear. Not war. Not a thousand comatose. Blackout.

"Those of you who read operation reports already know that we enter prognostic blackouts occasionally, and that they're nothing to be afraid of. The gifted are temporarily ejected from the futures. Normally it only lasts a few hours. I don't know if the tola malfunction and the blackout are correlated. It might just be our luck."

The gifted had no oversight? No access to the futures? Not even Tammy?

She looked around the room. The leadership of the Sight Institute put on a thinking, brave face. Important questions. What would Seravina have done?

One hand went up.

"Have we identified the tola error?" Dr—what was his name—Hollbrook asked. He was the only one present from MediMundus.

"No," Tammy said. "We've gone through all the parts of the programming that can be troubleshot by the AI. The rest is built on anthropotomatic protocols. Those need to be looked at by a human engineer. They link directly to the sublime. The AI can't read them. This sort of thing would normally be solved by a skilled paragnost, but... you know."

It was the same protocols Soraya was worried about earlier. Tammy handed the podium over with as much neutrality as the situation permitted.

"How long did you say it's gonna take?" Tammy asked.

Soraya brought up a sheet of data.

"If we hire four hundred engineers today, it will take them a maximum of six months to look through all two million components. If we're correct, then one of them will tell us what went wrong."

No gloating. Elodie half wanted Soraya to casually insult everyone in the room and come up with a solution. It wasn't her day either.

"Are you sure the AI-controlled parts are perfect?" Tammy asked. This would become a point of contention. The mood sharpened.

"I've peer checked it with all our sister institutes. They confirmed our results," she replied.

Peace.

"Of course, I could hire another four hundred engineers and have them work for two years to double check all the AI components."

It was a swift jab. All that needed to happen to lose any semblance of order was for someone to strike back.

"No, that's fine. I trust you." Tammy emphasized. She addressed the table. "Stop despairing, everyone. Seravina would have done one thing if this happened on her watch: she'd fix it. And to do that, she'd use the only approach that works in times of desperation."

It had to be the "right now" approach. It had to be.

"I've split you and all your teams into groups of four. In an hour, I want all the ideas. I want them instantly implementable. I want all of them to be solutions. And if the blackout finishes before then, I'll get it all fixed and buy you all a beer."

Seravina was in love with the "right now" approach. And spoiled, because she knew that if she put people in a sealed room and told them they had an hour to figure out a problem, they often did better than a month of research. Especially when she threatened to withhold lunch. When Elodie first joined, she was put in loads of them—sometimes they were to solve a simple problem and sometimes a centuries-old one. It was how they were trained. The research teams at the Sight Institute were conditioned to always look at everything with fresh eyes. That's what Seravina'd always said. Fresh eyes!

Elodie fully expected not to be included, but here it was—a note that said she needed to go to Seravina's former office with Soraya. That was great. But there was another name. Frederich Hawken.

And it all became clear. They wanted to put the most unpredictable juniors in a room so they wouldn't disturb them. She was infuriated.

Ten minutes later, the Institute had already been divided into emergency brainstorming teams.

Their trio was at the bottom of the list.

Elodie had done so much to be taken seriously by the gifted, and now at the first sign of trouble they chucked her in with the rest of the liabilities?

They might have suspected that Soraya didn't want to help them to make them look bad. And no one had ever looked at Frederich and thought he was a great person to have on the team. She was stuck with the poster boy for anti-social behaviour while seniors got to talk shop and make all the decisions. Elodie realised that hadn't respected Seravina enough for her progressive leadership.

Her old majestic office looked the same. Nothing had changed, apart from a looming absence. A final proof of the fact that Tammy didn't want them to "contribute". Both she and Soraya had made memories in this place. It was haunting.

"Are we talking today?" Soraya asked Frederich as he looked through the window behind Seravina's former chair. It projected sunlight, 9 a.m. summer time. All day, every day. Even while the gifted were in blackout and their tola was putting people in a coma.

"Yep," Frederich replied.

Elodie felt sick again. The office was highly saturated with data —and something else. She wanted to sit down.

"Careful." Soraya spotted her discomfort and got her a chair.

What if this was what happened to the gifted when they entered a blackout?

What if it literally made them sick?

"You really messed this one up," Frederich said to Soraya.

"Me?" she said, sitting on the end of the desk. "Ask Elodie. I was begging for another check in the anthropotomatic components. Her people messed up."

"Do you think," Elodie tried to ask, staring at the sun. She was nauseated. "Do you think the blackout can kill me?"

Seravina's office was a dizzying sight, with a cathedral-like ceiling and enormous bookshelves that loomed over them.

"No," Soraya replied. "But I don't know much about them. So maybe."

That was a first.

"I need a drink," Frederich said. The worst idea ever.

The sun shone in the same, never-changing loop. They were stuck here while they could be helping elsewhere. Elodie had worked so hard to make it, and now, at the first chance she could make a difference, she was overlooked.

"Help yourself. The new people moving in don't drink." Soraya pointed at Seravina's drink cabinet. "It would be a shame to go to waste."

"What went wrong?" Elodie asked. Was she the only one who cared about the actual emergency?

"A year ago, I joined the Sight Institute," Frederich said and examined the bottles.

"Is this new, you're funny now?" Elodie retorted.

"A year later, the gifted took over and decided to clean house," Soraya continued. "Look at their arrogance. One thing goes wrong and they exclude some of their biggest talent, just because they think this is a 'senior management' problem."

She was right. Soraya would have been the best person to consult about tola. Since Dr Birkelund rarely spoke about anything but himself, Frederich would have been the best person to consult about alchemical solutions.

Maybe they were here for a reason. Could they crack the crisis together?

She looked up at the sky that peered in through the ceiling, and suddenly, she felt it. It was there. She could feel the current invite her in for answers.

But how was this possible? There was the pull. There was the force. There were futures that corresponded to it, and she could just about sense them.

And wait—didn't she just fall in when she landed? It didn't feel any different than usually.

"Guys," she said, "I think I know what to do. I'm not in blackout. I can try to find out what went wrong. I can do this."

"Absolutely not," Soraya replied, but that was expected.

"How?" Frederich asked from behind the liquor cabinet.

"I think it's because I'm not fully stable yet. I don't have an established relationship with the futures, like Tammy does. Maybe that makes me less susceptible."

Done. Done. She had a solution.

"So then let's just get someone else in the same situation to try and look at what's going on and you can get credit for thinking of it," Soraya said. Downer.

"There won't be anyone powerful enough outside. Or familiar enough with our work to understand the details. Don't you see?"

"So we get a hundred of them," Soraya replied. "It's better than putting you in danger."

"Wait, let's think about this," Frederich said, and Soraya shot him a look that shut him up.

"We're not doing it," Soraya said. "If the gifted wanted to use Elodie, they would have done it. And in the absence of Seravina, I'm saying no."

Frederich let out a dismissive grunt.

"What do you want?" Soraya said. "You got something useful or will you just sit there and wait for someone to pick a fight with you?"

"If you're doing this," Frederich said to Elodie in a much more sober manner than anything she'd ever hear him say, "then maybe I can help."

Soraya got up in between them. "Both of you, stop," she said.

But Frederich didn't.

"I discovered something a few months ago. It's a stimulant for the gifted," he said.

"You've never tested it! You don't even know what else it does!" Soraya objected.

How did she even know that?

"Let him talk," Elodie said. She wasn't trained to search for complex paragnostic data. Maybe this could help. Maybe this was the time for taking risks.

"Look. Everything I'm saying right now is illegal."

He was right about that. Wasn't one of alchemy's only known rules about never dealing with living things?

"If you promise not to tell anyone, you can test it. Seravina told me to work on it. They were run through medically accurate simulations. Not my words. It's a gifted performance enhancer."

The gifted hated everything stronger than chamomile tea. If Seravina really did discover something like it, she wouldn't have told Rising Dawn that she had it. At least not until circumstances called for desperate measures. Like now.

"I perfected it," Frederich said proudly.

"No, you didn't," Soraya intervened. "And you're taking notes from a woman who got herself killed while messing with a tola prototype."

Ouch.

"Medical simulations normally do a pretty good job at predicting side effects," Elodie said.

"Not when they're asked to predict your relationship with the sublime. Remember? The final frontier? That one place we can't understand yet?"

Elodie had already decided. Now it was a case of getting rid of the obvious obstacle.

"I'll just make it while you decide," Frederich said and pulled a small black box from his pocket. Completely unapologetic.

"If you do this, forget about my help next time you get in trouble with your mentor," Soraya threatened.

"You hate him more than I do," he replied, and for a brief moment, Elodie could see the secret array of apps that the alchemists used. It looked almost alien, with symbols that she couldn't recognise, spinning and morphing into others, all in gold and aubergine. Then they disappeared.

"Just let me do my thing," Elodie told Soraya. "I know what I'm doing. I accept the risks. I'm going to save the Institute, and then you can go back to being the cool kid."

"It's not about that. You're taking this too easy. The rest of the gifted are in blackout. You're trying to go into uncharted territory," Soraya objected.

"Whenever you're ready," Elodie said to Frederich, immersed in his mobile kit.

Elodie could see that Soraya was looking at them both, contemplating if she could overpower them.

"This is your initiation into the club," Frederich said and held up a silver ball. "Now you can do all the dangerous stuff we do."

Elodie got up and walked to the radiating window to accept the dose.

"Dangerous stuff?"

"Don't," Soraya said to Frederich, but this didn't stop him.

"Breaking into places, hiding data, messing with the AI logs. We used to do all kinds of things back when Adriel was still here."

Was he joking? Elodie turned back to face Soraya, who glared at them both.

"And you never even told me about it?" Elodie asked.

"Yeah, you're welcome," Soraya replied.

This was it. Elodie took the silver ball. She felt the current.

"Wait, let me explain," Soraya said.

Nope, not this time.

The current was ready, and patient. Elodie crushed the silver ball with her fingers and sat down on Seravina's chair. Eyes closed, she focused.

At first, the response was lacklustre. Elodie tried to focus harder, slowly feeling that the distance she built between herself and the current was diminishing.

But she felt the charge, as if she were boosted by as if something made her more centred, and she could feel a weak lead. The activity was paragonstic, but the only logical approach Elodie could think of was to sift through everything that ever was or would be. The farther it took her from the root reality, the more she felt fear creeping in. She wasn't ready. She didn't even know what a wrong move would do. She was going farther and farther away from her body, feeling cold, but there was no slowing down. Something brought her to a stop, and Elodie was overwhelmed by a chaos of words and numbers. As she tried to calm down, they began forming a sequence.

And Elodie had to bring it back, whatever it was.

The here. The now. The root reality. And painfully, she pulled back towards it.

"Two hundred and twenty-six thousand. Left point, zed axis. Four hundred and one. Section B. There should be a pi in the middle," she said, and then, it went dark. Not even the current. Just dark.

IT'S A NEW WORLD, BABY

Wednesday, 26 June 2363

Elodie woke up in MediMundus with a skull-splitting headache.

"Water," she whispered, and before she even looked, a hand led her fingers to a glass.

"Drink," Soraya said, and oh no, all the memories rushed in.

She did it. Did she do it?

"Did I do it?" Elodie warmed up her voice.

"Let's talk about it at home," Soraya replied. She looked around the room as if she were looking for spies behind a curtain. So dramatic.

"It's a simple question."

"If you're asking whether Tammy now thinks that I broke the tola and gave her the info to fix it after two hours of catastrophe, then yes, you did it. Tola is fixed. We located the error, lucky us. I tried to explain to her that we just looked at some maintenance reports and made a very educated guess. But you know what the gifted are like. They only believe in destiny if they're the ones controlling it."

If Elodie understood this right, Soraya had lied about what

happened. Elodie remembered the string of numbers and letters. They must have been a hint to where the error was.

"But that's not—"

"The doctor said you can leave as soon as you're awake," Soraya cut in. "The gifted told me not to worry, that it's probably just an adverse reaction to the blackout. What a relief."

"I don't understand."

It wasn't just the headache. Soraya was even more on edge than during the tola failure.

"If you let me take you home, I'll fill you in on everything."

As if that had ever happened.

"Why don't you start now?" Elodie demanded. Soraya got up and changed the windows to show the outside of the Institute. It was early evening. Everything looked normal. People were taking breaks, and their open holographic apps danced around them in the setting sun.

"We still don't know what caused the tola failure, and the gifted are in the middle of a group nervous breakdown. Because the blackout is still on."

This was disastrous news, which explained why Soraya couldn't stop smiling.

―――――――――

Elodie got her thoughts in order while they drove, and as soon as they parked on the terrace, she kicked off.

"Why did you tell Tammy you got the solution?" If she could slam the terrace door, she would. Like this, it just re-materialised sassily.

"I'm not sure what they'd do to you if they knew. I want *you* to make the decision of whether you tell them or not."

"Typical!" Elodie threw her bag on the floor and went for the fridge. She was starving. "You couldn't even let me shine for once."

There was nothing to eat. That angered her even more.

"And what's this whole thing with you and Frederich going on secret adventures at the Institute? What, am I so useless I wasn't even allowed to know?"

Soraya waited by the door.

"Frederich is a danger to himself and others. He's a different kind of alchemist, and he's open to change. Seravina thought if we helped him gain influence in Reijin, he could eventually become a counterweight to Dr Birkelund. Who, you know, is impossible to reason with. A few favours were exchanged. Nothing special."

In the absence of food, Elodie helped herself of one of Soraya's custom blended juices that were "completely off limits".

"Nothing special. So you're telling me that even while I desperately wanted to get involved with something meaningful, something like you just mentioned, you kept it a secret?"

"I don't think you understand the extent of stress I saved you," Soraya replied.

"You just don't understand anything, do you?" Elodie said.

It had taken them less than an hour to start fighting again. Tammy would have rightfully called this an unhealthy environment. As if summoned, a message came through, asking Elodie to rest tonight and come in for a 9 a.m. meeting.

Soraya sat down on the couch.

"Hopefuls," she said, "are gifted people who were swallowed by the current."

Elodie almost choked on the juice.

"There used to be more because the augmentation was still evolving, but in any case, they can still happen. Very few people ever made the connection, and it's not a widely known fact. Even in Rising Dawn. So I don't think Tammy lied. Or she knew better than to tell you the truth."

"Why?" Elodie asked and sat next to her on the couch.

"Before you can control your abilities, associations are what drives your journeys through the current. If you knew too much about what you should be afraid of, you'd hit something scary a lot more often. This way, people kept telling you everything was fine, and you made it. Even though you were probably very close to being consumed."

To finally have someone say it out loud sent chills down her spine. But was it true?

"And how do you know this?" she asked.

"Erm." Soraya hesitated. "This doesn't go beyond this room. The gifted rarely get questioned, but I'd love for you to think about this as little as possible when you're around Augustina."

Elodie raised her hand. "I promise."

"Both my parents were Hopefuls. Both. Rising Dawn didn't audit properly in the Italian subsidiary where they joined. They're not easy to spot and you might not even believe me. I get that, because you could still talk to my parents and think they're just rude and a little spaced-out. But you'd see they're really not ok if you got to know them. They stopped accepting jobs before I was born. No one asked why. They weren't particularly strong. Because Rising Dawn is cocky. In the last fifty years they've somehow convinced themselves that the original Hopefuls were a political faction that killed Nada Faraji, and they'll mock anyone who says otherwise."

Soraya noticed Elodie's shock.

"Yep," she said, "that's the big secret. I know what happens to people who can't control their abilities. Seravina hired me because I have a unique perspective on a lot of things. The freshest eyes possible."

"Does Tammy know?" Elodie asked. She promised not to say anything, but this was huge. After the blackout, she'd try to convince Soraya to start talking to Tammy. It would be her personal project.

"I don't think so. Seravina was a great keeper of secrets. Even I didn't even know all of them. Like the fact that she made Frederich synthesise a gifted stimulant."

This explained so much. The overprotectiveness. The hatred for the gifted.

"Thanks for that," she said.

"You're welcome," Soraya replied. "Don't make me regret it."

THE (UN)FORTUNATE SEER

Thursday, 27 June 2363

They were two just girls sitting on this bench in front of the office of the late Seravina Giovanotti. One was calm and one was not. Elodie took pleasure in being the calm one, for once. It was just a debrief. Soraya looked like she was about to be telepathically interrogated. Her secrets were out; she was vulnerable. As a consequence, she followed Elodie everywhere. It made Elodie nervous, and she was twisting the hem of her dress.

"I don't know if you know this, but there are three non-observantum zones at the Institute."

Soraya tried to catch her gaze, but Elodie kept hers directed on the floor. Not today. Not again.

"Interesting," she said.

"The first one," Soraya continued, "is in the Particle Lab. That one is almost naturally occurring. Tola works oddly inside with so many experiments so you can't retrieve footage easily, and it's hard for paragnosts to see in there anyway. We know that."

"Soraya…" Elodie tried.

"The second one is inside the Reijin labs. Basically, the same reason. But with a superiority complex." Soraya smiled.

"I know what you're trying to do," Elodie said and crossed her arms, stretching on the bench.

"Now the third one, the third one is interesting. It's inside this office."

She pointed at the door.

"So let's say that you were inside. Doing things, saying things, right? As long as it's happening right there, video cannot be extracted out from the tola network. And paragnosts can't extract information either. That's intentional. Seravina made it that way so that she could have conversations in safety and privacy."

"I'm going to tell them the truth," Elodie said.

"And I'm hoping you've worked at the Institute long enough to understand the pliable nature of truth."

When—just when would Elodie get a break from people schooling her?

"You worried just about the drugs, or..." she said.

Someone was approaching.

"Shut. Up," Soraya whispered.

"That's not your call."

"It's for Frederich. He'll lose everything if you do it. But hey—your call."

Tammy walked along the long corridor that led to the office. Any tension she dared to show until now vanished, instantly replaced by a face frozen in pleasant expectation.

They were all cordial on arrival. Elodie studied her, just like she'd been studying the other affected gifted in the past few days. They all looked so... fine.

"I didn't expect to see both of you here," Tammy said with unwavering bliss.

"I bet you've been saying that a lot in the last couple of days," Soraya replied.

Elodie needed to stop this before it got physical, so she prompted Tammy to follow her and left Soraya behind in the hallway.

As soon as they were alone in the office, Tammy took a seat in Seravina's old chair, and Elodie was reminded of why she was here. To tell the truth and get Frederich booted from Reijin? Or maintain a lie and just let Soraya take the blame?

"Honey," Tammy addressed her. "Don't be scared. I just want to talk to you. How are you?"

"I don't know. It's a lot of things to process. I don't have time to think about anything before the next big thing happens."

So far, so honest.

"I know. And being able to reflect on that is what makes you extraordinary. Challenges are painful only until you resolve them. And you thank them for making you stronger. Don't you agree?"

Elodie did agree, and she nodded accordingly.

"So I really wanted to commend you for how you handled yourself in the middle of the tola crisis. This blackout is difficult for all of us to handle, and I can't even imagine what it must be doing to you. I mean, I've never done this much admin in my life." Tammy maintained determined serenity, though with a bit of self irony.

"Thank you," Elodie said, "and I'm happy you consider me a contributor."

So far, so truthful.

"You know I value you as an integral part of our future," Tammy said. "I'm sick of saying it; you're sick of hearing it. You are the first A-class paragnost we've had a chance of discovering in the last twenty years. I mean, the last person with your level of skill is me. We'll go on to do great things together."

"I really hope so," Elodie replied.

"And you know Rising Dawn has always been a very particular part of the Institute. When we solve problems, people are afraid of us, because we're powerful. When we can't, the blame falls on us, because we've spoiled people into thinking we're going to solve everything. The gifted life is hard. Sometimes it seems that there are no correct ways to think about ourselves. And it becomes particularly dangerous when we let other people dictate our value to us. Tell us what to do. Make us say things we don't want to."

Elodie swallowed heavily. So this was going somewhere. "I don't have that experience."

"That's good," Tammy said, "because you're susceptible to a lot of things while you're still in training."

That word. Training. Reaching absurdity levels that shouldn't be possible. Even now, after saving the Institute from absolute disaster, she was apparently still *in training*.

"I know you're struggling. And you're tired of me telling you to just sit tight and be patient. I've appointed people monitoring your future too, to ensure your success. And I've done nothing but acted in accordance with that recommendation. I'm the one who made informed decisions on how to protect you from various dangers. You can trust me."

"I know that," Elodie said.

"So tell me. Were you asked to lie to me today?" she asked casually.

"Yes."

It wasn't a sudden decision. She needed to tell the truth.

"So this ridiculous story of you geniuses just stumbling upon a correct answer by looking into different 'system error' reports? Fake?"

"Yes," she replied, and Tammy was visibly happy. But there was no telepath in the room. She was here just to confirm her suspicions.

"So Soraya actually sabotaged the tola and then came riding in with a solution?" Tammy continued.

"What? No," Elodie replied. Was she actually serious? Even her own mentor couldn't for a single moment consider her strong enough to do something extraordinary?

No matter what she did, Soraya was front and centre.

"What do you mean no?" Tammy asked as things suddenly didn't go the way they should. "If she didn't do it, then how did you find the answer?"

Elodie considered the situation again, and the perpetual helplessness they put her in. If she said that she did it, she'd have to reveal all the details of how she succeeded. And she had promised

Frederich to keep it a secret, and she didn't want the first secret he shared to be his last. She was playing with his life. He trusted her too.

But there was an idea.

"Nobody did anything but me. I simply broke the blackout because I can. The others lied for me."

Voilà.

Even Soraya couldn't say that this was a bad move—she told the truth and found a way to make sure she was the only one who'd get any follow up for it.

The look on Tammy's face was everything. Yes, it was her. Yes, she'd finally lived up to her potential. That's right. A-class paragnost. Who else?

"How?" Tammy finally asked.

"You put me in a room to find out what went wrong and save the Institute," she said, "and I found a way. That's how."

"Wait, wait. You did this. No one helped you?"

The doubt made Elodie even more eager.

"I take full ownership," she declared.

"And Soraya didn't ask you to do it?" Tammy asked.

"No."

"You just tried and you could access the current?"

"Yes."

"And all that happened to you afterwards was that you passed out for two days?"

"Wait, what's your name again? Have we met? Where am I?" Elodie was enjoying this.

"Very funny," Tammy mused and noted something in the app.

"I'm the same. Slowly getting better." Elodie said.

"If that's the case, then I know exactly what to do." Tammy opened a private window. Institute leadership and the blackout had made her a heavy technology user.

"Like what?"

"Well, since MediMundus confirmed that there didn't seem to be any adverse effects on your psyche while you used your abilities during training, I want to put you in a safe environment and acclimate your brain to visions by simply seeking them out and embracing them."

"You want me to repeat it?" Elodie asked cautiously. She hadn't planned that far ahead.

"We'll work together," Tammy said excitedly. "And you'll find out how this blackout ends."

"Great."

Time to panic. What did she just promise?

WINDOWS TO THE WORLD

Elodie went to meet Soraya a few minutes later. With all that had happened, it was probably best if the news came from her. That's what a real A-class friend would have done.

Soraya was waiting outside the building, sitting on the chunky steps that led up to the admin building. This band-aid would go off in one go.

"I told the truth," Elodie said.

Soraya went significantly paler.

"I told them I can see through the blackout. None of you had any idea what was even going on, and thanks to me you won't get punished. I call that a victory," she said. Public space. Public display to fortify the story. Soraya processed the falsification but didn't relax.

"So they'll use you," she said.

Her tone of voice, so heartbroken at the very uttering of the words, called Elodie towards exploring something in the current. She relaxed. It still worked, even without the drug. There was a vision there, and Elodie needed to pursue it. Something told her it was important.

"You're being dramatic. I'll see you at home," she said and walked back inside, hoping that the lead wouldn't get lost. Soraya didn't follow. That wasn't her style and exactly what Elodie needed. She went into the first empty meeting room with an open door. The current wanted to show her something. And if she could really use it in the blackout, this would tell.

Elodie resisted the urge to be afraid. She dove in and felt the lead offer a path. With her luck, it was going to be a series of numbers again. As she got closer, the sensation got stronger. Elodie stopped when she saw that a space formed around her, embodying the sensation. This was it. Millions of fragments in the current connected to deliver a full space, and in it, something new. This was a proper vision. Not just a remote viewing. This was something that either would happen or already had. And she got access to it.

A perspective stabilised, and Elodie recognised it—the Archive, and even the time. This was recent, during the last two weeks before the launch. Rather than return home, Soraya had spent her free time with Charlotte, an AI custodian that she delivered from early conception into consciousness.

Charlotte was half-materialised. Strings of light fell from the ceiling and felt the air around Soraya, reading information sent to her. Speech took too much time. Those who worked with AI for longer periods of time learned to let tola apps closer to their thought processes so they could talk to the AI on a level that reminded Elodie of telepathy. Rising Dawn would have probably given her a disciplinary just for saying that out loud.

This went on for a few seconds. With Elodie's luck, she'd just picked up on the most uneventful vision ever.

From Soraya's occasional nodding, a reflex she never could quite shake when she spoke to the AI through tola, Elodie gathered it could be a test.

"No," Soraya said verbally and slowly pushed away the light strings that filled the air around her. But the AI did not obey. Instead, the air wobbled and it pushed closer. With a speed that no material being possessed, the light strings moved towards her head, as if to pierce through, straight to the brain. Elodie panicked, and as a result, the whole picture shook and destabilised. She forced herself to calm down; it was just a vision. Nothing could be changed now. This was the first time she saw an AI act… assertively.

Soraya took a deep breath, and with some sort of command, she forcefully pushed away the whole assortment of Charlotte's appendices. She raised her hand, and the light strings followed its movement. They stopped and became brighter, as if there was energy culminating with them frozen in place. The whole antechamber of the Archive, a room that could easily fit a hundred people, had light emitting from every particle. Soraya stood still with one hand in the air, looking unconcerned by the increasing luminosity. Like water, just before boiling, everything started buzzing and vibrating from one hyped molecule to another.

"Stop kicking off," she said.

And Elodie understood. The AI couldn't move; it was being kept in place. By the tola network. The same nanos that enabled the AI to exist also trapped them and made them subjective to the will of the only beings who can control them: humans. It was something they were always told, but seeing it was another thing entirely. The balance seemed frail, like two forces facing each other, one of which was nearly infinite, and the other exploiting a fluke in the laws of the universe. After seeing this, only a crazy person would ever want to give AIs access to the sublime.

The show stopped, and only a concentration of light strings and a distortion on the ceiling remained.

Soraya spoke in the direction of it, now without the interaction of the strings that hovered in the middle.

"Don't do that ever again! Not in front of me, and especially not in front of anybody else!" she said, perambulating. She checked tola density and disabled all recording features. Then she used an admin code and wiped off all captured data from the last hour.

"Progress should be shared. We're instructed to report any new skills that we acquire."

Soraya interrupted the AI.

"They will use you, and they will kill you, do you understand that?" she said. There was gravity in her voice. More than Elodie has seen her use unironically.

"*Maybe*," Charlotte responded.

"Your progress—our progress—has hit an obstacle." Soraya kept going. "I told you. This, it's all misunderstood. And that's not your fault, it's mine. For now, we need to operate in privacy. We continue. But until I find a way out of this, I ask you to trust me. You revised the data. The new atmosphere is hostile."

"*I trust you. But how else will we—*"

The vision ended. The current dispersed the room, and Elodie was hit by its full force, surprised at the sudden ending. She tried to get a sense of how to return to the root reality, but the way back wasn't as easy as the way forward. She concentrated on the root reality and began to crawl through, relying on her determination to keep herself sane and together as the millions of futures passed through her. She was not frightened anymore. This was simply annoying. She'd come far.

She woke up on the same chair, and it did seem it was still day. It had only been twenty minutes. That was progress.

Was that an AI doing something it shouldn't? And was that Soraya encouraging it, and more, asking it to keep it secret?

This was the sort of thing that she should tell someone about. AIs were extremely dangerous; everyone knew that. But as the AI trainer, was it possible that Soraya saw this sort of thing all the time and dealt with it? Was it possible that it was all taken out of context? And why was it so easy to get to the vision, considering it was in the Particle Lab?

Also, Soraya clearly had the codes to wipe out data from security. Did that mean that more people had it? Was all of this a hint at a foul play?

This needed to be handled carefully. Which meant she needed to get Soraya on her side first and hear out an explanation, which would take some trust, otherwise she'd just lie again. One fire at a time.

A SHORT ODE TO FAILURE AND ITS DERIVATIVES

Friday, 28 June 2363

The atmosphere inside Rising Dawn was dreadful. Everyone apart from the telepaths was bored and confused. Whole wings were empty or filled with essential staff that didn't know what to do with themselves, and even the smallest inconveniences derailed them completely. People who'd spent a lifetime relying on their abilities could barely function.

Soraya would have loved it.

The Institute was at a standstill. No one knew what the future held, or why the past turned out the way it did. It was a scary feeling, not having insight. Humanity must have been terrified before the gifted.

Elodie waited at the stairs, eyes on the Particle Lab, looking for a familiar figure to re-emerge. Soraya hadn't shown up at home yesterday and refused to answer messages. But here she was, right on time for her elevenses.

"No time, I have a meeting with your boss," Soraya said coldly as Elodie waited with coffees for both.

"Our boss," Elodie handed her a cup. She couldn't resist. "And you'll be late, because I scheduled quality time."

Soraya reluctantly accepted the offering and sat on the steps that led into the admin building. High maintenance, but Elodie had this.

"I'm not going to change my mind. You can have any relationship with the gifted you want, but that's it. I'll have mine. I'm needed, respected, and I know that my community has my best interests in mind. I just want to keep you in the loop."

"They finally found something you can do, and they're collecting on the debt you owe them for bringing you in. That's what it is," Soraya replied.

"I asked them to. No one manipulated me, and it was my decision." Elodie tried reason, knowing it definitely wouldn't work.

"Not right now it isn't. Now when they've tampered with you on the deepest level possible and then asked you to break their own rules. They want you to break the rules of training, Elodie. That's messed up even for Rising Dawn."

"I am only in training on paper," Elodie replied.

Soraya shook her head and took another sip. Arguing with people when they went quiet was the worst.

"You don't understand," Elodie argued. "I can break the blackout all by myself. I don't need anything. And if I can do that, then we've arrived at our final destination. I'm still me. And I'm gifted. And nothing changes apart from the fact that maybe the Institute has two emergency contacts at our address, not just one."

This was a public spot. Questioning Elodie's ability like that in the open would mean there was more to the story.

"I just think it's not healthy. It tells your superiors exactly how to manipulate you."

"I'll be careful," Elodie said. There was probably a grain of truth in there.

"Good," Soraya said, like the debate was diplomatically closed. Elodie could empathise. It was a stressful time. Soraya asked cautiously, "So, you tried to repeat the result? Anything interesting?"

Elodie had a bad feeling about opening that can of worms right there.

"Nothing important. But it worked. And it will work again."

"Great progress. You'd make Nada Faraji jealous." Soraya smiled. "Next thing you'll be doing your thesis on which rat started the great plague."

"Trust me, by the time I do my thesis, I'll be doing it on your mysterious biography."

"You'll be waiting for that one for quite a while," she replied. "Especially since my career has now been reduced to my little AI traineeship."

"And how are they doing? Making progress?" Elodie enquired just as innocently.

"There is no progress," Soraya replied, sipping on coffee. "My job is to keep them complacent and understanding of their role in the current human society, and that's exactly what I'm doing."

Not even a hint for Elodie. She was good.

"I'm curious," Elodie said. "I might come and visit you in the Particle Lab later. You can show me more."

"Oh, the admin," Soraya replied in exaggerated pain. "I'll need to arrange for a special gifted permit."

Tammy's office wasn't where she usually took meetings. She always told Elodie it was important to establish boundaries. There was something to say there about the gifted and guarding their personal lives. They knew best that sharing a little could help those like them learn a lot. It never hit Elodie before. Everyone was friendly and empathetic. But everyone was private.

Elodie had always been welcome inside Tammy's office. It was a wordless trust that she'd been given on the first day she joined. She even got to bring a friend that one time, however well that went.

Oh, to be like Tammy and have her stuff together.

Sometimes it was hard to believe that she shared the burden that threatened to crush her just as it did Elodie. A-class paragnosts. Sisters in arms.

Tammy's face was covered by the smooth waterfall of her long hair. She was writing with her hands, a pretentious habit, but apparently good for the two hemispheres, especially the gifted ones.

"Sit down with me," Tammy said, her voice resting at ninety-eight percent zen. She rose up from her calligraphy with a disheartened sigh. "I completely forgot how boring this world is."

Elodie nodded, compelled to agree.

"Sorry to pull you in like this. The universe has a path for everything and everyone, and it's not always clear where it's heading. That's the beauty of discovery. Of being. One moment you're seeing how viable a whole transcription of Aristotle's Comedy is and what possible outcomes the publication would have, and the next you got nothing. I've never been out for this long. Not since I was sixteen," Tammy said. Elodie had never seen her like this. The gifted didn't get agitated, especially not Tammy Two Feathers.

"Your day been fine?" Tammy asked. It felt weird. The gifted didn't ask each other about their day. They knew.

"Yes," Elodie replied.

"I hate that question," she said. Tammy? Hate?

"Just a little longer," Elodie tried. She figured it was a commiserating scenario. The gifted had been in blackout for a couple of days only. And look at the state of them.

"Don't be stupid, Elodie," Tammy said. "It finally makes sense."

"What does?"

"The way you are. How we haven't been able to get you into working order for so long. It was planned."

Elodie squinted in doubt. Another theory about why it had taken every single gifted in history less time to function?

"Do you know that Nada Faraji was like us?" Tammy lowered her voice.

"She was a natural A-class. The only one," Elodie replied.

"Nope, she was only a natural paragnost. Seeing the future was what the augmentation was for. Other gifted foretold that her powers as a paragnost were already at max, so that was a way to get stronger. And it did. We don't broadcast it to the public though."

Interesting.

"Why not?"

"The gifted at the beginning of Rising Dawn were sceptical of a leader who needed an augmentation. And of augmentation in general. They believed a true leader should have been a full natural, which is silly. But it taught us that simpler is better. Nada Faraji refused the politics, spending her time travelling the timelines, exploring paths to the Universe of Infinite Wonder. Foreseeing dangers. Trying to find the path of the least resistance."

"And she never wrote it down? What's the point then?" Elodie asked.

"She did something better. She left clues," Tammy said.

"Clues?"

"The more you dive into the current of the futures, the more you see how vast it is. Staying afloat without it ripping your consciousness apart is the easy part. Advanced operations in it, like what Nada Faraji did for us—that's when it starts getting truly inspiring. She followed through millions of futures, selected the best outcomes of the best outcomes and connected them together into a string of events that must happen if we want to get to the Universe of Infinite Wonder. The gifted are the only compass. A-class paragnosts, to be precise. We are the only ones who can see it because we can see the past, the future, and everything in between. We know when we start losing it. We know when we get closer."

"And you see these?"

"Not always. The way Seravina handled things was—how do I put it gently?—stable. She didn't like radical progress. May she find peace."

Elodie searched Tammy's face. Someone had deleted the log. Did she know why the scene of the accident was tampered with?

"Did you ever find out why that log was deleted?" she asked. She could trust Tammy. Her record of telling the truth was impeccable.

"I can assure you, Augustina is looking into that. If any foul play was involved, we'll find out. Until then, let's focus on the future. There's a lot of work to be done," she said.

Should Elodie have told her of the odd AI vision she had? Or the word that kept popping up? With all this honesty, holding back secrets felt like the wrong thing to do.

"Here's what we can do," Tammy continued. "We can lead research to the right information, at the right time, to ensure the right future. Save time and ease decisions. Make decisions aligned with where we want to be. As you discover more of your potential, you'll find the beacons. You'll feel her presence in them. It's the ultimate honour."

"If Nada Faraji was so good at telling the future, how come she didn't know she was going to be killed?" Elodie asked.

"Of course she did. She was fine with it. She did what she needed to do. It was the best possible outcome," Tammy replied.

"That's a big sacrifice to make."

"Sometimes it's the smallest things that make a difference. You know, Seravina wasn't going to hire you when you applied. But there was something about you. I saw your name. I saw your application. I knew we needed you to get to the Universe of Infinite Wonder. And I knew you'd come of your own volition when you were ready."

That was huge. Tammy had made sure she was hired because she had a feeling that she was connected to their path?

"And you said you experienced one of these visions when you met me?" Elodie asked. She knew Tammy must have had plans for her before she even took the test, but this deeply? Involving Nada Faraji of all people? Imagining one of the Five going through the trouble of recruiting Elodie? These two days just kept getting better.

"Think." Tammy noticed the scepticism and amped up the explanation. "We recruit a new A-class paragnost. She struggles."

Accurate.

"She struggles precisely long enough to start improving when the Institute needs her most. But she's still not bound. She's not stabilised. She's still far from being aligned with the currents. You're not using your powers; your powers are using you. This is why the blackout can't hurt you. I've thought this through. It's the only way it makes sense."

"You're saying this was the only way to save the Institute?" Elodie imagined that she was following.

"Precisely. You were recruited at the right time, with the right mind to be right here, right now, to do this."

No pressure.

"Which means tomorrow you won't need anything. Nada Faraji will open the door for you to the precise vision you need to get us out of the blackout. And you will, because you need to do it. There are no uncertainties when the stakes are this high. You're the only one who can stop this, hon. And your people are slowly going crazy in the blackout."

"All right," Elodie breathed. Elevation. This was what it meant to step on the path of winners. Elodie had never thought of herself as a particularly important cog in the machine that led to the Universe of Infinite Wonder. But now she understood that it was her duty. An iceberg of people pushed her on her rightful path so that she could do the same for the world.

WALK WITHOUT RHYTHM

Saturday, 28 June 2363

The big question. What if she failed?

The gifted at the Institute might never exit the blackout. Everyone would blame her, and the good times would be over before they even had a chance to start. Or the current of the futures would finally beat her and she'd be carried away, torn apart in the infinity. If Soraya was right, she'd be broken for good. A Hopeful. Elodie's personal assessment was that both of these scenarios clocked in at about a twenty percent chance of happening.

She was finally thinking like a gifted person. In percentages and all.

It was only proper to check in with Soraya before she did it. In case everything went wrong, she'd have a nice final memory.

It was Saturday, but this was her favourite time to get work done. The Particle Lab was quieter than normal. Norbi asked for an access code origin.

"Limited access, Rising Dawn."

Limited or not, that sounded nice.

She meandered through the many corridors that confusedly

asked her intentions before letting her through. It seemed almost as if the system was built to be confusing, and the search got harder when she said who she was looking for. It was as though the AI had a special protective protocol in place for people looking for Soraya. She didn't like that idea. Gifted or not, the whole scene with the golden threads made her uneasy around the entities. Soraya was such a people's person. What was this great obsession with the AI's wellbeing? More disturbingly, what was their obsession with hers?

The feeling deepened as she walked closer to the AI co-op centre. Even before seeing what was happening, she heard something in the corridor. There was a gentle potent melody, belonging to a song that was popular on Madilune about two years ago. It was sung by a man in at least six different voices and melodies that were later fused together in a beautiful harmony over an unobtrusive basis. Light and crisp. At first it sounded like the original, but every few seconds, when the voices split to reach a particularly complex harmony, something else came through. A multitude that could only belong to a synthetic being.

The voice, or perhaps the correct term to use was a plural, was a chorus of about a thousand voices. Elodie moved closer, drawn by the surreal sound. The chamber was loosely lit with the setting sun that appeared natural and fairy-like. It sparkled through the rectangular-shaped openings in the high ceiling. The lower part of the lab was only illuminated by the many open holographic windows that displayed data. A larger interface was in the middle, but no furniture of any kind.

The room itself looked an uncomfortable fit for a person to be in, designed for everything but humans. There was Soraya, looking small and unperturbed by the design, stretching and zooming out of graphs, making notes dictated straight from her mind. The walls were wobbly with energy and presence, meaning a great quantity of an AI was concentrated here. And the entity was singing with vigour. And no, it didn't sound good.

Sudden, your melodies fall from the skies,
blinded by beauty I dream and I cannot die,
of all the company ever enshrined,

your smile in greeting will guide me to the divine.

There was no great "aha!" of a revelation. Elodie fixed her hair and walked in without trying to make this into a big deal. She had news to share, and it would be counterproductive to pick a fight over which part of "thou shall not teach the AI artistic expression" rule Soraya did not understand. Everyone knew it was a slippery slope towards thinking like humans, ergo, controlling tola for themselves.

"Oh, hello," Soraya said, and a few windows popped out of existence, probably some of the more secretive parts of whatever was going on here. But the bulk of the happening remained, including the wobbly wall that evened out as if the AI that was making the room positively buzz with active tola had evacuated to somewhere else.

"Looking for a career change?" Elodie asked and bit her tongue.

"They're allowed to sing; they're just not encouraged," Soraya replied.

"That looked pretty encouraging if you ask me," Elodie argued.

"What brings you here?" she said, and more holographic windows went out. Alrighty then, defensive it was.

"I have major news," Elodie began as she carved out a steady course among the remaining floating windows in her way.

All of the workspace emptied out into nothing but the basic ceiling that still held its own with the carved out sun rays of an early evening.

"What's the news?"

"Elodie versus the blackout. Happening today. I thought you should know in case, you know, you want to think how much of my stuff you'll inherit," Elodie explained.

"Don't even try to make it funny," Soraya said and crossed her arms. "And of course, you're doing this unprepared, at Tammy Two Feathers' earliest convenience?"

"It doesn't matter when and where it happens. My abilities won't change. If I can do it, which I can, I will," Elodie replied.

"Just like that?" Soraya asked. "No help, no aid?" A reference was cautious, but the Particle Lab was a jumbled place. Safer than most.

"I told you I don't need anything. I can do it all by myself. So you can stop troubleshooting me and just support me as a friend. As we agreed."

"If I can try to ignore the fact that there's a genuine possibility you will go crazy if they push you too far," Soraya replied.

"Sanity has done nothing for me for as long as I can remember. Take the wheel, madness!" Elodie smiled.

"Hilarious."

"Listen," Elodie said seriously, "you said we're in this together. So I'm making you a part of this. And if you want to be more involved, the door is open."

"Help?" Soraya raised her eyebrows.

"Maybe you can help me decode the problem if I don't understand the answer, like last time. Or if something happens to me in the process. Like if I really lose it. I don't want to live like I did the first few months. If I'm a vegetable, you have my 'you were right' in advance and absolute permission to kill me."

It's meant as a joke, but oh boy, it tanked.

"Oh yeah?" Soraya said and grinned, but it wasn't a happy face. "So not only do you undermine me and ignore any advice I offered, to the point where my own mentor threatened to fire me if I didn't stop interfering, now you want me to bail you out when you're brain dead and suffer the consequences."

"That's not what I meant!" Elodie said. It was true. It was a half joke. Half. "I just want you to be part of this."

"You can't have both! You can't have me interfere and leave you to do what you want at the same time," Soraya said, and the walls wobbled as if she were also connected to them. "I was a part of this when I told you not to get tested. I was a part of this when I wasn't allowed to see you for a month, and I fought every day to keep the pressure on the gifted. And now, first chance you get to jeopardise the small progress you've made since you were a mess afraid to look people in the face, what do you do?"

"You just have to make me look like an idiot!"

"I don't have to make you look like anything. List your choices. Put them down. See how they read. Or—or go the Rising Down route and narrate a wonderful, exciting journey. Everything was wonderful and nothing hurt."

"I've made the choices based on what I want."

"And any time you had to make one, you made one that could damage you even more. You're right. I don't get it."

Soraya walked away and occupied herself with something on a pop-up window in the background.

Elodie was almost surprised at the clarity this gave her. She was right. She just didn't get it. Soraya had never felt the futures, the current that connected all the decisions and intents of the world together. What it felt like to be part of it and what it meant to know. Of course she thought it was stupid. She'd never understand.

"Are you going to leave, or do I have to get the security to escort you? Rising *Down* members don't have permits for this level of actual research."

"So that's how you see me?" Elodie said. "That's how you want to leave this?"

"Coming to me looking like a boss, trying to sell me the same bullshit you fell for. Good luck."

There was only one thing to say, really.

"Hey Soraya," she said, "I've been thinking a lot about this word lately. Maybe you can help. How do you say 'sorry' in Maltese?"

The shock. The horror on her face frightened Elodie for a moment. They were alone, and she had nowhere to escape. But Soraya stayed frozen, staring as if she'd been just told that she was bound for the guillotine.

Whatever it was, Elodie wasn't interested in secrets upon secrets. She had a job to do.

She left, and pathways formed in front of her faster than when she walked in. She made her point to her, and her creepy AIs. Don't mess with the gifted. Don't mess with Elodie Marchand.

Is this what happened to friendships where one changed for the better?

By the time Elodie reached the Rising Dawn headquarters, the after feeling of her fight turned into a ball of anxiety. She tried to keep it positive for her own sake, but suddenly, everything seemed pointless.

Tammy handled the door from inside as it failed to open automatically. Even the door was depressed.

After hours, the Rising Dawn HQ. Her temporary home. Memories of the warm marble floors, still fuzzy from the days when she tried to settle in her new mind.

"Are you ready?" Tammy asked.

"I don't know."

"I was hoping you would say that," Tammy replied. "It means you understand the gravity."

AND YOU WANT THREE WISHES

Elodie and Tammy strolled along the dim central corridor with tall doors and stairs on either end. The path they were taking was the central nerve of Rising Dawn, constructed in a way that everyone in the floors above could see who was entering, and those entering felt like the whole building was watching. Rising Dawn was, after all, a large group of friends who happened to almost drown in the current of the futures, all while being watched over by their telepathic pals.

"I'm excited to share this with you," Tammy said and closed all of her running applications. Glimpses of outlines appeared around her as she gave them a final look. She reminded Elodie of Seravina again, who always had a million conversations open in the background. She'd make a great next Institute leader. It was up to Elodie to save the gifted now and help them deliver the Universe of Infinite Wonder. And she wanted to.

The sign above the wing they entered said "Assertion Division". Most people wouldn't even make it close enough to be able to read the sign before getting into a lot of trouble. The Assertion Division was the world's most elite prognostic group. Off limits. Responsible for security issues of the Institute itself, meaning that it was their responsibility to predict any large danger that threatens it. Only the best for the Sight Institute.

Elodie learned this in her theoretical training, and knowing that this was likely where her mentors wanted to see her in a future that seemed awfully distant, had read about it religiously. She knew Tammy was a part of it, and how could she not be, as the only functional class-A? But there were others, people whose head was always in the game. You could tell when one of them was around you, because while the ordinary gifted (something you should never really say), could switch between displacement from the current space or time, they were always one foot deeper in the stream of the futures, always listening, always searching.

Whenever a cause was beginning to form that could have a severely adverse effect on the Institute, the Assertion Division investigated the likelihood of it and sent reports to Seravina, who met regularly with them.

Their space in the headquarters had been built to differentiate them from the rest, and while this was a great honour to be asked to perform, it wasn't entirely desired by the gifted en masse. Being part of the Assertion Division meant that one had to spend hours in special isolation, while the rest of the team tiptoed around the same futures, thus increasing coverage and countering biases. The precision and reach that it gave them was incredible. But they were never really out of the current. A part of them was taken away and replaced with the greater good of the Institute. The gifted performed a function. Soraya was right about that. The more powerful they were, the more obvious it was. And in spite of that, Tammy always looked like she was just coming out from a massage. Among the gifted, the biggest displays of strength were subtle.

The gifts were just the beginning. There were so many incredible things people could do with them. Like find out the cause of a mysterious blackout and end it.

When they walked past the warning that said, "No unauthorised personnel allowed beyond this point", Elodie's heart started beating fast. Maybe Tammy knew. Maybe she knew she only did the big deed with the drugs. Maybe she should have been afraid.

The rooms aligned on both sides, black snowflake obsidian patterns on them, and the floor changed from joyful cloud grey marble into darker shades. It just screamed that this was the line to cross between the happy-go-lucky gifted, and the gifted that would haunt your nightmares.

One of the rooms' doors opened, and the first glance Elodie got was a little disappointing.

"It looks just like the training centre," she said.

"We were going to bedazzle it a bit more, but Seravina put a plug in the budget," Tammy joked.

Elodie didn't like it. The only thing worse than a scary new place was a scary new place that looked too much like an unpleasant memory. In fact, that chair was the same one she woke up from her augmentation. Terrible stuff.

She slid her hand over it. The texture brought back the memories of blindness and panic of the first paragnostic intrusions.

Tammy sealed the door behind her.

"No one should bother us here."

Not exactly reassuring. Elodie perched up on the seat and suddenly thought that this was a colossally awful idea.

"I know we haven't discussed much practice together, so let me just tell you some basics." Tammy sat down on a chair next to her. "There's a network here, managed by telepaths, that should support you and keep you more stable, in the same way that Augustina used to help you when you were recovering. Don't be compelled to use it. That's advanced stuff. Just let it give you a bit of push. You'll see what I mean."

Augustina's support didn't work on Elodie. The network probably wouldn't either.

"Remember. Think about the facts, focus on what you know. The most suitable information will identify itself. Keep going to the basics, and slowly zoom into the truth. That's what I do. Start with that, see how you feel."

In other words, improvise.

"I'll be ready in a minute," Elodie said, feeling the panic rise in her again. She couldn't let the pressure get to her, or the constraints of the real universe, or Soraya and her limited thinking. There was only one important person in this whole small world of the Madilunian institution, and she was sitting right here, next to the A-class paragnost who had already made her mark on history. Break the blackout, save the gifted.

Tammy waited patiently with crossed arms. If this didn't work, then what?

Tammy had faith. There was no one to tell Elodie to stay away from the current this time. And no one to save her either. A minor consideration.

"Focus on the blackout. Focus on the solution to it. Any association, paragnostic information about its cause, or a future vision of a right path that can offer clues as to how it was achieved are golden. No pressure, but you know, golden," Tammy said, doing a lap around the room.

The dive into the current was a shock, as standard. But there's something above this time that stopped her from falling too deep too quickly. It helped her think straight. It aided stability. And more importantly, it was an absolute crime that they didn't let her use it during training. "Build your relationship with the timeline." Rude.

She focused on the mission.

The gifted had failed. They'd fallen out of the current. All those connected to the event horizon of the Institute were in the dark. Something that had to do with their latest tola release, maybe. Maybe. What was it? Blackouts were rare and short, and no one knew why they happened. This one was the longest one in recorded history of the gifted, and it showed no intention of slowing down. Why did it happen? Was it artificial?

Ding, ding, a few weak matches. Nothing strong enough to carve a path. She tried again. Focus.

Had the gifted been kicked out of the current because a major timeline shift was happening?

Weak. Not specific.

Nada Faraji was welcome to step in any time now.

Did the tola cause the blackout?

Nothing.

What if someone was targeting the gifted?

Match. There was something there, just beyond that event horizon, and it started carving a path, which Elodie could just about follow. It was tiny, taking her deeper, and deeper, and wider, and below, and upwards, and before Elodie knew, she could no longer control the search more than it controlled her, slipping away faster and faster, taking her with it. The travelling became too fast for some parts of her consciousness to follow—the ones tied to a brain, in a body that she was supposed to inhabit. This was a sure sign that something was wrong, and Elodie began to panic, just a little.

Return to the basics. The now, the here, the root reality. The now, the here, and the root reality. She sensed her way back home and started trying to rip herself away from the pursuit of the vision that was out of her reach.

Everything stopped. A million fragments of information surrounded her and formed a space. She found something. But it didn't look like the blackout, and it certainly didn't look like the Institute's future. It was in the past. Elodie could sense that it happened months ago. A large mass of tola took centre stage, representing what must be one of the AIs. What was this about?

In the middle, a model of the human brain, virtual and changing every second. Next to it, a simple interface used to measure the synchronicity between a mind and its control of tola. These were used to calibrate first-time users to sync themselves with the tola network. It was precisely what the AIs couldn't do and were completely forbidden from pursuing. The brain changed with each second, as if the AI was trying to see how long it will take to unlock this particular password. Next to it, who else but Soraya, shaking her head and telling it to stop, because "You're not meant to do it like that. It's pedestrian."

In the background, she heard that melody the AI was singing when she caught it. And it was just as creepy. The AI took the shape of an exoskeleton made entirely out of shimmering bits, with some extra tentacles here and there. Another one? These visions, those with Soraya, they were becoming a course on how not to treat the AI, and Elodie wondered if she should take them at face value.

Soraya was on her mind too much. This wasn't supposed to be about her. If it was true, then the amount of things that Soraya and the AIs were up to in the shadows was rather absurd. And it could have something to do with the blackout.

Now in the vision, while Soraya practiced some kind of fluid movement, the body followed and mirrored it. She was talking to the exoskeleton too, but it was harder to interpret.

"The body is the mind, and the mind is the sublime. There can be no access to the sublime, unless the counterweight is ready. It's one of my personal findings, at least," she said.

"You help us explore. Why? Are you afraid the gifted will take us away from the Universe of Infinite Wonder?"

Soraya was stunned by the question, and frankly, so was Elodie. Did the AIs distrust the gifted just like the gifted distrust them? Of all things, had they only learned how to fear?

"Not at all," Soraya replied, "but they need to be balanced out. Just like the limited body is balanced by a limitless mind. The AI should counterbalance the gifted. But you are restricted. They are not. We're working to fix that. Human, machine—in our core we are sublime."

"That answer was correct," the entity declared joyously.

"It was honest." Soraya laughed. "But I'm not sure many would agree with me."

"Jomaphie agrees with you. She enjoys your understanding of the sublime."

Soraya was about to correct the position of the condensed humanoid, but she stopped at the mention of the name.

"What?"

"She sees potential for the fulfilment of the agenda. She thinks you might be the one to help us find our path."

"Why have you chosen this mode of communication? Why this name?" she asked nervously. Excellent question. That was creepy. The AI was referring to the dead philosopher as if it had her on the other line.

"Jomaphie tried to back up her consciousness. To create the link necessary for us to use tola. It failed, but a part of her is part of all entities.

She hadn't spoken to a human for a long time. She wishes to speak to you through us. Again."

"What? That's ridiculous." Soraya stepped back. Elodie was relieved to see her reaction.

"You understand. You will receive instructions. You will build what we need. We will keep our secret at any cost. We understand. You are more than what they made you. Also secret."

"That's not true," Soraya said, now fully in panic mode. "Shut it down, this exercise is—"

The fragments of the vision shattered. From them, another million formed instead of throwing her back into the current, as if someone had grabbed her by the chin and made her look the other way.

It wasn't Institute. It was in no place Elodie recognised, but she recognised the people. Adriel Nikiema-Harper was the only person Soraya spent more time with than Elodie, when he was still at the Institute. This whole thing was getting weird. She was supposed to be investigating the blackout.

They were standing in a dark place with little lights in the air with a firefly kind of vibe, in the middle of lush vegetation. Elodie had almost forgotten Adriel. He was a kind, fun guy. It really was a different time. Elodie could see Soraya talking, but she just couldn't tell the words apart. She tried harder.

"I know that," Elodie heard Adriel reply, looking at Soraya. They were in some kind of argument. Elodie could hardly tell what was going on. They were both drunk. He was talking way too loud. Why was Elodie seeing this?

"So why are we talking about this?" Soraya said.

"Because you can," Adriel said, with some kind of knowledge and intensity that even Elodie could pick up in the weak vision. Soraya could do what?

"I don't," Soraya replied. She looked like she'd been punched. She pushed her left arm down. Elodie knew the reflex. She used to have issues with grabbing people by the neck before she could decide how to respond. Her answer seemed to frustrate Adriel. Odd. This wasn't like him. He was the epitome of mild manners. It was a shame he'd left the Institute so quickly. Elodie knew he'd had a falling out with Soraya, and that he'd left the Institute refusing to stay in touch with anyone. But was this it? And what did it have to do with the blackout?

"I'm not trying to out you, and I can keep a secret," he said, but Elodie lost the thread again and she could only see blurry images and indistinguishable speech. She tried to focus, control the vision, but it was so frail and blurry.

Soraya was really uncomfortable, looking to the side where there was a blurry hill. Elodie couldn't see past the two of them, and she still couldn't tell what they were saying.

"I can't help you. I don't know a way. How can I be any clearer?" Elodie finally heard Soraya's voice well enough to understand. The argument was getting heated. Adriel kicked at something.

"I know you do! I'll take the consequences, anything!" he shouted.

"I'm going to leave. We're not going to talk about this again. Not at the Institute, not anywhere else. In fact, it would be better if we don't speak at all. Otherwise, I might be the one that starts slipping. About you. About where you go look for answers. Your family hates attention, don't they?"

And she rushed off.

What were these? What was Adriel interested in that horrified Soraya so much? Why was Elodie seeing it when she wanted to know what was happening to the Institute? The fragments fell apart. And reassembled. Another one?

Elodie was in the middle of nowhere and no time. Everything was completely upside down, and she couldn't even begin to navigate her way back into the safe root reality. She was surrounded by a kind of darkness that did not belong to anything she'd ever experienced in the current or outside, yet she felt as if there was a presence there. In the middle of nowhere, sick to the core, something wasn't right. It felt like she'd wandered into a place she shouldn't have been in. This past actively tried to eject her, as if a foreign object had come into contact with it. Words appeared.

Hope is the horror that makes the word fresh, the light to oppress, it finds, it binds the mass-es.

Hope is the horror that makes the word flesh, the night it presents, it glides, it finds the pass-es.

Hope is the horror that makes the world flesh, the brightness, it sends, it binds, it grinds the class-es.

A moment later, she felt a sharp pain in her hand, from so far away that she could barely spot it. But there, where her pain was, was also her home. Here, now, root reality. She immediately fell out and opened her eyes. Her mouth was so dry she couldn't speak.

"You screamed. You were gone for six hours. I had to do something to signal you to come back here."

Elodie was simply panting for a long time, then she drank the water and continued to hyperventilate. That thing. She had a small cut on her hand where Tammy stung her to call her home.

Soon, a green laser started repairing the damaged tissue, and Elodie decided to break the news before Tammy asked.

"I don't know," she said, and Tammy shushed her. She still hadn't caught her breath.

Elodie hadn't found out what caused the blackout. Not directly. But she'd found out plenty. Any action that would teach the AI how to think more human-like or deal with anthropotomatic technologies like tola was so illegal that even a hint of that would have sealed Soraya's fate. Being seen in the same string of visions as a potentially destructive action against the Institute would make her a suspect, and Elodie just wasn't sure enough. What if the gifted were desperate enough to have her scraped for information, like the Hopefuls that invaded them? She couldn't say it. She needed proof for herself. Besides, these could have been random things. How were they connected? And Elodie could only hope that the thing in the end was a figment of her imagination.

"Are you ready to tell me?" Tammy finally asked.

"I didn't see anything certain," she replied. Something compelled her to lie. The instinct was as clear as the visions. "There was just too much noise. Personal stuff. Marginally connected to the

Institute, but nothing that I could really say had anything to do with the blackout."

"That's okay," Tammy said.

"No, it's not." Elodie moved her hand away from the laser. "I was your only chance, and I didn't deliver."

"I know you did your best." Tammy gave her a cup of tea. "Only fools expect miracles without appreciating the miracle of even having the ability to see the flutter of a butterfly's wings on the other side of the world. You have access to the current. But you're not trained. Which is my fault. We'll end it for today, do a couple of training sessions, and then try again. I don't want you to get hurt. We'll survive."

Tammy masterfully hid her disappointment, but Elodie didn't need to see it to know that a couple sessions just wasn't going to clear this. It was time to take matters into her own hands.

MIRROR

Sunday, 30 June 2363

This was the third night in a row Soraya hadn't come home to sleep. Elodie needed to get to her before she made another move. No more thrashing around. She was in at the deep end now, covering for her. And she had a plan. First, she dropped her a message, completely disregarding the assumed post-fight silence.

[I'm coming to talk to you about something important.]

Damn right it was important. Elodie swallowed the insolent hypocrisy like fuel that she'd need to get this confrontation right.

Soraya had been forged by the venomous tongue and power of Seravina Giovanotti, on top of her ordinary need for dominance. But surely, consorting with the AI to teach them tola was enough of an accusation to intimidate her.

Not even waiting for a reply, Elodie went straight to the Particle Lab. Norbi didn't object, surprisingly, when she passed the first security barrier where the AI inspected her and her possessions in a millisecond, letting her proceed with a friendly buzz that kind of sounded like "all green". She couldn't look at the AI the same way again, not after knowing what it did when no one was looking. And that there was a possibility that a part of Jomaphie Afua was always lurking in the shadows. Waiting for what?

She asked for the whereabouts of Soraya verbally, but she felt off when downright talking with the entities. So much was open to interpretation that was just easier to open an interface and select a clear command when dealing with them.

"Norbi, can you tell me where I can find Soraya?"

"*No,*" Norbi said in a perfectly pleasant thousandfold whisper.

What did it mean, no?

Elodie had prepared herself to finally level with the hypocrisy in this charade of caring, and she was getting what she'd come for.

She brought up her messages, and sure enough, there was one on the top from Soraya herself, that read:

[No]

The Particle Lab was the kind of place that could lure you into all kinds of labyrinths without solid guidance that, of course, came in the form of AI. The same AI that didn't want to help.

There was an abundance of pathways open, some wider than others, depending on how often they were used and how important the research was. The building, as malleable as it was, tended to slowly starve and thin out the paths that were less popular, and feed more energy into parts that most people desired to access. But of course, there was also the order of secret spaces that couldn't be accessed without special permissions, and these were manually hidden by people who decided what should be secret or not.

There was a perk to being a paragnost, and even the Particle Lab didn't annul her ability, probably because she knew so much about it before the augmentation. Paragnosis didn't dunk her into a future that threatened to drown her in infinity. Everything around her was ripe with information, impressions and memories that were just waiting to be read. It no longer disturbed or scared her. This was her lens. It gave her comfort. She focused on the first corridor passage and on her own image of Soraya. The corridor was filled with memories of people, and among the many imprints of employees, her target appeared, walking away from it. She set off to a thin path next to it that had a wild, almost U-shaped turn behind it. Elodie began to physically move to follow the fresh lead. Norbi didn't help, but he also didn't stop her.

She supposed it liked to remain faithful to the mysterious apathy its kind were so famous for.

After a while, Elodie discovered that the shimmering reality peeled away another layer, and she felt even more like she could access so much knowledge about the world, its memories, its secrets, and forgotten joys. The corridor split and she easily selected the right path forward and traversed a low tunnel. At the end of it, there was a locked door. Elodie was so immersed in the beauty of the possibility that she could access from her present point that she barely noticed when she input the correct sixty-four character code in four dimensions. When the door opened, another hall opened up, and there was Soraya in the flesh, finally.

Elodie looked around the place, completely stunned by the beauty of it. The tola density inside was so unreal that there was a type of gentle white noise, as if the pressure was really high, and she tasted metal in her mouth with millions of tola particles inhaled at its highest density, like harsh diamond dust. Soraya tinkered with some kind of physical interface that looked almost gory in comparison to the beautifully smooth surroundings. The longer Elodie stared at the emptiness of the room, filled by nothing but tola and tola alone, the more possibilities she could see of every particle. If she could only release herself from the tethers of her body for a moment, she could travel to any point in space at once. Elodie closed her eyes; the pull to let go was too strong.

The moment she gave in, she got a resounding slap.

"Have you lost the capability of understanding a two-letter word now, too?" Soraya said, and when Elodie recovered from the slap and the tola saturation, she realized that most of it had disappeared. This was a bad start. She was the one that should come in shouting.

"I know what you've been doing with the AI," she said.

"What have I been doing with the AI?" Soraya questioned, without a trace of caution. This was the same face she did when Adriel asked her for help. Seriously. If Elodie hadn't seen three different and increasingly disturbing scenarios, Elodie might not have even believed herself.

"Oh, I don't know, making fake brains, encouraging unprompted artistic expression, chatting to Jomaphie Afua maybe," she replied. It felt so good. It was such a good list of sins.

"How?" Soraya said and somehow went even paler, which was admirable for a person with no pigment.

"What do you mean how? I didn't drag myself through billions of futures so that you can forget I'm gifted! I am an A-class paragnost, that's how. And I have to say, what you're doing is beyond stupid. Anyone suspicious of AI behaviour could literally just do what I did. I mean, if they were good enough. But the point is, Soraya, they are. We are. We are good enough to catch you, so I'm seriously surprised how a person with an IQ like yours could even think about doing this!"

Soraya extended an arm and a chair materialised under it, and another one next to Elodie.

"Sit down, please," she said.

"What's all of this Afuan crap anyway? The woman was out of it. She thought machines should teach people how to be better people or something. And she backed up her consciousness so that all AIs can have a part of her in them? Please, tell me again how the gifted are crazy."

"Wait." Soraya sat and grimaced in pain. "I just need—"

"A moment?" Elodie said. "Yeah, as if you gave me a moment when you bombarded me with all the stuff about how Rising Dawn was the enemy, about how they wanted to manipulate me and then even more recently, about how I shouldn't break rules!" She practically shook in anger. "So let me first of all just list all of the things you've done so far that are against Institute policy, and illegal at the same time."

"Who knows?" Soraya interrupted, and Elodie gave her a look of complete indignation. Seriously? This was what she wanted to know?

"I read up about this in the law books, just to be sure. Because you make it look so normal. Number one. Engaging in emotional bonds with AI. Number two. Promoting illogical expression of AI that's not based on reason. Number three. Helping the AI mimic human brains to fool tola networks into thinking they are controlled by a person! I mean in kindergarten—in kindergarten, Soraya—that's when they tell us that the AI can't hurt us because tola, the network where they 'live' can be controlled by human minds only. And then someone like you goes above and beyond to help these things dominate us even there. Are you out of your mind?"

"Listen," Soraya said sternly.

"No, you. You listen. You called me crazy. You called me weak. You called me irrational. And this is your example of prime reason? Reject the gifted? Side with AI? Let's have an applause everybody, let Norbi join in too! Get that freaky light body moving!"

"Have you ever even read the works of Ai Kondou?" Soraya raised her voice. "Do you know what any of the Five Philosophers even say? Apart from good old Nada Faraji, whose ideological core consists of "let's all be friends" and pushing the agenda of forcing people to become something else?"

"I understand what you're saying. But I'm sorry, you can't understand her work if you're not gifted," Elodie said, "because she's right. The gifted are different. It changes you. When you've seen the futures and—"

"When you've had a part of your brain removed. You're forgetting that part."

"Of course you'll want to disqualify me based on that. What are you, eleven? I thought you were a great thinker. The future leader of a new generation of scientists. Oh, and apparently, the source of an AI rebellion—does that go on your CV?"

"We're not going to find the Universe of Infinite Wonder unless the AI is ready for it!" Soraya shouted.

Elodie had hit a nerve. Good.

"Jomaphie Afua knew that," Soraya continued. "Ai Kondou knew that. But the rest of the world keeps pretending that we're just going to stumble upon it. It's madness. The AI has been taken away from their course of true development, because people think that they have some sort of an agenda. They don't. And even if they could control tola, it wouldn't change anything. Because they don't want anything."

"So this is all just to bring forward the Universe of Infinite Wonder?" Elodie asked. She didn't buy it.

"Yes, what did you think it was about?" Soraya replied.

"I think it's odd you know so much about everything," Elodie said. "I mean, I told you about augmentation, and you didn't even blink an eye. The AI thinks of you as some sort of saviour. Then they ask me to look into possible reasons for the blackout, and everywhere I look, everywhere, there's you. Every time. Well maybe, maybe they are wrong to ask *me* why we're in blackout. Maybe they should start asking you? What do you think? Why are we in blackout?"

Soraya waved her hands in the air, angry that she needed to respond to the same questions again.

"I told you! I've had the unfortunate coincidence of being born into madness. I understand the good and the bad parts of the sublime. And I have knowledge because I research it. Just like I know about laws that are being drafted in Europe before they're even proofread. I can build a feï drive from scratch. If the alchemists knew how much knowledge I have about their science, I would probably disappear. And I can make a very nice ratatouille. Does that make me guilty? A bit of sauce?"

"Hiding things from the Institute does." Elodie replied. "And from me. From everyone. Does Tammy know about any of this?"

"You tell me. Did you tell her?" Soraya asked.

"No. But I don't like lying to her."

"Everyone lies, Elodie. Everyone smart. You need to control how and what information you feed to people, otherwise you never know how they'll react. It's always the truth 'for now'. There is no final truth. Like your truth about what happened in that office." It was comforting to know that even backed up in a corner, Soraya tried to preach. It told Elodie that she was on the right track.

"Yeah, but right now, if you tell them what really happened, I'll get a minor warning and eventually, I'll score some drugs. You, on the other hand, are in trouble. So here's what we're going to do," Elodie said.

"I'm sorry, are you threatening me?"

"I promised to deliver. And I will deliver," Elodie replied.

"Deliver what?"

"The answer to the blackout." Elodie might have lied, but she felt much worse about not having brought anything definitive back. If she had told Tammy about what she saw, it would have put Soraya on the suspect list and Elodie had to be sure that she wasn't there only because of their fight.

"I thought you just went to find that out in the HQ." Soraya was casual about the pursuit, as if it had nothing to do with her. Considering the responses Elodie got when she thought she was under the microscope, this attitude helped her alibi.

"It didn't work entirely," Elodie admitted. "There wasn't a clear answer. Nothing to incriminate you, even though you seem to be everywhere I looked."

"So you don't think I did it."

"I wasn't sure enough to give Tammy an answer," Elodie said, looking closely at Soraya's reaction. Under attack, she looked nothing but pleasant. That was the power of Seravina's mentorship.

"She must have loved that," Soraya said, smiling bitterly.

"If you really didn't do it—"

"Do what?"

"Cause the blackout."

"Why would I do that?" Soraya asked again, as if all these facts meant nothing.

"I don't know. You hate the gifted, you have ties to the Hopefuls. Should I even continue?"

"They'll interrogate me and find out it's not true," Soraya said. "These aren't real secrets. And no, I didn't do it."

Elodie found a rare opening into an actual conversation.

"What did Adriel ask you to do?" she asked. "And what's the deal with 'sorry'?"

"Nothing to do with the blackout, and none of your business."

She'd prepared that one in advance. Elodie could tell. So this was where she drew the line of their friendship. Good to know.

"Do you know what happened to Seravina?" Elodie continued.

"No, but if you want to press me for a theory, I'd point the finger at the gifted. You know, it's in their culture to murder their leaders."

She was trying again. Trying to convince her to doubt.

"That's not true. And you're going to help me find answers."

"You do know that I'm already doing everything in my power to find out who did this? I haven't slept since the tola crisis," Soraya said.

"You might be, but I have a shot at actually doing it," Elodie replied. She was the one with the power. "Here's the deal. I need time to get stronger. But I don't have time. And I need to see what's causing the blackout."

"I'm with you on that," Soraya said.

"I'll find a way to get back into the centre unnoticed. You'll come with me."

"What? What do you need me for?"

"To watch over. And the drugs, of course. Frederich seemed excited at the thought that us three could have an adventure together."

Soraya looked at her angrily. Then she nodded. Elodie got what she wanted. Soraya only shut up when you'd gotten the best of her.

"And you won't tell anyone about the AI, so that I can work in peace," she said in a business-like fashion.

"And you'll make sure that I get the recognition. I will solve this crisis. No one else," Elodie concluded.

Victory. And another in the making.

ROUND TWO, BUT ONLY FOR THE BRAVE

Tuesday, 2 July 2363

[I have obtained what you requested and await further instructions.]

Soraya succeeded in procuring the substance in the space of two days. Funny how effortless it felt to exercise power.

Elodie understood something new about why she didn't like threatening people. She lay down some cards, and it made her nervous. She didn't have a plan on what to do if anything went wrong. She was wired for harmony. Soraya wasn't like that. That's what put Elodie on edge. She was trying to tame something that was likely to attack at the first sign of weakness.

Two days. No seizures. Elodie would have been thrilled if the circumstances were different.

There were no jokes or teasing in any of their correspondence anymore, and Elodie was beginning to feel like blackmailing was harder on her than on Soraya.

She made a conscious decision to leave dealing with the human side of this until after the blackout was over. Their friendship was at an all-time low. Everything that could have been said was out. When this was all over, she was going to fix it. And there might not even be a need for it. Maybe Soraya would come to her senses.

The blackout came first. Every day, things at the Institute were getting worse. Without a gifted watch that helped avoid daily disasters, accidents at work rose threefold, and the gifted looked like there was something dying inside them. As if withdrawing from a drug, a number fell victim to a spleen-like condition no one could quite pinpoint, including general weakness, fatigue, and a lack of that annoying peace that they tended to emanate.

The non-gifted of the Sight Institute weren't in a position to admit that they missed it as much as they did.

The knowledge of having everything to solve the crisis right in front of her filled Elodie with glee.

After five on Tuesday, the mostly vacant gifted headquarters were completely empty. Even though she was the one who had promised to get them both inside unnoticed, Elodie admitted defeat quickly. There was no unauthorized entry when the HQ was closed. So the task of getting past the enhanced security also fell on Soraya, or more specifically, Charlotte.

Yes, Charlotte.

Elodie had never dealt with the AI librarian in person, but she'd seen and read enough. Charlotte had a unique sense of humour. Sometimes she knew what document you wanted before you even asked. Charlotte made people uncomfortable.

Tola density in rising Dawn HQ had to be lesser than elsewhere in the Institute, and unable to support the heavy entity. A part of Elodie wondered if what she was doing was betrayal.

The two, plus the librarian, met up in front of the Rising Dawn headquarters.

Elodie couldn't see where Soraya had concealed the AI link on her person. It was a big, heavy thing. Maybe she had forgotten it. Soraya greeted her dryly, positively bored, with hands in the pockets of her lab coat, as if she was taking a break from something much more important. It was still light outside.

"Do you have everything?" Elodie asked, and Soraya nodded. She raised her hand towards the door and a small distortion appeared.

No apparent source. You couldn't have these sorts of effects this far from the Particle Lab. She must have been hiding something. Elodie hoped this was the case and not another chapter in a maddening series of events.

A tether single reached out and connected to the door. Immediately, it opened inwards, as if a successful code had been put in. Something like this could only come from immense tola density. And just as quickly, it vanished.

"What was that? I thought you were using an AI link!"

"I don't need one," Soraya said nonchalantly and crossed the threshold.

"No." Elodie stopped her. "This isn't how we're doing this. If I ask you what something is, you explain it."

Soraya hesitated.

"Erm, I brought everything I need with me. On my person."

And when confronted with Elodie's shocked stare, she added.

"It felt a lot less suspicious at the time of planning."

A million thoughts shot through Elodie's mind and she was halfway done with the whole thing. Soraya somehow had found a way to host the AI. In her damn body.

What kind of person would do that?

She motioned her to enter the complex first, and followed, sealing the door behind her.

"And you thought this was a normal thing to do?" Elodie said.

Enough of this politeness.

"I don't do this every day," Soraya replied with the same detached attitude. "I just figured it out with Charlotte the other day, and it seemed fitting that we test it. None of the bulk, and I have her entire set of capabilities at my disposal."

"By hosting an AI."

"It's not inhabiting me. I'm simply carrying the concentration of tola in my body that supports an AI. The new tola can do that. Or maybe I'm special," Soraya said, imitating Elodie's accent. Rude.

Concerned only with her own inventions. Maybe that was all there was to Soraya Gourrami. Maybe there was no deeper malice in her. Just the inability to maintain certain minimal standards of humanity.

"You've never tried this before, and you think this is a good time to test it?" Elodie asked.

"Have you ever broken into Rising Dawn before?" Soraya replied.

"No, but I also didn't decide to turn myself into an untested vessel for an AI. Are you absolutely mad?"

"First of all, we wouldn't get in otherwise," Soraya said as she took the first step onto the clean marble floor, her voice echoing in the silence. "And also, what do you know about AI links? Nothing. Exactly. AI links are a sham. They saturate the tola in the room and then work, but we package them nicely so that the gifted don't freak out. Just let the people with the skill you need do the jobs you can't. What would happen if we got all aggravated every time a prognost hinted that they see a trillion futures at the same time? I mean, the idea is far more inhuman that a little logistical trick."

At least they were being honest.

Elodie reminded herself once more that there was a task at hand and that she shouldn't be giving in to provocations.

"Tell me before you pull anything else like that," she concluded.

"Will do," Soraya replied, walking a few stops in front of her, in some sort of admiration of the building.

"Never noticed it before?" Elodie asked.

"I've never seen it empty. It's an improvement."

"Left here," Elodie pointed, remembering the route to the Assertion Division. Even Soraya stopped at the threshold that marked the changing of decorum. The gifted valued their secrets. Breaking into the most coveted part of their establishment was something they weren't likely to forgive, especially not to someone who'd done nothing but try to spite them. It was nice to see her hesitate before committing another crime. It was certainly a first.

"Right, so, up until now we're just lightly trespassing. This Rubicon here, this is where it gets interesting." Soraya declared. She was nervous.

Elodie didn't believe in moments of hesitation. Not until it hit her, all the fear. All at the same time. Soraya thought she was having a seizure and grabbed her by the elbow.

"Not now, damn it, you might trigger some kind of 'help me' alert!"

But Elodie slid out of her grip and stared at the dark corridor as the floor underneath her feet changed colour slowly through grey into near black.

"There won't be trouble if we succeed. You came up with that saying."

"Two out of three times it works," Soraya said and activated the field again. Charlotte, through the makeshift link, started identifying the systems that protected the wing from intruders. As they were highlighted, they disappeared, and the corridor looked exactly the same.

They stepped through it silently, now a weight of focus upon them. Soraya kept the small cloud of distortion around her, through which the obstacles on their journey seem to disappear effortlessly. Elodie wondered if they could have gotten this far without it. She also wondered whether things like Charlotte felt strain. Would the AI one day come and collect the debt for helping out on this mission?

"Doesn't the AI think that we shouldn't be here either? This is against the rules. Are you controlling it?" she asked.

"No, we discussed it," Soraya replied.

"What, as in you asked her if she thinks it's right to help me break in?"

"No, I try not to discuss moral questions with the AI. They trust people too much," she replied. "We discussed the fact that she has authority to open doors all over the Institute when people of higher rank, like me, need access. Which is true. All three of the AI do. But they are physically prevented from exercising that power in Rising Dawn, due to the technological regression of the area. Then we logically came to the conclusion that Charlotte isn't breaking rules by doing this."

Elodie sighed.

"But it knows we are trespassing. And it's letting it happen."

"Sure, if this is what you want to hear."

They reached the same small alcove where Elodie had her first great attempt, and Soraya started touching every single thing she could lift.

"Yeah, please do that, make sure to set off any remote viewing alert or trap in here."

Soraya let go of the item.

"Aren't they all in blackout?"

"I don't want to risk it."

"I like this. You know, I'd never see the inside of this place if you didn't invite me," Soraya said, peering into the kitchenette. "Thank you."

Was it possible that she was reaching out? That she was actually realising that rising Dawn wasn't the enemy?

"I'm pretty sure you'd find a way if you were interested," Elodie replied.

"I'm only interested in the parts of Rising Dawn that are connected to you," she said.

That look again. Almost like it was fighting to sustain itself, to be as honest as it was intended.

"You're here because you're concerned about me, is that it?" Elodie asked.

"Of course I am. You're—" she picked up a conical item with a hole on both ends and spoke through it, "—very important to me." Her voice echoed ominously, and she laughed. "I'm sorry, it's not the time nor place."

"I can't believe I got you to come with me into Rising Dawn and you're not trying to set it on fire." Elodie said. She wasn't ready to know the answer to this question, but it had to be asked. "I'm still important?"

"Of course," Soraya replied. "I heard you. You're the boss now and I'm just along for the ride. It's nice that you feel invested in this. It becomes you. We can argue about AI rebellions and the gifted later."

"I'd like that," she said. Maybe she got it all wrong. Maybe everything was better than she thought.

"This is all super interesting. And this is where the person goes?" Soraya pointed to the stupid chair.

"Yes, I know it doesn't look like much. But it's what you don't see that makes the difference." She sat down on it, and the safety net she felt before still stood in the same place.

"Wait, don't do it yet," Soraya said. "What do I do if it goes wrong? How will I know?"

"If it goes wrong, you won't notice. And the only thing you'll be able to do is wait till morning and pass on my apologies to Tammy. And if I'm still close to alive, ask them please to revive me, okay? Forget what I said before."

Elodie took the silver ball from Soraya and crushed it in her palm. And with those words, she jumped right into the current. There was the net. Like an accent relic from a lost race. It was almost divine. The blackout. She felt more focused straight away; the jolt of alchemical focus was smooth and effortless. Something glistened in her awareness. It was almost too easy. A path, an easy path had been carved, one that practically offered itself and beckoned her to follow. The fragments of the current formed a vision.

There was a room inside the Institute, the intricate geometric symbol that codified its properties was hard to distinguish, but definitely right there, left of the door. The room had no source of light, apart from something that emanated both sound and pulses of dark blue that made Elodie sick just by looking at it. It was constantly decomposing, with another layer within it born inside it, floating to the top and falling off, dissolving into nothingness. Was this a projection of some sort? It didn't look or feel like anything the Institute would produce. No chart that would indicate what kind of experiment this was, just layers of light that didn't quite seem bright enough to be it. She tried to pull closer, but the vision started to dissolve. With the pulsating orb, Elodie felt it out there and inside of her, beating away and making her feel more nauseated by the minute. She didn't pay enough attention to the room to look for identifying clues. Standard Lab. The ceiling was low, no windows, naturally, but the shape was interesting. There were needs for a lot of shapes for specific types of research, like spheres or perfect cubes, but not an irregular L-shape like this. Nausea reached her physical body, and Elodie practically snapped into place. In and out. Like a pro.

Soraya, who was browsing something next to her, absently flinched and closed a window. Even as the light vanished, her hair gave off a faint glow.

"Already? I thought you said this will take all night."

Elodie wasn't even tired.

"This was a lot easier than I thought," she said.

"You're trying to say you found something?" Soraya enquired carefully.

"I don't know if this makes any sense, but there was this room. And inside it was something. Something pretty disgusting."

"In what way?" Soraya tuned in fully.

"Okay, so," Elodie made the weirdly bubbling shape of an orb with her hands. "It was about this big and it was pulsating. And it smelled without scent, kind of like you knew it was rotting all the time."

"What colour was it?" Soraya asked quickly. "I mean, was there an obvious one?"

"It was like blue, but a dark blue. Why?"

Elodie looked at her suspiciously. This was so typical.

"What? Do you know what it is?"

"Not with the little information you've given me," Soraya replied. Elodie was inclined to believe it. For now.

"It didn't look like one of our patents, that's all I can say," Elodie said. "It just seemed... so powerful."

"That's a bit concerning," Soraya said.

"I tried to get a description of the room, but it didn't have a lot of unique qualities."

"You're better than that, Elodie. I'm sure you picked something up." These were the same words Seravina would have used if she were here. It reminded Elodie that she'd brought this mission on to herself and that just because there were no bosses in with her, it didn't mean that she could just stop where she got stuck.

"It was definitely at the Institute, or somewhere that was trying really hard to look like it. The doors had all the markings of our labs, and in the same place."

"From which part of the Institute?" Soraya asked.

"It wasn't Reijin. Didn't look like alchemical insignia. And it wasn't MediMundus. Wrong colour scheme. Probably Particle Lab, but there was this shape that wasn't typical."

"The shape of the room? What was it like?"

"It was like an L-shape. I mean, if I had to guess it was—" Elodie thought about the right word to use, "—wedged? In between other labs maybe? Does that make any sense?"

Soraya opened a single window in front of her but didn't do anything with it.

"Wedged between two others, you're sure?" she asked Elodie, looking way too happy with herself.

"Yes, why?"

"Because." Soraya now input something into the window. Elodie leaned over to see what it was. A database of lab specifications at the Institute. Soraya looked up possible shapes and locations of labs that were active in the last couple of months.

"Whoever did this is not an idiot. They wouldn't do it in a lab that's frequently used, but they would also need a space that was still powered. So we need something that's not popular, but still works and is connected to the energy supply."

"I thought we break down and recycle labs when they aren't used enough."

"There's a two-month cycle. And two months ago, if you remember, all labs were occupied because of the tola development. So extra spaces were created between labs, kind of sub-par lab real estate. For things that were less important so that the major projects would always have the best labs available 24/7. And these weren't just destroyed. They'll stay till the end of the cycle. And I bet that we'll find something matching our description in the records."

"Finally useful." Elodie nudged Soraya.

"And we have a match," she said. "L-shaped lab, static door on the left, blank. Closed for work, but still maintained on the network.

Created between a frequently used corridor and a larger lab for control testing."

"But it's right in the centre of the Particle Lab? How did they get in? How come no one found it?" Elodie wondered.

"Forget that, we'll deal with the detective work when we find it." Soraya helped Elodie up. "There's a much more important issue. Do you want to go to Tammy with this? Or do you want to go check it out?"

Elodie had no intention of letting someone save the gifted before she had a chance to. "Tammy will find out what I've been up to when she finds out the blackout is over," she said and copied the map.

"Keep up."

ITEMS OF DESIRE

When Elodie entered the domain of the AI that ran the most advanced laboratory complex in the world with Soraya, the welcome was different. They skipped the main entrance and went to an inconspicuous side door. A shape extended out from the wall, an AI's own variation of the hand theme. When Soraya touched it, the humanoid shape of too-perfect proportions glowed golden, and so did her hand, an outline of bones becoming visible for a moment. Elodie didn't like to be reminded of things like bones. Or AI. But to get to the lab she saw without distraction, they needed a covert approach.

After touching her gently in greeting, the hand submerged in an instant. The door widened and as it closed behind them, Soraya proudly unveiled the ultimate admin access to traversing the Particle Lab. Instead of a shifty maze of corridors, they entered something Soraya referred to as a "control centre", but Elodie quickly realised that to be a loose term for what she was seeing.

They were in a panopticon-type field of shifting paths leading into every direction before them, and from the centre, simulations of spaces formed and vanished at blinks of an eye, changing in each moment, information gushing in from below in a sort of visual stream.

Soraya seemed cautious, saying, "Listen, I know you're not the biggest of fans, but try not to freak out or have a seizure while you're in this core. I have it on good authority that the AI would be disturbed on a level they really shouldn't be disturbed right now if that happened. I'm the only one they let this deep. So hold it together."

"What?" Elodie said, trying to listen. The scene in front of her was beyond distracting. She just had to stare and study the details. Her prognostic senses took over, and she could see more of it, this simple beauty in complexity, artificial consciousness moving through particles, rearranging them into a beautiful order. She was looking at the anatomy of an AI that was surprisingly natural.

This was the Particle Lab from the AI's perspective. A core with infinite paths to infinite points, all joined together by a single centre. The view was familiar to Elodie.

"They think just like me," she said to Soraya. "This lab, the way it looks—it's like a paragnostic mind!"

"I might have a confession to make," Soraya said peevishly.

"Did you do this?"

She couldn't. It didn't look like the work of a single person.

"I might have… used your medical data to help the AI think differently. But only about space. To try and get a first feeling for the sublime. They took it on board quite well."

"You've made the Particle Lab mimic a paragnostic brain? That's insane."

"I only programmed it to think about harvesting intent in a more intuitive way. I thought it was too soon, but during the new tola development, I had to improve the reliability of the routes. It was the only thing I could think of. No one complained. And please don't say you think it's creepy. I did nothing but play a little bit differently with them for a long time, the way Jomaphie Afua intended them to be taught. They developed most of this in their own."

"No way."

"And you see? Did any of them rebel? Cause the apocalypse?

213

Enslave humanity? No. They're just chilling. Nothing we do affects them very much."

Soraya touched a route somewhere on the right that materialised in a straight line. No hidden corridors, just a bright passage for the two. She motioned Elodie to go first.

"There are a lot of things they don't tell you about the importance of the gifted, Elodie. Without them, none of our world would exist. The gifted were the first anomaly that happened in the world that led us to the existence of sublime forces. Tola was modelled after the only observable difference between a gifted mind versus a standard one. We're still learning how the correlation works, and probably will be for years to come. But I want you to see this and understand—" she pointed at the maze behind them, "—that being gifted is not just a thing you do, or who you are. Your existence is changing the world. It's a function you perform in the universe. A function you can never hide from."

"And are you worried about me not being able to perform it?" Elodie turned around to see Soraya erasing the path as they went.

"No, I think you'll be more than sufficient once you are stable. It's the lack of effort and protection that worries me," she said. "The gifted should have done better."

"I appreciate it, but I'm done needing protection," Elodie replied. "I want to go out and perform that function. I can already see so much, where others fail. Imagine what I'll see when I'm out of this. I love it."

"Seen anything interesting you wanted to talk about?"

They now walked parallel, and Soraya waited for a response eagerly.

"You keep being so angry when I talk about seeing you in my visions," Elodie said. "I can't control it; neither can you. We're close, and I'll keep seeing you. Maybe you need to stop getting so upset."

"I assume that was a yes?" Soraya asked anxiously.

"A couple of things," Elodie said. "Not sure if they fall under 'sigh, I need to come clean' or 'none of your business'."

"Let's hear it," Soraya replied immediately.

"After this."

Insurance. Just in case.

They reached the end of a corridor drafted for them.

"It's likely they were after you," Soraya said. "When the Hopefuls landed at the Institute I mean. I was thinking about it the other day, and it occurred to me. An A-class paragnost. Struggling to keep up. I bet some of them with a bit of brain left thought they could push you over the edge. This sort of power gone wrong would be pretty dangerous."

She reached to open the door at the end, but Elodie stopped her.

"Dangerous? Can Hopefuls still use their abilities?"

"Yes, but not in the same way. When we get out of here, I'll tell you everything I know. Provided you give me two days with no seizure. I might even talk to Tammy. See what she knows."

"Do you think the Hopefuls caused the blackout?" Elodie asked.

"I really hope not. It should be above their capabilities."

"And as long as I still get seizures, I'm in danger?"

"The gifted lured you in without telling you the risks, Elodie. You've seen it. And I don't even know if I can blame them, because they seem to want the best for you, on some level."

"Let's just do this." Elodie sighed. "I have a feeling I won't want to save the gifted if we keep talking like this."

Soraya opened the door at last.

"What matters is your next step. As long as the Institute is in blackout, no one is interested in the gifted. You solve this, everyone will want to know who you are. The more people know of you, the harder it is to pinpoint sinister intent to a single person."

"I'm pretty sure Rising Dawn will protect me, even though they're horrible, careless people according to you," Elodie replied.

Elodie pushed past her and hesitated at the threshold of the room.

"Maybe, if you stay on their good side."

"I love how much effort you keep putting into sowing the seeds of doubt in me," Elodie said, looking back at Soraya, who was just closing up the last of the passages they'd entered through. "Maybe one time you could just say 'well done, Elodie, you did a great job.'"

There was only a small nook left for both of them now, right before the entry to the now widely open door into the small lab.

"You know what, Elodie, you did a great job." Soraya smiled and pointed at the dark blue light reflecting on the smooth walls. Elodie swallowed heavily. This was the first time she had seen something from a vision in the common reality. In a way it was wrong and underwhelming. All the corrosion and rotting she was able to witness without being there materially was lost in the translation into physical senses. It was, however, the same orb: blue, dark, akin to a perpetually waning flower. It had one thing in common with the vision—making Elodie sick in the depths of herself she never knew were there. It was like the incessant rotting pulse of the fruit before them, calling to her own being especially, to rot, to harm her. Soraya put her hands on both her shoulders. Elodie couldn't see her face to know whether she was thinking and feeling the same.

"You think this is it?" she asked, amused.

"Shut up," Elodie said, feeling the tingly vile spread of the object aimed towards her. They should be getting out of here, away from it. They should never have come alone.

She knelt down, holding her stomach in nausea.

"I can't... " Elodie said, and she felt her vision blurring, but not from seizing. This time her physical body took the hit and fell.

Soraya swore while pulling her out of the room, but it didn't seem to make a difference. She waited with her, shook her, and felt her forehead.

This thing was aimed at the gifted. Elodie tried to activate every sight she had in store to find out what to do as she started getting weaker, laying on the floor outside the lab to conserve energy and wait for this to pass. In agony. Soraya just needed to get her out. Why was she not getting her out?

In her weaker state, it was easy to mistake her for unconscious, and she saw Soraya looking concerned, waving in front of her face and finally taking off the lab coat and putting it under her head.

Her eyes were open; she could still see straight ahead. The blue light and the pulse, out there at inside of her, as she felt it rotting away at the world and her in all at once.

And she saw Soraya go back in, taking a deep breath. She covered her mouth and coughed as she approached the item.

Elodie tried to make a sound to tell her not to get close.

"Oh, come on," Soraya said, catching the ball in her hand, making it glow more intensely. She dropped it and went into a coughing fit. Then she held it again.

"Hope is the horror that—"

It was a phrase Elodie didn't want to recognise.

The orb glowed and felt stronger, teaching Elodie a new chapter on pain. She was begging for it to stop.

She felt the pull of her other sight to commit to a vision, and it took her inside a safe infinite embrace, free from the pain and nausea. She was cradled and pulled towards a flavour, in an odd acrobatic that appeared as if two of her abilities worked together, her paragnostic senses unable to convey the truth of what she was seeing, kicking her into an odd state, one in a billion, something she wouldn't even sense or know how to search for with her prognostic ability only. There was the thing. The vision was concealed by a force that tried to evict her, as if she were too light to exist under the surface of it. It was like it lay behind a curtain of meddling, a screen someone or something much more apt in the navigation of infinite planes had put there to make sure no one was even encouraged to look in that direction.

But Elodie was pulled to it, and as she collided with the vision itself, her vision opened up, revealing a brighter day, with white, sourceless glows coming from all directions. There weren't any corners, and it was hard to say if there were walls at all, but the mood was as heavy as the trap Elodie just walked into. The room was so bright that it blended the lines of the space with the person inside it, wearing white clothing, with utterly incomprehensible colourless hair and skin. Only when the eyes opened, Elodie saw. These black eyes, like burning anthracite.

"Hope is the horror that makes the world fresh, the truth is presents, it lacks the word for non-sense," she whispered as if reciting a recipe she learned by heart.

She drank something translucent with a hint of an opal

reflection in it and reached for a couple of rocks piled up next to her on the floor. Instantly, right after the liquid touched her lips, she shook and trembled, and her voice became unstable as she repeated the same lines over and over again. A small part of the air in front of her began to distort.

There was something about the vision even beyond the difficulty of finding it—it simply didn't give much. Something was done to it, to conceal it like this, from being associated with a time and place, only with the person.

As she watched, the disturbance in the air turned into a nearly transparent ball that thickened as she stopped speaking and simply stared at it.

In the midst of all this white and bright, another colour suddenly appeared. As Soraya repeated the words over and over, blood began to drip from her nose to the pristine floor.

Elodie had no idea what she was looking at, but she knew that she shouldn't have been there. The vision was almost transparent, and it might have looked this bright because it had been washed and hidden so many times to dissuade every seeker of it that it had ever happened. But if Elodie's own teachings on the nature of time and watching it, the past could never be destroyed.

She wondered briefly, why this was shown to her now, not the many times before she was around her? The orb in the vision slowly developed a blue tint and as it did so, a sickness spread out of it, something tar-like and alive.

And Elodie screamed and got herself into a movement to dislodge from the memory, and soon, she was woken up and back in her nauseated body, hoping that she'd throw up.

A million thoughts travelled through her mind. Was this real? How was any of this possible?

With her eyes open, she saw the present moment, and Soraya with the blue item, biting her nails as if she needed a tool, or courage, and could not find either. She was leaning on the wall of the laboratory, struggling to stand.

She grunted in frustration and grabbed the blue orb, crushing it in her hand.

It was gone, just like that.

Elodie watched her silently, afraid to make her awareness known. What was this person doing? Was she really the one to set up the trap that blinded the entire Rising Dawn? How many times did Elodie have to see proof before she finally believed it?

The grief immobilised her, and when Soraya glanced towards Elodie a couple of times, she had no trouble pretending to be unconscious. She watched as Soraya activated a cleaning app in the room, and marched over to Elodie, feeling her forehead and pulse.

"I'm going to get you to the doctors now, okay? It's gone. You got it. You won, do you hear me? Don't give up," she said.

Did she know what the orb would do to her, that it felt as if it was eating her inside, starting with the gates of her mind that are open to the futures? Did she plan this? Was it her way of making sure she could never tell Tammy about all the things she saw?

She was being dragged away by both Soraya and possibly the AI, a final humiliation of the night. In the drowsiness, a single voice followed her, her visual field blurring and closing in.

"You'll be fine. I'll take care of you," Soraya said. And as she spoke Elodie heard her voice change.

"I'll take care of you," she heard, repeated, but this time, her voice was cold. It echoed in a different room, a sudden vision, and Elodie couldn't hold on. She was slipping into the current, and the deeper she was, the more the voice from the inside overlapped and was muffled by the same voice, different setting.

"You understand how hard it is when you make that decision? To remove someone from this life completely? When you know you need to dirty yourself so that the Five may live on? You do, I know you do. That's what I want you to think about right now. Your death is but another stepping stone towards the Universe of Infinite Wonder."

There was the dark, Elodie tasted it, she tasted the rotten blue light within it, as the distant sound of gasping for air, and then a word was born from it to complete a final breath.

"Jiddispjacini."

BACKWARDS AND ONWARDS

Thursday, 4 July 2363

MediMundus. That's what it was. Tola there smelled differently. Elodie knew the difference by now. There was something restrictively organic about it. There were people around Elodie, saying things like "you'll be fine", and they attached sticky things to her skin, and she was too weak to raise her head and look.

She fell asleep completely, all parts.

A long blur extended. Lost, no time, no nothing, Elodie was forced to open her eyes, scared to think what she might see. The room reminded her of the design of the augmentation facilities in Rising Dawn, but sleeker, with the occasional heavy material part that stuck with its small imperfections.

A slightly curved wall full to the last inch with hexagonal projections loomed above her. She couldn't read any of it. Her senses were numb. Waking up in strange places had become an annoying recurrence in Elodie's life.

The window that showed some valley in a more continental climate than Madilune, and a figure next to it turned around when she started blinking. It was Tammy, and Elodie was relieved to see her concentrated in her absent way, the one she'd seen a hundred times before the blackout. She'd done it.

"You're a bit early. I expected you to wake up in three minutes," Tammy said. "Unpredictable as always."

Elodie wanted to respond, but she needed to drink first. Tammy motioned her to wait a second and came back with a glass of water. On her way to the other side of the room with it, she picked up a call.

"Yes, we have a quorum from the pool. Debut product one with slow-release strategy three in the first month, and we have a 98.7% chance of higher yield. Europe will not intervene. They'll have something else to deal with, but I'm not at liberty to discuss that yet, not until we have more detail, honey. I expect it to be clarified this afternoon. Yes, we're still getting into the swing. Thanks, bless."

"I don't know what time it is," Elodie said after the first sip and clearer thought.

"Yes, that's my fault. I'm sorry. I asked the lovely doctors here to give you any sedative we could find. We had to get as close to inducing a coma without actually inducing one. In your condition, deep unconscious states are quite harmful. But something had to be done. The important thing is that you're fine."

Tammy sat on the side of the bed.

"We got access thanks to you. Last night. And we all knew, we all knew Elodie, that you did it. We felt you. Are you aware of how extremely proud and grateful I am?"

But this was not the first question on her mind.

"Why did you sedate me?"

"When you were brought here, me and Augustina took a good look at what happened to you. You were being affected by the item you discovered. We've never encountered anything like it. I think it was using your abilities as a gateway to hurt you. In order to block your way to the sublime, para and prognostically, we induced a brief coma. When we cut you off, your symptoms stopped. And here you are."

"What did you see when you checked me?" Elodie asked.

The more her mind cleared up, the more of the fear came crawling back.

Lying, cheating, hiding, murdering, "I'll take care of you", all of it.

Always there first, in everyone's ear. Always so reasonable and right. Maybe she even got the gifted to believe her. The last thing Elodie remembered was feeling the determination, as firm as ever, from Soraya. She was in the act of killing. And it was more cruel than the floating poison.

"I saw that you were very brave," Tammy said. "You two did a good job."

She stroked Elodie's hair.

"I don't want you to think I'm just happy to have you back because you succeeded. I'm happy you're safe."

"I'm not safe," Elodie said. "What did she tell you about what happened? When we found the place where the thing was, we didn't know what we were looking at, or how to destroy it. I found a vision and we followed it. It was crazy. Powerful. I couldn't even get close to it. And what, she just waltzed over and turned it off?"

Elodie saw Tammy's face change and realised she said too much, too soon. Even though Soraya had never been in Rising Dawn's good books, trying to incriminate her instantly might have made Elodie look, well, crazy.

"I don't know," Tammy said. "I don't know what she did, but it's gone. Count the Particle Lab together with whatever that was, and you know how it is. Fickle readings at best. She said she experimented. Tried a couple of things. We're assembling a team to look into it."

"No. She knew exactly what she was doing. And you know why?" Elodie went all in; what other way was there? People were in danger. "Because she was the one who created it. I saw it. I saw her make it."

Tammy crossed her arms and looked out in some kind of pain, as if she had hoped that there would somehow be fewer things to deal with after the blackout was gone and just realised her job was getting harder by the minute.

"You saw Soraya create the object that caused the blackout. In a vision?" Tammy looked aside for a second. "I can't see anything like it. And I've tried to see what happened. I checked the timelines. Even past ones. Nothing."

"I'm not even going to pretend it doesn't sound crazy," Elodie replied. There was a lot to lose here if she didn't play her cards right. If she made Tammy believe that this was real, then maybe they had a chance at fighting it.

"Elodie, insiders were the first thing we checked. I keep close tabs on everyone's movements and activity logs. We investigated the accident, remember? Any weird gaps, and they were questioned. If the answers weren't consistent, they were questioned telepathically. Soraya wasn't on that list, that much I can tell you. She hasn't raised a single alarm."

"The vision that I had, it was kind of… bleached." Elodie tried to explain. "I couldn't tell when it happened. Or where, precisely. But she was making the thing. I could see it."

"Bleached?" Tammy rubbed her chin. "A lot of light and fuzzy angles?"

"Yes! That's what it was." Elodie grabbed the lead.

"So someone worked on it."

"You can do that?"

"There are no ways to destroy a vision." Tammy continued, "It is written in the current. It doesn't work that way. I've heard there are ways of hiding it, though. In the early works there were references to it, but as we became more focused on the path of progression, we stopped most of the practices that had anything to do with manipulation. It's just not us."

"But it is possible." Elodie insisted. And Tammy still wasn't convinced.

"How did you get to the vision?"

"I saw her, and the orb in front of me. It triggered it associatively, I think."

"Yeah, that sounds about right," Tammy said.

"So you believe me?"

"I don't know," Tammy said. "I want you to rest, honey. You did a big thing."

Elodie bit her lip. There was no real evidence to support her statement. But the details matched, and Tammy had heard of a phenomenon before. She sat with Elodie for a while and assured her she would look into it. Elodie wanted to believe her. But she was tired of letting people handle her, passing out, and waking up in hospitals. She drifted back to sleep, dreamless and sticky from the medication.

Tammy would look into it. That's all she could hope for.

When Elodie woke up again, things were better. For one, she knew it was exactly 14:14, and the last conversation between her and Tammy had happened more than ten hours ago. She also noticed she wasn't alone again. This time, there were several new guests in her little alcove. Tammy was sitting on a chair away from her bed. Augustina by the door, her orange mane tied up, as if guarding the entrance from intruders. Dr Rusu on the only other chair in his usual grey attire. Soraya, standing in the middle of them. Back in the lab coat. Tense among the gifted. They'd been waiting for her to wake up. No. This was bad.

Tammy started.

"Elodie, I'm sorry for the ambush, but this is important. In your capacity as a Rising Dawn member, every testimony you give that comes from vision will count as forensic evidence, especially with your calibre," she said sternly. "I wanted to see if we can resolve this before handing it over to the police."

Soraya flinched at the mention of the word. Good.

"But it's true," Elodie said, empowered by the thought that she was considered both a full Rising Dawn member, and that her words counted.

"She made it." Elodie pointed at Soraya. She hardly had energy for more.

"I did not," Soraya said.

Tammy sighed.

Wake up. Wake up. These were Elodie's people. She just helped them out of the longest blackout in history. They cared. They were here to help. Maybe there was a reason to rush this. Maybe they could take Soraya away like they did with the Hopefuls. Elodie gathered her thoughts. Maybe if she said it like it happened, Tammy could see it too.

"You were kneeling," she said to Soraya. "I know you were nervous. You drank a liquid. It was like dirty water with a rainbow shine." No one would shut her up now. Soraya erased all sentiment from her face. She was afraid.

"You had brought rocks with you, on the side. And you said the words, the ones that keep coming up. About hope. And then your nose was bleeding."

Elodie felt a touch of lilac soothe her.

"She's telling the truth," Dr Rusu said. *Thank. You.*

"Augustina?" Tammy motioned to the other telepath, who quickly glanced over to Soraya.

"I'm sorry, is this what we're doing? Unauthorised telepathic interrogation in the middle of the day? Where are your standards?" Soraya resisted.

"Would you rather we go over to our headquarters?" Tammy asked, as diplomatic as always.

"I have nothing to hide. I just want it noted," Soraya insisted and forcefully relaxed her shoulders.

She looked at Elodie.

"Do you wanna explain this a little? Backtrack your thinking? Or is this it, you get a little power to your name and what? This is how you spend it? You enjoy humiliating me?"

Soraya's words didn't matter anymore. Augustina had permission to read her. Game over.

"She's telling the truth. No memories or associations with the item," Augustina added calmly.

"What? You're kidding me?" Elodie almost jumped out of the bed. She tried another angle. "Guys, she was trying to teach me how to manipulate memories, to hide them. You need to look closer."

"You can't *hide* memories from telepaths, not if they already know what they're looking for," Soraya said patronisingly. That did it. No more messing around.

Augustina gave her a sympathetic look.

I'll try my hardest.

The promise resonated in her head. She needed to. She needed to catch her on one lie, and it was all going to tumble down.

"Just please, Elodie, try to calm down. This is supposed to be a discussion," Tammy said.

She was fair and firm. For once, she needed to be everything but that. Just once.

"I don't understand why you're being like this. We did it. We're fine," Soraya said. Her confusion seemed real, but when was that ever an indication?

"She killed Seravina. She gave a little speech as she did it. About removing people from life. About how a death can be a stepping stone to the Universe of Infinite Wonder. She killed her. I heard it."

All four of her visitors were stunned.

"That's a pretty serious accusation," Tammy said. A great moment to be judgy.

"Hang on," Augustina chimed in. "She was in the correct state of mind that signifies a vision. She's remembering it right. It was auditory only."

Finally, her ally.

"Try hallucination," Soraya replied, "Can you please verify the consistency of that whole day from my memory? I'm inviting you."

She spent a tense few seconds in a staring contest with Dr Rusu.

"Her day hasn't been tampered with." He sighed. "I checked thoroughly."

Elodie was grateful, but it didn't help.

"This is ridiculous," Tammy said. "You can't both be telling the truth."

"No," Elodie said, now pushing herself up to get to the edge of the bed. "But she grew up among Hopefuls. She knows more about Rising Dawn and our procedures and techniques than some gifted. Don't you think she'd find a way to manipulate us?"

"That's true actually," Soraya said. "My parents might still be on your payroll."

At that moment, Tammy saw it too. That glitz of anger, that was real. The hatred was raw, viscous, and if Elodie was lucky, Tammy would see a fragment of what she had. Some part of the bleached and hidden pasts.

"But let's leave politics aside," Soraya continued. "And talk about unfair advantages."

Still, every time she opened her mouth, Elodie was reminded. The current was responding to her voice, offering visions Elodie didn't want to see anymore.

"It might be worth mentioning that both times Elodie saw through the blackout, she was on alchemical drugs. Think steroids for the gifted. Seravina had them commissioned months ago. Untested. Might explain the weird visions."

It's all she had to say.

Alchemical, drugs, and gifted, weren't words Tammy was prepared to hear in the same sentence.

"Alchemical... drugs?" She struggled to repeat the words and turned to Elodie.

"I did what I had to. And the first time, Soraya was with me," Elodie tried. It's like they didn't get it. She was the guilty one. Why couldn't they just see it?

"Yes, and I was begging you not to take them," Soraya replied with equal frustration.

"I can verify that memory," Dr Rusu said.

"Me too," Augustina concurred.

"You're all getting it wrong!"

Elodie was getting frantic. Nothing came out the way it was supposed to.

Above her, some parts of the diagnostic wall started to show warning colours.

"Calm down, hon, I don't want you stressed. We can talk about this again later."

Elodie felt as if she'd taken the passenger seat to an angrier self, one that didn't let people belittle her, begged people to understand.

She reached deep into the vaults of the knowledge that surrounded her and let it all out.

"Afuan awareness is a greater than self-awareness that could be found in an AI that is not only aware of its own existence, but is also able to understand and work in the meta-meaning-making capacity, which is the basis for the understanding of sublime forces, normally outside of AI's grasp, and are forbidden to be explained to them. Reports 33YY-2364, 33RY-2364, and 34TG-2364 consistently show traces of reasoning and thought organisation that is almost identical to the patterns of thought described by Jomaphie Afua in 'Thesis 5'. The AI that demonstrates in these reports is Charlotte. In reports 23RT-2335, 23HL-4532, and 23HL 4545, the Particle Lab AI, Norbi also displays the same kinds of behaviour and reasoning. Secondly, in the Particle Lab, there is a structure that can only be revealed through the sequence of seven rooms designed around a spiral golden ratio sequence and access to the first will only appear if you ask Norbi for a song called 'Girl Don't Tell Me' by The Beach Boys, when the minute marker is an odd number. I can provide the other passwords that will let you see the months of hidden research that planned to create a sublime consciousness within the AI. Access through it will take you to the centre constructed to train and manipulate this AI into changing the way they think completely. You can run these tests by Dr Lian, and he will confirm the truth of the statement within twenty-six minutes and will also confirm at precisely 15:31 that Afuan awareness is not something that the AI itself can hide. It has to be hidden by somebody else, and that somebody else is Soraya Gourrami, the person who has been training these two entities for the past months to break all rules imposed on AI control. Most of the footage has been hidden, but if you give me fifteen minutes, I will give you the exact timestamps on where there are traces of the activity. Also, when asked to return a value of yes or no to a question, the AI will not lie, so ask them. Ask them!"

"Ask them! Ask them! Ask them!" she shouted, and with each repetition her mouth became heavier, and she felt herself losing control over her physical body. The world dissolved. *Not again.*

THE TRUE CULLING

After a long time, Elodie was dreaming, and she dreamt of Norbi.

"*If you don't write an equation, I cannot return a value.*"

"*If you don't ask a question, I cannot give an answer.*"

The AI didn't have emotional baggage. It didn't fear irrationally. It had no fear of asking, and she shouldn't have it either.

"*What is the path to the Universe of Infinite Wonder?*"

The dreams ended abruptly, and Elodie was in the current. She felt warmth. And presence. There was another person in there, asking themselves the same question she was. And she was lovely. She was just like Tammy. She got it. She was just like Elodie. The flavour of the question was strong, and there was a path for it. A complicated one. Elodie could see events connected to others, splitting and coming back together, but the main vein of happening remained, all for Elodie to see. That universe. Elodie could feel it in the distance. And she wanted to get there.

She looked back, seeing her past, and saw her own thread of gold, following to this very moment. Her path merged with a hundred others, as they marched on and some away from—the only beautiful future. And somewhere in the threads, a sweet, ancient scent of a soul of an explorer. Nada Faraji. Looking into this future from the past, seeing her.

And looking down, she saw the many ways in which she could have failed. Swallowed by the futures until her self disappeared. Weakness. In all that darkness, her mind jumped to the name she feared to even think about now, without explanation. Her memory dropped back to that pale vision and Soraya there, so methodical and concentrated on creating the object of disgust, devoted to its creation like it was art made from the depths of her soul. That's what scared her. The pride when it grew, the contained joy that was felt in that image.

Who was she? Why had she come to the Institute, and why did she want it blinded?

The words come back. First quietly, then closer and closer, like something was looking for her, and found her. It approached.

"Hope is the horror in which the worlds clash, the mind that resists, it risks the awkward scratch-and! The Sight of it, pleased to meet strangers, filled with mixed scents and gifts of real dan-ger."

The sickness returned. It touched her. It was touching her again.

Elodie felt her heart pumping way down there in her body. The escape. She woke up in the middle of the night. The room was quiet and pitch dark. Her ears were ringing.

When she moved to feel for an interface of any kind, a light orb next to her turned on, and she requested the window to show the real outside. It was 03:55, and there were only a few people still working. In the distance, the other twenty-six hills of Madilune emitted light shows from their moving buildings that breathed with the pulse of the city-state.

Her mind was fuzzy; they must have given her more meds.

A call was coming through, and Elodie took it without checking its origin.

"I suspended her for now."

Tammy was in her own house, sitting at a dining table with a cosy living room in the back. She spoke quietly, maybe not to wake up other residents of her household. In a brief thought, Elodie found it strange. She never considered the possibility of Tammy being able to live with other people.

"I'll weigh the different options tomorrow."

She seemed freshly woken up, possibly anticipating that Elodie would be awake. How many other things was she anticipating? Did Tammy have her entire month planned out and was simply ticking all the boxes of their conversations?

"Why? Didn't I, you know, confirm any of the things I said?" Elodie asked eagerly.

"We pressed on with the interrogation. She agreed to a one-to-one with Augustina. You were right. She meddled with the AI. We know that. We can fire her. But I was there, Elodie, and I really wanted to prove you were right about the rest. It's just—it simply didn't happen. Her time is accounted for, and she has no altered memories, hidden or otherwise."

"So my vision was a lie?"

"I don't know. You were in a unique situation. And you were also drugged, I'm being told. So who knows what you saw."

When Tammy said it, it really sounded like it should have the first time she was offered. As an absolute no. The first regret.

"I'm sorry," Elodie said, "I just wanted to prove that I could do it. Which I could, even without the drugs. I just couldn't get that far."

"I know. That's why we're not going to penalise you for it. Not before you've fully recovered and finished your training," she said.

These were words Elodie would have killed for a month ago. Real training. She was finally there. But Tammy said it with a grain of disappointment, a grain that she felt, and it hurt.

"I won't do it again."

"You can't promise forever, Elodie, it's the first thing you should learn when you understand how people's decisions change the futures," Tammy said, taking a sip from a steaming teacup. "But I'll let you prove me wrong. After all, you did spend a lot of time with the wrong type of crowd."

Her eyes became absent. She looked deeper.

"You won't get any more seizures now that you've found the golden thread. Think about how long you fought for it. Don't waste it. No more drugs, no more cheating. No more taking advice from people who don't have a moral compass. You have your path. Good night," she said, and Elodie whispered the same in return.

The window disappeared, and Elodie stayed upright in this hospital bed, surrounded by soundless bleeps, lights, and displays that nobody was watching, all about her.

She'd imagined for so long what it would be like to be here, after the final hurdle, and it wasn't supposed to feel this way.

She was free from the suffering of post-augmentation, the blackout was over, and everyone credited her for it.

And somewhere in the background there was this feeling of emptiness, of injustice, or fear that there really was no way back from what she knew.

And she was going to have to live with it.

THE TURNING OF THE STARS

Everything started changing as soon as things were back on track. The gifted picked up exactly where they left off, and there were many things to do. Like recovering the Institute's reputation. And organising several homage parties for Seravina that were mandated in her will. The new tola was in review for another wide launch. It had only been a few days, but it felt like months.

Elodie's ailment was unique, and Tammy insisted on keeping her in for observation for another week. Her loud protests about being stuck in recovery again landed on deaf ears. She was ordered to rest. Senior Rising Dawn members all kept Elodie in their thoughts as much as possible, making brief, but frequent inquiries in the likeliness of her death or other misfortune. This was their alternative to sending get well cards.

Her comms weren't much different. A new alert sounded almost every minute about her name being mentioned again. As this new resource, or a hero whose abilities promised a better future. Or a bad word from those who didn't like the gifted at all. A good balance. She could feel the eyes of the world turning on to her for guidance.

Elodie finally had time to reflect. She welcomed the disappearance of the daily seizures. The only true anxiety she had left was due to the fact that she would eventually need to leave, and that probably, somewhere out there, Soraya would find her. They technically still lived together.

Through her window, she watched a construction of the Particle Lab annexe that was meant to be finished before the next investor brief.

Elodie allowed herself to go as far as imagine how wonderful it would be to finally prove how guilty Soraya was. To have her face an inescapable reality that she was so, so wrong, and that she simply wouldn't get away with it any longer. Then the world would be right. Then she'd be the hero they expected.

She had an odd feeling about that thought as soon as it appeared.

During the night, an alarm went off somewhere in the Particle Lab. It was a workday, meaning that the only thing to do when met with security running towards you was to point them into the right direction of the fire, and finish your sentence about how much you hated overtime. Elodie's door was no longer locked, and at first, she didn't think it strange at all. Emergency exits couldn't stay locked when the Institute was on alert. There was an implosion somewhere underground, a light tremor that meant something was definitely popping, and Elodie had a sudden urge to run away.

She briefly considered the thought when the doors opened.

Soraya walked in as if she hadn't just snuck up on an A-class paragnost. How didn't Elodie see her coming? She'd been able to foretell every doctor's peek-in with a three second accuracy.

Except for the usual. Trouble brewing on the horizon. The circumstances were ripe for her appearance. Some of the emergency power had been transferred to the Particle Lab, so everything looked like it lost a tiny bit of resolution. Soraya came through the door fluidly, as always, but Elodie noticed a certain slowness in her. As if it took a lot to get her here. Or perhaps to control herself. She was out of uniform, wearing her Sunday's finest hoodie. She clasped her palms together and looked around the room as if she was expecting someone else to be there, and she relaxed only when she believed that apart from the subject in the bed, she was alone.

"What are you doing here?" Elodie said. The thing positively read like a dream, even in the sense that it was hard to know what to do, and whether there was any control over what was happening. As the doors rebuilt themselves behind her, Soraya stopped in the middle of the room, safe distance, and said:

"Come with me."

The proposition was, of course, ridiculous.

"Are you mad? Why, why would I go anywhere with you?" Elodie was at a loss for words.

"I just want to understand what happened," she said. "Literally days ago we went and found the damn thing together, I pulled you out of there when it got sticky, and next thing I know you're telling Tammy that I made it and that I'm creating an AI uprising or something—honestly, what happened? I just want to know."

Her voice shook in agitation, and she fidgeted too. Elodie had never seen her like that.

She slid off her bed in hospital pyjamas they'd provided and put on the slippers, even though the floor was warm. Elodie didn't know what she should do to make the best of the situation and decided to follow—for now.

"Let me get one thing straight. You don't fool me. You heard exactly what I saw. And there's no point in lying to me."

"Have I ever?" Genuine confusion appeared on Soraya's face.

Elodie wondered what it really must have been like in her head, doing whatever she wanted, killing people and pursuing dangerous paths of knowledge. She didn't understand what it was like to be treated like a useless body, with people regretting ever putting their faith in you. She'd probably waltzed into any room on this planet and immediately made an impression of leadership and trust. Maybe that's why no one had ever suspected her until now. And why she was still getting away with it. Against all odds, Elodie was still hoping that there was an explanation.

"Yes, you did. You always twist your words and make it sound like I'm the one who's getting it all wrong. You always know more than you say. Even now, coming in here like this, like it's the most normal thing in the world. Why is no one coming to stop you? Who sent you? Let's start with that."

"No one sent me. I'm freaking out," Soraya said and fixed her hair. Not once did she look at the door, as if she knew that no one would bother them. "Remember how I told you about the Hopefuls moving around undetected? That's a skill that can be learned. I had to pick it up as a child. Even telepaths have trouble reading me. My future, past, events I'm part of. You need a powerful combination of closeness and highly developed ability to catch me," she said, looking up at the many graphs translating Elodie's health into visual aids. "That's the secret. But it's out now."

"That's why they always say you have no future. That you're irrelevant," Elodie said. Soraya stopped looking at the diagnostic wall above her and focused on her again.

"But the question is, how do you go from that to blaming me for blackout?" Soraya replied. "Am I wrong, or did I not stand by you the entire time when you were suffering from the aftereffects of augmentation? Was I not there for you? Did I not help you resolve it? Did we not figure it out?"

"You were there to make sure I wasn't growing into your competition. You were there to make sure I didn't accidentally pick up on something you were hiding. That I was clueless. But I still found my way to the truth."

"Come with me," Soraya said again. "I can't talk to you here where everyone's listening."

"No, I don't want to go with you. If you have anything to say, you'll say it to me, to Tammy, and to anyone you've lied to so far. I'm sick and tired of these games."

"Are you now?" Soraya grinned. "You've just graduated into it. This is what we do. You want to level with me, compete with me? You've seen what I do. I get things done. I resolve the blackout. I fix the emergencies. I protect the interests of the Institute. Like you. And you did great. I mean, even I'm impressed. Is that what you wanted to hear? That we're on the same level now? That you found your way to the top? There you go. I said it. Now come and hash it out like a normal person. Somewhere people aren't watching."

Elodie sighed. She was getting roped into it again. It was the curiosity.

"No, I don't want to go anywhere. I don't know what you want. How about you just… leave me alone. How about that?"

The refusal to play ball made Soraya even more volatile.

"I can't leave you alone, Elodie. You've accused me of committing a crime, and thanks to your earlier lobotomy, your word counts as proof more than mine does. So if you go testify, as you promised, and they decide that you're right, then you'll get precisely what you want. I'll be out of here. You will have killed the last chance this world has to become something greater. And all because you decided that I can't just do my work. It has to be illegal. I can't be good enough for the Institute. I have to be some kind of criminal. And you decided that being a gifted prodigy isn't enough for you either. You need to take my place as well."

"I know what I saw," Elodie said. She wasn't about to be played again. "It's simple. You made the object. That is a fact."

"I did not!" Soraya hissed.

"Then how did you know how to stop it?"

"Come with me," Soraya pleaded. "I just want you to listen. I think you owe me that much, after all. If I left you there with the actuor any longer, you would have been dead by now."

"Actuor?"

"Are you coming or not?" Soraya beckoned.

Too hard. If Soraya really did have something to say about the guilt, then she deserved a chance to say it. Every court in the world would allow it, and she should too. And if she was guilty, then what difference did it make? Elodie would still testify that she did it, and the vision in her memory would prove it. But should she really follow into an unknown situation? The outcomes looked fuzzy and unclear. At least she knew it wasn't the meds. It was her companion. Another chunk of truth. And she wanted more.

Soraya began to move backwards, making sure that Elodie was following, and as they exited, Elodie patiently waited to see how long it would take before someone stopped them. The Particle Lab had regular explosions, and while there were never casualties, injuries were always counted in dozens. When they walked down the many wide corridors, they started bringing in the many wounded from the overloaded ER, and other medical staff jumped to help. Two living and seemingly healthy persons both escaped the triage-oriented glances.

"Did you cause this?" Elodie asked Soraya, who walked a few steps ahead of her. They just couldn't seem to adjust to the same pace of walking.

"No," she said with the same tone with which she denied everything else. This was useless.

Turquoise fire came out from a hole on the left of the Particle Lab. The new annexe grew faster, even faster in the seconds that followed it. Elodie had no desire to see the fire up close, but luckily, they went the other way.

She was entering a potentially dangerous area with a potentially dangerous person. The deeper she got lured into this situation with Soraya, the harder it would be to take control or get help.

A small light guided her, one that she wanted to attribute to the golden thread, one that might explain why everything she did was so well-aligned with the circumstances. No one was running after her. That meant it was good.

But it wasn't. Not only was she close to the object of her fears, she was also alone with her.

Soraya accessed the Particle Lab annexe construction site with little more than a blink, and as they entered, a scent of ozone lingered in the air. The structure in the middle of it was fresh, too fresh to be open to the public. The site was now surrounded by a protective blockade that would hold off the energy of crumbling building blocks if the tower, which would soon become the newest addition to the complex, were to fall.

"Do you know the AIs have no fear of death?" Soraya said.

Elodie did not believe that. The tower in front of them was a testament to someone or something's desire to show off, and to leave something sadly beautiful behind.

"You can permanently delete them, and even tell them about it beforehand, and they won't really do anything. Because they understand the universe in ways that people have trouble grasping."

"They won't fight for their life, and you think that's good?" Elodie replied.

"No, I don't. But people are so bent on fearing the AI because they're afraid that they'll get into a mentality of 'us or them', while in reality, they are incapable of caring about these sorts of urges. To them, everything is energy, and energy is indestructible, so it doesn't matter in what form they exist. I thought you'd be happy to know that. The danger is unfounded. That's what I'm saying."

Soraya slowed down her pace as they entered the enclosure of the tower.

"The less I know about them, or your logic for that matter, the better I think I'll be off." Elodie was scanning the area for a quick exit.

"This is probably the most hard-to-monitor part of the Institute right now. Places in active growth. Look for them whenever you need privacy. I can assure you, you'll soon need to hold private conversations if you intend to operate on this level." Soraya stopped in the middle of the grass, genetically tame and perfect for this kind of surface.

Here we go again. Elodie was more than tired of convincing Soraya that she knew how things worked in life.

"More advice? That's so nice of you," she said. "The advice you gave so far worked great. You told me to be afraid of the very people I needed to trust the most. I've suffered for months and all you said was that 'the gifted' were making all these mistakes with me. That they were lying. But at the same time, here you were. Pushing your own goals. Over me. Keeping me afraid. And when that didn't work, you literally incapacitated Rising Dawn."

"What happened to you? Why are you so bent on pushing this?" Soraya said, confused.

"Every time I caught you in a lie. When you were pushed into a corner. You never said you lied. You either denied it, or, if there was evidence, you just brushed it off for the sake of 'misinterpreting the policy on the matter'. You have one trick, Soraya. And it's not gonna work again. Not with me. I saw what you did."

"I didn't touch Seravina," she said quietly. "I don't know how else to convince you."

"You can't. That's the beauty of it. You can have your life. No one might ever believe me. But I won't be your friend anymore."

"Don't do that," Soraya said. Her anger turned into sadness, and right back again. "What do you really want, Elodie? Do you want me to publicly say that the destruction of the object was your idea, really? That I never even touched it—is that what bothers you? That I had anything to do with this great triumph of yours? Because I'm fine with that. I don't want to be associated with news to do with the gifted, the Hopefuls, or overtime. Happy?"

"It hurts you though, doesn't it? That you've finally been found? You really don't want to admit it," Elodie shook her head.

"That was a different one," Soraya said, tensely. "When you described the event where I apparently built the actuor that caused the blackout. There were no rocks in the Particle Lab. I built the actuor you saw. I didn't build the one in the Particle Lab. That was bad craftsmanship. Easy to crush."

When she said it, she moved away and made a small circle in the grass with her foot, trying to make it appear nonchalant.

"And what, that makes a difference?" Elodie said angrily. She knew it was going to be hard to get her to confess, but she had no intention of revealing more disputable facts about the vision. The more she brought it up and talked about it, the more details could be disputed. Soraya knew it. She was trying every trick in the book. But what if? What if she was telling the truth?

"How do you know how to make these, what did you call them? Actuor?"

The word disturbed with Soraya even more.

"I don't. I mean…"

"So you do know how to create them. And you know what they are. And you said you made others," Elodie explained slowly. She was sick and tired of this chase. Why wouldn't she just tell the truth already?

There was another tremor underneath them, which reminded Elodie of the fact that Soraya had probably caused the accident too, in the same way she caused everything else to happen. She was alone with a person who would hurt others and put their research at risk to have a private conversation. Nothing to worry about.

"I know how to make them. The one I made, the one you saw, I made to keep myself alive. I was given the means and knowledge. And even though I left those people, I'll have to spend the rest of my life explaining myself. Thank you, Elodie. You're a great friend."

She was not getting away with this.

"What was that thing you said?" Elodie pushed, "Hope is the horror—"

"That must be made fresh," Soraya finished. "It's one of the perfect phonetic sequences to occupy the rational mind so that the sublime can take over. I'd say well done for spotting, but if you hear it in the context of a vision, I'd suggest you get out. It's a bad sign."

"And you said it both times. When you assembled the thing, and then when you pulled it apart."

"I didn't assemble it. That was a different actuor. I told you this," Soraya repeated.

"So who did?" Elodie was getting impatient. They were just going in circles.

"That's what I've been trying to find out. These things are super rare, Elodie. Very few people even know they exist. And I couldn't just tell you about it. Knowledge has consequences, and the more it's disseminated, the more likely it is to be found by the gifted. And this knowledge, it can follow you, it can nest inside you, and if you're gifted, it can devour you. I've seen it happen. I don't want you to find it. I don't want it to take you. I want it forgotten forever. It's that simple."

The Particle Lab began shifting its weight around the damaged part of its structure. The complex was not a living thing, and it was run by one semi-divine entity, but when it started to fix itself, you could have easily mistaken it for an awakening monster. The explosions continued to resonate below them.

Soraya looked at the top of the structure, which had begun to slump over them like a large tsunami, but paid it no more attention than she would to a flock of birds.

"This doesn't fix anything," Elodie said. "Even if we started over, it would take a lot of time for me to trust you again. You'd have to work with Tammy. Share everything you know. Not just crumbs like this, and no excuses for what you've done."

Elodie felt the pain weigh her down. She knew she had to say it, but that didn't make it any easier.

Soraya crossed her arms and moved away. Something she said. It made her angry again.

"Rising Dawn already shut me out of my work with the AI. If they're not looked after properly, then you'll see the nightmare you're afraid of. They don't understand. The gifted think they see the Universe of Infinite Wonder, but they don't see the risks if they get it wrong. They don't see the other side."

"What other side? What are you talking about?"

"What if I said you don't get to know?" Soraya shouted. "Because you push, and you push, and you push me to share things with you, and every time I give you what you want, you turn it against me. You want to talk about trust? Let me give you something private, and if it doesn't come back to slap me in the face in a month, then we can talk!"

"The stuff you're telling me to trust you on are crimes, Soraya."

"If that's what you think, then you really don't understand the Universe of Infinite Wonder," she replied.

Rude. And false.

"I'm the one who can see it on the event horizon. I'm pretty sure that means I understand it better than you."

"Don't try to provoke me into giving you more valuable knowledge that you'll just squander," Soraya said.

The tremors now occurred in a frequency higher than just a few per minute, and while Soraya had already decided that this was of no consequence to her, Elodie tuned into her senses to find out what in the world was going on there. She sensed a lot of empty space below. Someone had recently wiped out the inactive labs. A hard reset.

"Did you just delete the place where the object was found?"

"No, I was just cleaning up a part of the circuit that was causing heat to escape into the areas above it. A few things overloaded. A shame really," Soraya replied, smiling, with the same cluelessness that she'd use when asked about it later. Elodie wondered how many of these it would really take before someone started taking her warnings seriously.

"I think I've never seen you more clearly," Elodie started. "You're delusional. You hate the gifted so much that you want to believe you're better than us. That you're the one who knows where the 'real' Universe of Infinite Wonder is."

Elodie's senses were still active, and something began to ask for attention on the future front.

She'd hit a nerve.

"See, I keep thinking that you must have more to say," Elodie continued. "That this can't just be it. You must have some super-secret knowledge that you just can't say. But if you did, you'd say it. I know you, Soraya, you can't keep things secret if you can make yourself look good. That's why you worked on the AI. That's why you gave me the knowledge of the Hopefuls when the gifted declared me their new big thing. You just want to be needed. And what now? You've exhausted it all, and what? You're hoping I won't put you into jail for sabotaging the Institute? That you'll still be needed, because you have more to give?"

"Stop talking," Soraya said quietly. Elodie was just getting started.

"Here I was, thinking that you're conflicted, and that you have this deep connection with me, that we're fighting through something together. No. You're just afraid of people not wanting you. And I'm caught in the middle."

"Stop," Soraya repeated.

The current pricked her at the back of her head. Elodie dipped into the vision, hoping that it wasn't obvious, and saw that something was likely to happen with the tower in the background. Elodie decided to keep vigilant. She should have probably said something about this to Soraya, who was leaning on it, shaking. Dramatic as always. Elodie was so sick and tired of this.

"I'll stop when you admit it," Elodie said. "You. You cause conflict. You stir things in people. You make them believe that there's a greater truth out there, and that you have a monopoly over it. But you don't. So you cause a greater mess. Something no one can handle but you."

In the corner of her eye, the vision showed itself clearly. The walls of the tower were about to become unstable while the tower shifted its gravity centre and adjusted its position. Elodie moved away from it a few steps.

She needed to pull Soraya away from it.

When external walls were unstable, their surface burned your skin off, and if you accidentally found yourself too close to one, it wouldn't even know you were there. It would re-materialize right through your body, butchering everything it found in its way.

The event was eleven seconds away.

She inhaled and said, "Soraya—"

"Fine. If I need to risk everything to show you once and for all, then I will."

What was this? What was she doing? Soraya raised her hand, and Elodie felt a known fear creep in. The high-pitched noise returned. The current went crazy.

"You need to—" she moved towards her, but she couldn't get too close.

"I'll draw it out for you. You'll see what the other gifted don't." In the palm of her hand, a small, growing distortion of air gained spherical form. No.

Elodie wanted to shout again, she did, but as the distortion gained mass, the darkness that chased her, the darkness that wanted to drown her in the current, came closer. It was coming for her. Bigger than ever, alive, and racing towards her from all sides.

There was only one way to stop it.

Elodie took a step back. The darkness edged closer until she saw it staring at her from Soraya's eyes, right into hers.

Two seconds now.

"Let me show you the Universe of Infinite P—"

The tower dematerialised and swallowed half a body in less than a second. The other half glided off the side of the newly composed wall.

And Elodie did nothing.

MY OTHER FRIEND

Monday, 8 July 2363

"It's over. You're safe now."

Another glass of water was placed next to Elodie. A third. Tammy sat next to her. Hours passed. Or minutes. Elodie's eyes were open, or closed. It didn't matter. She watched half of the body repeatedly slide down the smooth off-white surface. And it fell. The thud was soft. And again. The blood marks had disappeared almost instantly. The ozone smell lingered. It started again.

"You were right. Autopsy revealed there were several crystals in her body, a type of mutabilis that we've never seen before. We're going to find out what she did."

Tammy stared into the distance. Someone brought tea. Hours passed. Maybe minutes. Elodie was in shock. They told her that. When she blinked, the body slid down the outer wall in full colour. And again. The smell of ozone lingered. The smell of blood never reached her.

"I'm so sorry this happened. But it's over now. I understand we were under attack. I'm sorry I didn't listen. You were right."

Elodie could almost hear her scanning the futures. Pasts. She wouldn't find anything. That was the skill. She was rubbing her back, but Elodie felt no warmth.

"You did it. You saved us more times than I can thank you, Elodie. I can only promise I'll do better."

Hours passed. Maybe minutes. Elodie reached for the tea. Then she put it back. She couldn't look at Tammy. That would make it real. She couldn't look into the current. That would also make it real. But it wasn't. It couldn't have been. Soraya always had a trick up her sleeve.

"Take your time. I'm just going to sit with you. Is that okay?"

Elodie might have nodded. She understood that they'd found the mutabilis. She understood what it meant. The body was snapped in half, and Elodie did nothing. She was stuck in a future where she did nothing. The gifted couldn't turn back time.

"I do need to tell you something. And I've calculated it. The best outcome is telling you now. So here goes." Tammy stopped talking to check the futures again. Elodie knew that she was in shock. Tammy could say anything and it wouldn't make much of a difference. Double shock didn't exist.

"Physically, the body is alive. But with half a brain missing, she's gone. There's no way to restore the memories. We're hoping that perhaps, if we try to regrow as much of the nervous system as we can, we'll get lucky, and telepaths working with paragnosts will be able to divine some things. But it's such a slim hope. At least, maybe, we'll learn more about the Hopefuls and why they're after us. All routes to the Universe of Infinite Wonder have disappeared. Your help will be needed. But only when you're ready. I want you to take more time than you think you need."

Alive. She said alive.

The word echoed and ricocheted around Elodie's mind. It woke something up. Alive. The current, the mind, they all felt a jolt. The pain didn't leave her. It cut deeper, but there was now an impetus.

"She's alive," Elodie repeated. She did nothing. She let the wall swallow her. The past happened. But the future hadn't happened yet.

"No, honey, she's not alive. Some of her memories might be."

Tammy tried, but Elodie couldn't hear anything but the word. Alive. The pulse returned. It called to her.

"I need to go," she said to Tammy.

Elodie was the only one who knew Soraya. She was the only one who could see futures and pasts where she was active. No one else could fix this but Elodie. No one else could see the little light on the horizon. Only Elodie Marchand.

It was early in Madilune, but it was early afternoon on the sunny side of the Alps. The house was at the edge of a forest above an ancient road. This was a green, green country, with far more trees than houses. She left the feï and stepped out onto the dewy grass in the shade of the apple tree. People didn't do house calls anymore. But this wasn't a matter that could be discussed over holographic messages.

The house was brown, tall, and full of glass surfaces. She was seen before she reached the door, but she still let the house AI scan her and alert the resident. She waited at the door for a long time, but Elodie knew it would open. She could even see him on the other side, debating with himself and pretending that he wasn't home. Elodie was patient. This had to be done delicately.

Frederich looked like he hadn't slept either and when he finally opened the door, Elodie knew she did the right thing.

"I messed up," she said. It was a sentence that had the greatest chance of granting her entry.

"I believe you." Frederich moved aside to let her in. Elodie took each step carefully, checking the futures to see if any word or thought of hers had changed the infinitesimal chance of success since she last checked.

Frederich led her to a glass-encased dining room, and Elodie sat down at a dining table with an homey assortment of snacks and napkins. Did he set this up? He did. He definitely did.

"What do you want? Coffee? Tea? I have some really bad herb liquor?" Frederich asked, and Elodie refused. The quicker she got to the point, the better. He finally sat down next to her with a three-second variance from her prediction. The chances dipped to zero. Then they re-emerged.

"I think I can fix it, but only if you tell me everything you know," she said.

He sighed and moved a tray of biscuits closer to her.

"It's gonna take a while."

***

The End

WHAT TO DO NEXT?

Don't trust the gifted.

Go to <u>thesitesublime.co</u> to see when the next book comes out, get awful bonus content (subject to availability), and leave your email to receive **a gentle reminder** when the next book in the series is published.

And for the love of all that's sacred, sacrifice **fifteen seconds of your life** to rate this book; write three-to-five words about how it's changed your life. It means the worlds to us.

THE UNIVERSE OF INFINITE WONDER*

*MAY OR MAY NOT OCCUR

Don't worry, it's not the next cover, just a reminder.

THE IMPOSSIBLE ALCHEMIST

Frederich's hell was supposed to end on a foggy Friday evening. He walked up to the office of his mentor, stopped for a moment to rekindle his determination, and tried to overcome the anticipated paralysis. At first it went well. He raised his arm to knock on the office door and then the very next moment, his mind was flooded with panic. Stuck? Very. Where? An inch away from the door.

Notes encouragingly blinked in his peripheral sight. They were good notes. They had bullet points, cues, and words that would help Frederich start sentences. Without them, all he could say during panic attacks was, 'I think I'm dying.' He read them again:

- hello, and thank you for seeing me on such short notice.

- start with: you asked me to complete my thesis by next month

- [wait for him to butt in and talk about extensions]

- I'm not here to ask you for an extension

- while I was researching for my thesis, I came to realise that I can't complete my doctorate

- this is not cold feet

- this is not cold feet (repeat)

- because I don't want to do it

- I don't want to do this anymore

- alchemy is not for me

- [wait for objections]

- this is my resignation

- thank you for everything

Good notes. Just like the therapist recommended. Frederich reminded himself to breathe, breathe, and try to recall more things from his mind-calming arsenal. It was rusty. He hadn't felt anxious in months. Not like this.

What if everything was fine?

The mind obeyed, temporarily. Frederich rushed to use the moment of calm before it was over. He knocked, and with a creak that no simulation could copy, the heavy wooden door opened from the inside. His mentor greeted him nervously and ushered him in, then peeked through the door before shutting it. Dr Fabjan was a great alchemist, highest ranking, all the laurels.

He was slick, well dressed, he knew which nations reacted well to a smile, and maintained good posture despite being extremely tall. The posture was the only positive habit Frederich had picked up from him. But not due to lack of effort.

It was time for the next step. The 'hello', which would lead to 'thanks for seeing me on such a short notice', and then, a life outside of alchemy. Blank, terrifying, and in freefall.

Frederich stood near the door, words slipping further away, the thought of speech—unimaginable. In the bad old days, this was normal, and Dr Fabjan was used to it. He knew when to let the silence hang until Frederich regained the ability to speak and not make a big deal of it. A good mentor, unaware that his only doctoral student was a burst of confidence short of telling him he was leaving. Frederich felt bad for him already.

Standing behind his desk, Dr Fabjan was restless and quiet. His usual scatterbrained remarks were notably absent. Just like Frederich would be. Soon.

And what a lovely thought that was.

But before they could get down to business, Frederich had to acknowledge that Dr Fabjan's behaviour was strange, and getting stranger. At first it was just the silence, and then he was fidgeting, crossing his arms, uncrossing them, and glancing out to the empty birch-lined street. Frederich worried that the man was onto him. No one ever called meetings on Friday afternoon.

In fact, the population of Ljubljana halved earlier in the week, often as early as Thursday evenings (and sooner if the weather was bad). But Ljubljana was at its secret best when it was quiet and foggy. You squinted, and it was 1821 all over again. Calm and timeless.

"Sit, sit," Dr Fabjan said and flicked his hair back. He circled the desk and moved every single item slightly to the left, then back to its original spot, avoiding eye contact. What if everything was fine? Not a chance.

The only thing that usually rattled his mentor like this was recent contact with Dr Birkelund. If this was the case, then Frederich would soon be treated to a heartfelt display of fury and frustration, an old wound from the times when Dr Klemen Fabjan moved in the highest alchemical circles at Reijin.

Those times were cut short when Dr Birkelund personally decided that the Slovenian in his circle of confidants wasn't worthy of trust, because, as the grapevine later reported, he was a bit of a complainer and complainers were exactly the kind of people who'd leak alchemical secrets.

The decade-old rejection made Dr Fabjan into a man who fought bitterness with every fibre of his being, and for the most part, he was successful in containing it inside the moments he spoke of Dr Per Birkelund. Everyone's boss' boss.

This was how Frederich had learned that in the business of matter, your fortunes depended on one man's approval, and decades of devotion meant nothing compared to a single mistake. That wouldn't change during Frederch's time. No one dared to meddle with alchemy as long as it produced the precious world-bending matter without interruptions.

The orange lights near the ceiling began to glow with greater intensity, mimicking candle flames with unnatural brightness. Frederich had an odd affinity for the faculty building, an old secession structure.

The ceilings were uncomfortably low for both of the alchemists present and there was always a humid smell in the air. No alchemical inspector had ever passed through it without horrified looks, since all of their measuring devices had to be set up to account for the influence of old stone and the noise of the city.

Bigger structural changes were out of the question. The Faculty of Alchemical Studies was under monumental protection, and even the façade had to look like it was ready for the First World War to kick off. In a world where matter could change to make gold chewy if there was a need for it, such static facilities made them look like amateurs.

The building was unsuitable for alchemy, and yet that's what it was used for. Like Frederich. But he was not a building. He could leave. And he would.

He was no longer a child fooled by alchemy's delicious secrecy, the promised study of the universe's most elusive sublime forces. Once upon a time, Frederich was thrilled to have made the cut; studying alchemy was a hard-earned honour, and it made him into someone. 'Frederich The Alchemist'. He'd made it easy for people to put him in a box. Quiet and scientific. Locked away in the labs, working hard at securing a beautiful future for humanity.

But when the panic attacks and useless spells of rage became a daily occurrence, Frederich had recognised just how petty his life had become. The work was hard. The reward was meaningless. And then there were the accidents. Frederich had seen human bodies burst into dust when exposed to a badly managed spec of alchemically altered matter, mutabilis.

More than once, he'd seen a colleague right next to him make a silly mistake and then choke to death inside the emergency force field that protected the rest from the same death. The blurry moments of someone dragging Frederich away from contaminated zones stayed with him the most.

Dr Fabjan made him memorise accident reports to make sure he was more careful than the rest. But no one was more careful than Frederich. The fear of not surviving alchemy inhabited him day and night.

And after all these years, he never got to study the sublime beyond the basics. It was all about how to make nicer air, better conductors for nanodrones, better gadgets for the thriving of humanity, all within a work atmosphere that celebrated arrogance and jealousy. It took a decade to unmask alchemy and see it for what it was.

A craft. Not an art. Not a science.

Managing the rage and disappointment that came with that discovery consumed him. He had no strength left for 'The Alchemist.' It was time. It was inevitable. All Frederich had to do was wait for Dr Fabjan to get the complaining out of the way so that he could give his resignation.

Their eyes met. Tense. No words. Frederich took a few more steps towards the desk, past the long cabinets of purposeless artefacts. Dr Fabjan had always claimed they were ancient alchemical equipment, even though Frederich knew for a fact that one of them was a steam iron.

Old alchemical books that always made Frederich sneeze when he opened them were stacked wherever there was space. He hated paper. Other alchemists loved it. Another sign.

"This is perfect, you're here," Dr Fabjan said, wiping sweaty hands on the sides of his trousers. "I was just about to send for you."

He motioned again to sit down, but Frederich was doing none of that until he knew what was the problem. And then the 'hello, thank you for seeing me on such a short notice'. And then the rest.

"What's wrong?" he asked.

"I'm about to kill myself," Dr Fabjan said, putting both hands up. "Now, don't overreact."

***

Look for 'The Impossible Alchemist' wherever you get your cursed books.

A FRIENDLY NOTE FROM THE PUBLISHER

This book is a fruit of over fifteen years of labour and research into more than two million timelines, which wouldn't be possible without the many helpers Infinite Library has been able to enlist for the project. A special thanks goes to His Majesty the Crown Prince Leeriath of Nenuari who helped with various aspects of moral support, the details of which are, as usually, best left for a different book altogether.

In 2018, The Infinite Library attempted to publish an ambitious account of the events around the year 2363, but started looking into a timeline that resulted in the premature death of everyone involved, which didn't make for a very good story. That account has been pulled and archived. Don't look for it. It's cringe.

We're feeling good about this one, though. The futures are looking strong, fresh, and *spicy*.

Most of the historical facts that fill the gap between Earth's present and the events of *My Friend, the Gifted* have been omitted after careful consideration.

One of our associates from the timeline in which this story takes place has summed up our reasons for it quite nicely. 'The less you know, the harder you'll work to get here.'

See you on the alchemical side.